Return to Promise Cove

by

Casey Dawes

Mountain Vines Publishing

Copyright 2021 by Casey Dawes LLC.
All rights reserved.

No part of this book may be reproduced in any form or by any electronic or mechanical means, including information storage and retrieval systems, without permission in writing from the publisher, except by reviewers, who may quote brief passages in a review.

Some characters and events in this book are fictitious. Any similarity to real persons, living or dead, is coincidental and not intended by the author.

Book cover design by GetCovers
Edited by CEO Editor (ceoeditor.com)
Interior design by Concierge Self-Publishing
(www.ConciergeSelfPublishing.com)

Published by Mountain Vines Publishing
Missoula, MT
Contact email: info@ConciergeSelfPublishing.com

Chapter One

Kelly Richards recognized the envelope at the top of the mail at once: heavy, cream stock, with a firm name and address embossed in blue in the upper left corner. Even the addressee was embossed. How did anyone do that these days? Most of her mail, what few pieces she got, was clearly computer generated.

More importantly, what did her in-laws' firm want with her son?

She closed the metal box, once more vowing to zap it with a strong bug spray to decimate the nest of whatever was growing in the far corner, and headed up the walkway and stairs to her glass-fronted house overlooking the Pacific Ocean. Once she entered, she tossed Peter's envelope on the gleaming table by the front door and took the rest of the mail with her to the kitchen. Whatever her in-laws wanted could wait.

From the noise coming from the upstairs, Peter and his friend Jake were heavily into some action video game. She should probably nudge them outside. The pool begged for swimmers this late May afternoon. But the outdoors had never drawn seventeen-year-old Peter. He much preferred a dark room and a gleaming screen.

He was his father's clone.

As usual when Kelly thought of her late husband, her heart ached. The pain was growing less over time, but it was still there. They thought they'd had forever, but a faulty heart valve had taken John late last summer when he was coming home from work. Fortunately, he'd been pulled off the road, talking on the phone to one of his hedge fund clients, no doubt.

A flash of irritation sparked through her as she pulled the iced tea pitcher from the refrigerator. Over the years, John's clients had taken a top priority in their lives, ahead of her, and even ahead of the children. Oh, he'd loved them, she was sure of that, but a client phone call or a trip across the continent to New York to meet with one of them always took priority. She'd asked him more than once to get a dedicated phone for work so she could reach him more easily, but he'd always said a second phone was more trouble than it was worth.

Kelly shrugged off the memories and took her tea out to the backyard, giving a small glance to the gleaming baby grand in the living room. The cleaning lady had done a good job with it today. Not a speck of dust on the black surface.

Outside, she sank into one of the Adirondack chairs that surrounded a firepit beyond the pool. A soft breeze cooled her skin as she stared out at the water. By this time in the school year she was exhausted, and she needed these moments to let all the noise and drama of teaching middle school music seep away. By and large, her students were good kids. They were in music because they wanted to be, like she had been. At least she didn't have reams of homework to correct or artwork to evaluate like her friend, Gail.

Her brain nibbled on the envelope sitting on the front table. What did they want with Peter? Had John put something in motion before he died? Or was it just his parents' doing? They'd never particularly liked her, although they thought her of suitable breeding for their son, at least on her father's side.

Kelly had actually heard herself discussed in exactly those terms when she'd first been dating John. She'd thought it hysterically funny then, but over the decades the joke became stale. His family was Beacon Hill Boston, with family dating back to the *Mayflower* and relatives serving in Boston and Massachusetts politics, either in office or manipulating it from behind the scenes. They were part of the upper crust memorialized in an old toast: "The Lowells talk to the Cabots, and the Cabots talk only to God." Kelly had met plenty of Lowells, Cabots, and Kennedys at the Richards' parties, although the Kennedys were only allowed because Ted had been a powerful influence before his death.

She'd been grateful when John had been offered, and he'd accepted, a job on the West Coast. Kelly didn't want their daughter, Lisa, brought up in the constricted society of his in-laws and her parents. Kelly's mother, despite being raised in Montana, could out-Boston the matrons.

A group of brown pelicans skimmed low across the water below. Kelly took a deep breath. She loved the ocean—water of any kind, really. Her best memories had been of summers at her grandmother's house on a lake in Montana. She'd learned to kayak in those waters, enjoying the solitude away from her parents and anyone else who wanted to disrupt her dreams. It had been there, out on that mountain lake, that she first realized she wanted to be a concert pianist. She'd imagined herself in a gorgeous gown, her auburn hair in a stylish updo, sitting down before a hushed audience to play the opening notes of the Moonlight Sonata.

There'd been a boy in Montana—Ryan. He was older, and she'd definitely had feelings for him. He'd been sweet to her, and he was the

Return to Promise Cove

only one she'd told her dream to. With a smile, he'd told her he'd be the first one to buy a ticket to see her play.

Even now, sitting beneath the California sun almost three decades later, she could feel the peace and happiness that being around Ryan had given her.

But her parents had declared she needed to get on with her life. They'd held a party in her honor for her sixteenth birthday, presenting her to people she needed to know.

None of her friends had been invited.

Kelly drained the last of her ice tea, the cubes clinking against the glass. Then she hoisted herself up and headed back to the house. Dinner needed starting; she had to prepare for the next day's class and make sure Peter had done his English and history homework along with his math.

Once Peter's friend left, Kelly checked on his homework status. As befitted a senior who'd already gotten into Boston College, there wasn't much. "There's a letter for you on the front table," she said after he put the settings on the counter dividing the kitchen from the rest of the living area. After John died, and with Lisa at college most of the year, they'd taken to eating here rather than bothering with the dining room.

"Mom!" Peter yelled as he stood before her, waving the letter in his hand. "I've got an internship for the summer. At Dad's company."

"What? I didn't know you were applying." The serving spoon thudded back into the casserole dish.

"I didn't really. Grandfather said not to say anything until it was a done deal."

I bet.

"But you can't go," she said. "We've got our city trip planned— San Francisco, Chicago, Atlanta, and New York." She'd designed the trip especially around things he liked: museums, aquariums, zoos.

"Mom, this is really important. Grandfather says it can give me a real leg up when I start looking for work."

"You aren't getting a job for another four years. This is the last summer we have together."

"I know, Mom. And I'm sorry. Maybe we can see New York at Christmastime. I'll have a whole month off. We can see the tree, the shops, and go to all the museums. It'll be fun."

Even by then Peter would have new friends and a new view of

life. He just didn't know it yet. Once Lisa had gone, she came home only for short spurts. After she'd gotten a boyfriend last fall, even those had fallen off. She'd declared him "the one" and spent all her spare time with his family in San Francisco.

Now Peter was going. Soon she would be alone in this big, rambling, gleaming house with ten years to go before she could even think about early retirement.

"Mom, don't look like that. It's not the end of the world."

"You're putting me out of a job," she said, forcing a smile. She was being melodramatic, but the looming loss hurt more than she'd anticipated. "I'll have to join that organization: Mothers Whose Children Have Left Home."

"There's no such thing."

"There should be."

"It won't be that bad," he said, laying the letter on the counter. "You can have wild parties and stay up all night."

"I didn't even do that when I was your age."

"Well, you can find out what it's like." He gave her his best smile.

Her son had learned how to cajole her at an early age.

She picked up the spoon, doled out the casserole she'd made, and placed the plates on the counter. "Dinner is served. So tell me about this internship."

"You'll let me go?"

"I haven't said that yet. I've already started making reservations for our trip. All of that is going to have to be undone."

"I'm sorry. But this is really important to me." And he launched off into a description of all the things he thought he'd be doing.

Reality was probably going to be more reined in, but she'd let his grandparents dim his enthusiasm.

The ache in her heart from John's death cracked open again. Her son was really going to leave. And she was going to let him. She'd always put her children first, and that wasn't going to change. If Boston was what he wanted, she would let him go.

She stared at the stainless steel appliances and white counters. This house hadn't been her choice. She'd gone along with John, as she always did. Maybe her son did have an element of wisdom. It might be time to find out what her life was all about. She'd set it aside to have a family, but now her time was all hers. John was gone; it was time to start cleaning out his things. Maybe she'd downsize, sell the house, get a smaller one somewhere like Redondo Beach.

She was on her own now. All she had to decide was what kind of life she wanted to live.

Chapter Two

Kelly waited until Saturday morning to call her in-laws to discuss their plans. By that time, she was convinced she could act professionally, not reveal the pain she was feeling as the last of her children left the nest.

She sat at the kitchen counter, her planner and notepad in front of her. Paper was more natural for notes and initial thoughts.

"Good morning, Ruth," she said to her mother-in-law when she answered. "Peter got your company's letter a few days ago. I wanted to call to discuss arrangements with you for the summer. I assume he'll be staying with you?"

A formal way to begin, but it was best. California breezy didn't work on Boston uptight.

"Yes, my dear," Ruth answered. "We are delighted to have Peter. Why don't you come as well? It would be great to have you in the city. It would be good for you to get out after the unfortunate event. Almost a year has passed. It's time to re-enter society."

"I'm afraid that won't be possible. Thank you, though," she added belatedly.

"Oh? Do you have other plans?"

"Well, I had hoped to take Peter on one last trip before he went to college."

"You can certainly take some trips from here. The house on The Vineyard would be available. Perhaps Lisa can come as well."

For thirty seconds, she was tempted. The house, more a mansion, on the island was beautiful, and island life peaceful.

But the cost was too high.

"No, that's fine. Since we received the letter, I've been making plans for myself. To go to Europe. Italy, maybe."

"Italy is all the rage these days. We will miss you. Though I know Peter will be very busy learning the ropes at the business and finding his way around Boston. We will have some parties for him as well. It will be a great opportunity for him to become part of the family operation."

And for the Richards clan to get their claws into her son. Unfortunately, it couldn't be helped. John had groomed Peter for his eventual role, and her son had taken to it like the proverbial duck in water.

She nailed down the details with Ruth. She'd have exactly one week with Peter after school ended, and having gone through it with Lisa, she knew he'd want to spend that time with his friends. It was going to be a long summer and fall until they came home for Thanksgiving.

Ruth tried once more to get Kelly to come to Boston, but Kelly wanted no part of the routine, in spite of the fact she'd been born and raised in the city. Somehow, her spirit had never taken up residence there.

She hung up the phone and completed her notes. There were things that she'd need to go over with Peter: making sure he knew about his medical insurance, setting up an account for him to draw from for books, food, and other essentials. He would need to learn to budget, but they'd funded both kids' college funds well.

She closed the notebook and looked around. The house was still in good shape from the cleaning firm's job. A little pickup was all she needed to do before the end-of-year teacher gathering in her house. She often hosted, as she had one of the larger places. The pool was always a draw.

Only a few others lived in the pricy town. John's salary and stock income had paid for the house. On a teacher's salary, she would have been relegated with the others to a small apartment or repurposed beach shack.

Peter was spending the day with a few friends, so she had the house to herself. She wandered to the piano, sat, and opened the lid. Tentatively, she played a few scales. Every once in a while, she pulled out a book with a yellow cover and attempted one of Chopin's études. She could hear her last piano teacher, a Greek woman with a book-crammed studio in her house. The space barely contained enough room for the piano, a white bust of Beethoven, and the woman's larger-than-life gestures.

"Caress the keys," she would tell her. "With Chopin, you must always caress. Bach requires you to have a drumbeat in your head, and Beethoven needs your soul. But Chopin is a man caressing the skin of his lover."

The words had made her uncomfortable at the time, but they'd stuck.

But today she didn't have the patience for Chopin. Instead, she plunked out a few choruses of "Chopsticks," stood, and bowed to the imaginary audience. Then she closed the lid and turned to face John's office.

Ruth was right about one thing: it was time to start moving on. Oh, not drastically. At forty-four, it was too late to change the trajectory of her life. Being a concert pianist was out. Instead she'd learned the rules for being a good wife, mother, and teacher and obeyed them all. It had been simpler that way. There was no drama. And after living with her parents, she'd been very tired of the conflict her mother seemed to consider an art form.

No, it was time to clean out John's office. Could she make it her own? She'd always done her work at the dining room table or kitchen counter. Officially, she had an office upstairs that contained piles and drawers of music, lesson plans, and handouts from long-over courses. But she preferred to do her planning in the middle of her family, there when either of her children needed her.

If she did move her work in here, she'd need new furniture. John's sharp-angled desk with its single drawer didn't appeal to her. The white surface was covered over with papers she'd gotten from the various agencies. She'd read through them, made her decisions, then tossed them on his desk, like they were unfinished business for him to handle.

Somewhere in that pile was the unopened manila envelope the police had given her when they'd finished their investigation. One of the things in there was his wallet, an expensive leather billfold she'd given him as a gift one Christmas when Lisa was about ten.

There was something about a man's wallet that seemed to contain his essence. Maybe because he carried it so close to him and opened it multiple times a day. Unlike women's purses, a man held onto his wallet until it was barely usable, a familiar piece of him.

Kelly knew if she held that object in her hand, she would collapse into grief, regressing months in the cycle. The envelope would be the last thing she opened.

She sat in his desk chair and tried the lone drawer. Locked. She didn't remember a key anywhere. It might be in the envelope, too.

She glanced at the functional but up-to-date filing cabinets. Their keys were hanging from their locks. It was as good a place to start as any. Most of it could go back to his corporate office, where someone else would deal with it.

Retrieving the boxes she'd stored in the utility room, she opened the top drawer and began.

"Do you need any help?" Kelly's friend Gail asked as she

followed her into the kitchen, carrying an artfully created vegetable platter with scattered petunias and a radish rose centerpiece.

"I think I have it all under control. Drinks are in here, along with glasses. I'm leaving the food, plates, and cutlery on the dining room table so the wind doesn't get to them. Tables and chairs are set up outside. I've laid a stack of beach towels for anyone who wants to swim."

"Prepared as always—you have the precision of a marching band."

"Funny."

"I try." Gail grinned.

Although Kelly was close to many of the teachers she'd taught with over the last almost twenty years, Gail was the one she confided in the most. They had lunches out at least once a month, often down at one of the touristy beach towns where they could amble through the shops afterward. Most of the time they came home with a seashell creation of some kind or another. They declared it was in support of the local art community.

"More like the support of your local beach bum," John had commented more than once. He'd had a dim view of the surfing crowd.

"So what are you going to do now that Peter won't be here for the summer?" Gail asked. "I'm guessing Lisa won't be either?"

Kelly shook her head. "She's got a job up in San Francisco and is staying with her boyfriend's family. Good thing. I don't know how she'd afford the rent otherwise."

"That was fast."

"She's head over heels, according to her. I hope it doesn't come crashing down. They're awfully young."

"Are you going east with Peter then?" Gail asked.

"Heaven forbid! I don't know. I guess I'll just stay around here. I told my in-laws I was going to Italy, but I'll tell them I couldn't get tickets."

"You should go somewhere."

"Uh-huh. Maybe we can do a long weekend at a spa or something."

"Not happening. I leave the week after school ends, remember? Our annual pilgrimage to the old country so my children can 'absorb their Japanese roots'— my mother-in-law's term for learning to be more obedient. They're both boys, so they don't have to change too much to make her happy. They learned how to fake it a long time ago."

"I thought you weren't comfortable there."

"I'm not. She doesn't think I'm a good influence—not traditional enough and too opinionated. But I do it for my husband. He's a man who honors his parents, so we go." She shrugged. "What can I say? After all these years, he still makes my heart go thumpity-thump."

Kelly laughed as the doorbell rang.

Soon the place was filled with chatter as the teachers told classroom tales and talked about summer plans. One or two of them actually were going to Europe, and Kelly found herself with the itch of jealousy. If only she'd known.

At one point, she found herself talking with one of the oldest teachers in the school. Tara Johnson had declared she wasn't retiring until she had to do so. Since all the kids adored her, no one was forcing her from the building.

"So how are you holding up?" Tara asked Kelly. "This is when it gets hard. Everyone else has moved on, but you're probably stuck with the grief that sneaks up on you now and then. I know it was that way when my husband died."

Kelly nodded, fighting back as her eyes watered. "It's weird," she said. "I mean, all my life I've known what to do. I was the support team. I made sure my husband's and kids' days ran smoothly. My story wasn't important, only theirs. And now it's like the book is closed and there's nothing more to read."

"Don't be ridiculous," Tara said. "Of course your story matters. What you do with your life matters. *You* matter."

Was the woman right? Was there life beyond an empty nest? Kelly blinked away her tear, as a glimmer of hope lit on the horizon.

Chapter Three

Kelly put her best face forward as she took Peter to LAX the following Friday.

"You're going to have a great time in Boston. I'm thinking about coming out right before you start school. I'll show you all my favorite places, and you can show me what you've discovered. Sound good?"

"Okay." The answer was more a yawn than a word. Like his father, Peter had never been much of a morning person.

"No more sunny days all summer," she said. "Thunderstorms can be wild in the east, especially during hurricane season. And snow … you'll need to deal with snow!"

She steered the Lexus onto the ramp to go the departures building. In the early years, she used to take John this way, dreading whenever he had to leave. She'd loved him so much then, she couldn't bear to let him go. As the years settled in, their relationship had shifted, and he took a limo there and back.

Their marriage hadn't been bad, but the passion of the early years had faded, just like it did for most people, based on what she heard in the teachers' lounge. But unlike some, she and John had become partners in raising the children and being there for each other. And she could never complain that he didn't provide for them.

These were supposed to be their golden years.

Now what was she going to do?

Stop the self-pity. There's a lot to be grateful for.

She headed for the right terminal for Peter's flight.

"Love you, Peter," she said when they pulled up to the doors.

He leapt from the car and stood by the trunk as she released it. He almost flung his bags on the sidewalk in his rush.

Ignoring his anxiety to get away, she pulled him into a hug.

"Make me proud, kid," she said, taking his face in her hands, just as she'd done when she sent him off to his first day in kindergarten.

"Okay, Mom," he said, and like he'd done then, his lower lip trembled, and he clamped his upper teeth on it to stop it. He pulled away and picked up his bags. "Love you, Mom."

"Call," she said as he turned.

"Text," he replied.

And then he was gone.

Kelly was almost grateful that the traffic was a snarl as she left the airport. There was no one at home, so when she got there didn't matter. It was going to be her first summer without John, her children, or Gail. What was she going to do with herself? The script on how to be a good wife and mother that her mother had drilled into her didn't include a scene for this part of the play.

Maybe she *should* to go Italy. Why not? Funds weren't a problem.

As she sat there in her air-conditioned bubble, surrounded by other drivers in theirs, she told her phone to call John's travel agent, a woman she knew well from the times they'd used her to plan family trips or getaways for the two of them.

"How are you, Kelly?" the agent asked after Kelly identified herself. "I'm so sorry to hear about John. How are you managing?"

"Okay. School kept me going. But now my children are gone for the summer, and I seem to be at loose ends. I'm thinking of going to Italy for a month."

"Lovely," the agent said. "Italy is so amazing! The markets, the coffee, and the art will inspire you. It's a perfect idea. I'm going to send a link to some information that will be helpful. I'll also courier over some brochures for tours I think are fabulous. A group might be exactly the right thing for you at this time of your life."

Kelly squashed the temptation to shout, "I'm only forty-four!" Instead, she said, "That would be very nice. Thank you."

They exchanged a few more pleasantries, then disconnected.

For a few miles, she daydreamed about going to Italy and connecting with an over-expressive Italian male given to grand gestures her husband, even in his most passionate moments, never would have imagined much less performed.

She'd have to create some grand gestures for herself. No need to rush, though. She could begin with little joys, like practicing the piano every day.

John had been understanding of her need to feel the keys under her fingers in the beginning of their marriage, but once the kids had come, there had always been somewhere for her to take them or something to do for John. It had been subtle at first, but gradually her time at the piano had been eroded by her duties until the only time she used it was to prepare for her classes or concerts.

Once again, she dreamed of herself on a concert stage in an elegant gown, playing to a crowd that cheered and applauded her.

Getting her skills back sounded wonderful in concept, but in reality? Was there really a point?

She pulled into the garage, then closed the door and entered the house.

The only way she was going to make it through the day was to keep busy. Pouring herself another cup of coffee, she turned on her latest collection from the Berlin Philharmonic full blast and headed to John's office. Time to finish the job.

She'd finish the file cabinets first. As she thumbed through the files, she realized that most of the files were what she'd surmised: client files John had worked on from home.

There were some other folders: household appliance information, insurance, financial records from companies that still insisted on doing things on paper. But she'd already been through most of these in the winter as she'd worked through the inevitable modern hassles of a person's death.

Why did things need to be so complicated and obtuse?

She boxed up the client files and put them by the door. The standard stuff she put back in the drawer. As she did so, she realized this would forever remain her husband's office. The furniture and décor was too sleek and modern for her. Rather than give her the focus John had claimed it gave him, it made her tense.

When she looked at the pile on his desk, her stress increased. The brown envelope in the middle of the stack seemed to be a ticking detonator, with the computer below it serving as the bomb material.

Once again she started with the familiar, filing the papers she'd thrown there into the folders she'd reloaded into the cabinet. Then there was nothing else to do.

She undid the clasp and slid the contents onto the now-clear surface.

Keys, sunglasses, folded notes of paper, coins, the expected wallet, and phone.

No. Two phones.

She sank into the office chair and stared at the items on the desk. Why two phones?

She picked up the one she recognized and turned it on. Nothing happened. She glanced around the room. The charger lay on the windowsill. She plugged it in.

Then she returned to stare at the other phone again.

After a few moments, she picked it up and turned it on. Once again, nothing, but this time her search for a charger failed. Maybe it was in the locked drawer.

Quickly, she pawed through the keys, identifying most of them and finally deciding on one that looked like it would fit the drawer.

Her hand shook as she inserted the key.

It's only a drawer.

It slid open.

The charger was there, so she set up the second phone. Would she have the courage to open it once it was ready?

The contents of the drawer were slim: a checkbook, a coaster from someplace called the Ascent Bar, and an envelope. She opened the envelope. A ticket to LaGuardia Airport in New York City for Monday the week after John had died, with a return the following Friday.

She searched her memory, trying to recall if he'd mentioned a trip. Was he going to tell her right before he left? He'd done that a few times.

And it had always been a trip to New York.

She picked up her own phone and searched for Ascent Bar. It turned out to be an upscale bar at the top of a building overlooking Central Park. What was he doing there? If he was with a client, why would he have brought home a coaster? That was the sort of thing a lovesick teenager might do.

Horror overwhelmed her. Had John been having an affair? How would she ever find out? Did she even want to?

She needed to talk to someone. But who? Did she want comfort or answers?

With anger flooding her body, she certainly didn't want comfort.

She dialed her mother.

"Hello, dear. How nice—and unexpected—for you to call."

"Was John having an affair?" Kelly got right to the point.

"John? For heaven's sake. Whyever would you think that?"

"I found a second phone. And tickets to New York. And a ... well, something else." The coaster seemed a prop in a bad comedy.

"It never does go well when a wife looks too closely at her husband's things."

There were a thousand things Kelly could ask after that statement, and all of them were things she didn't want to know.

"So he was having an affair."

"I haven't the faintest idea. Look, he left you well provided for, and he was always there for you and the kids. Let the poor man rest in peace. Why do you have to know?"

The question was good. John was dead. Why did it matter what he did when he was alive?

Because she needed to know if she had been living an illusion all those years, if she had been following the rule book all by herself. If he had been having an affair, she'd never be able to forgive him. Never. No matter how dead he was.

And she'd never again be able to give a man her full trust.

Chapter Four

The next morning, Kelly got up early and drove down to her favorite spot on the beach. There were a few people, regulars getting in their morning walk before the weekend crowd came from inland to crowd the space.

She took off her shoes at the beginning of the sand, wanting the rough, cool granules to connect her to the earth. The constant squawking of the gulls almost drowned out the swish of the occasional car on the pavement behind her. As she strolled closer to the water, the only sound was the pounding of the surf as it bombarded the land.

A plucky surfer was out early with a buddy, suited up against the chill of the ocean. She watched for a while as he, or she, glided in on a medium wave. It was not a sport she'd ever craved. Too many unknowns. In fact, she barely went into the ocean. She'd tried a few times, but things she couldn't see touching her, even if it was only seaweed, freaked her out. Somewhere in her twenties she'd realized she wasn't the adventurous sort, at least not anymore.

She walked north, the sun on her right and the water to her left. She let her attention drift back to what she'd found, and a wave took the opportunity to sneak over her feet. She shrieked a little but welcomed the jolt.

At least she felt alive.

She bent down and picked up a tiny clam shell, smaller than the tip of her index finger. So delicate and white. Slipping it into the pocket of her capris, she continued on. Soon she became used to the waves playing with her feet, relishing the smooth feel of the water as she walked. Ahead, sandpipers did their eternal dance back and forth, their tiny legs whirring in motion as they raced back and forth.

She stopped thinking at all, merely walked until some internal clock told her it was time to turn back.

She was halfway back when her brain flipped back into gear and the image of two phones reappeared in her mind's eye. What to do with the unknown? Let it be, like the depths of the ocean beside her? What would she gain from finding out John had been cheating on her? Her mother was right. There was no point in scratching that itch.

But what if he hadn't had an affair? Would she carry this suspicion with her for the rest of her life, believing her husband was something he wasn't? That wouldn't be fair to either of them.

It all came down to courage. Would she be able to face the truth, whatever it was?

And how would it impact what she did with the rest of her life?

Of course, she had no idea what she was going to do for the rest of her life. The only sameness would be her job and the house. Everything else had changed in an instant, like the stroke of midnight in the Cinderella story.

She headed back to the car, brushed her feet as best she could, then slipped on her sandals. A few particles of grit remained, but that was normal.

When she returned home, she took a long shower before changing into a pair of light blue wide-leg pants and white sleeveless T-shirt. Out of habit, she added a matching necklace and one of her favorite bangle bracelets with blue highlights. Even if her plan today was to do the sheets in Peter's room and give it a good cleaning, she didn't need to be a slob.

In some ways, she was definitely her mother's daughter.

But before anything, she was going to eat breakfast. A good one. A meal where she savored every bite instead of telling someone to hurry up, signing last-minute forms, and locating something that someone, usually her husband, had lost.

A few hours later she had completed the tasks she'd assigned herself and was back in the office chair in front of John's desk, deciding her next move.

Nothing had changed.

That was the problem with living alone. Nobody else moved things. Or made the choice she didn't want to make. It was all up to her.

But she wasn't ready to know one way or another. She needed to get her feet back under her first. There had been too much rapid change. Even though it had been almost a year since John died, there hadn't been time to really deal with it herself. Her children, grieving the loss of a father they'd loved, needed her first. Then school activities took over. Even the weeks off, scattered throughout the year, had been full of negotiating with Peter about where and when he could drive his father's car.

No, she needed more time. First she was going to set up a routine so she'd get through the summer. The walk this morning had been good. She'd make that part of her daily habit. Someone had once told her that a morning journal entry was ideal to get the cobwebs from her head, along with a glass of lemon water. Later today she'd buy a pretty notebook for the purpose. She'd make a good breakfast and then tackle the household chores. No use to keep the cleaning service. With only her to mess things up, it wouldn't take much to clean.

And it would give her something to do.

The thought did her in. Tears overwhelmed her, and she laid her head in her arms and let herself bawl. Great sobs came from her chest, but she didn't care. There was no one here to hear. It seemed like the crying jag would never end, but eventually a few halting breaths were all that remained.

After using her hands to wipe the ravages from her face, she put John's wallet and sunglasses in the top drawer with the phones, locked it, and dumped everything else but the keys and computer into the trash. Then she locked the office door and headed up the stairs. After putting the keys in what had been his top dresser drawer, she went into the bathroom to begin the day again.

After the trip to the bookstore to purchase her journal, Kelly sat in a lounge chair by the pool, indulging in a novel she'd also bought, *The Personal Librarian*, about J.P. Morgan's staff member. She loved historical fiction, but its 352 pages would have been daunting when her family was home.

She added it to the plus column of her new life.

When she was hot enough, she slipped into the pool and swam twenty laps before coming back and resuming the story and sipping the flavored sparkling water she'd placed on the table beside her.

Lovely indulgences, but she didn't want to think about how long she could bear doing them. She was a workhorse. Sitting idly did not come easily.

Play me, the piano beckoned from inside the house.

She ignored it.

But then she hear another sound: the front door opening and closing.

She shut the book and held it ready. It would be a tragic waste, but with a good heave, she could stop someone long enough to get out the front door and scream.

"Mom!" Lisa's voice made her drop the book with a thud.

Kelly stood.

"What are you doing home?" she asked when her daughter appeared on the patio.

"I thought you'd be happy to see me," Lisa said, her shoulders drooping a little. "I thought you'd be lonely, Andrew was busy, so I got on a flight and came down. Rented a car and everything. I must be an adult now!" Her easy grin was back.

Kelly had always been close to her daughter, who was a lot like her. Theirs was the easy relationship, unlike the somewhat tense one she had with Peter, mainly because she didn't really understand what made her son tick.

"I'm delighted to see you." She kissed her daughter on the cheek. "I'd give you a real hug, but I'm all wet."

"That's okay." Lisa pulled her in close. "How are you, Mom? Really."

"A little sad. It's an adjustment." Kelly gave her daughter a quick squeeze, then stepped back. "I'm working on a routine for the summer. That will get me through it."

"You should go somewhere," Lisa said, flopping into a nearby chair as Kelly sat down. "Think of the fun you could have not trying to corral everyone to get them to some educational place."

"Was I that bad?"

"No. You were … you are great, Mom. And you're young. Take a trip to Hawaii or Bali or somewhere. Maybe you'll meet someone amazing! You could walk around all day in a sarong with a flower behind your ear, and people would think you're exotic."

Kelly smiled but shook her head. "I'm not ready for that big a change." Lisa looked good, but a little throb in her daughter's temple told her Lisa was tense. "What's up?" she asked. "Everything okay?"

"Sure. Andrew's great. His parents are okay with me being there, and I like my job." Lisa had taken an intern position at a major computer science company.

"Then what's the problem?"

"There's no problem. Can't a girl come see her mother?"

"Did you bring your laundry?" Kelly asked.

Lisa laughed. "Really, Mom, I'm just here to see you."

She'd taught her daughter well. Never confess that anything was wrong.

"Okay. Get into your swimsuit and we'll sit for a while and catch up."

"Got it."

Chapter Five

It wasn't until Kelly poured them each a second glass of wine that the truth began to trickle out.

"I mean," Lisa said, "Andrew's parents are fine with me being there. I bring home groceries now and then because they don't want me to pay rent. I tried to cook for them once, but they never let me again. They said they had too many restrictions in their diets for me to remember them all."

"Sounds complicated," Kelly murmured as she sipped her wine. It was good to be needed again, if only as a listener.

"I keep telling myself it's only eight more weeks before the internship ends, but sometimes I think I'm going to go crazy. I try to be really quiet because it doesn't seem like any of them—even Andrew—talk above a whisper."

"Difficult."

"But I'll stick it out. I've joined a gym, and I've gotten tickets for a couple of plays that are coming through. Did you know *Wicked* is back? I love that show." She sang a few bars of "Defying Gravity." Lisa cut off another piece of pizza and waved it around on her fork as she spoke. "I tried out for a couple of plays last year. I only made it into the chorus, but it was so much fun!"

"Why didn't you tell me? I would have come to see you."

"Because I was in the *chorus*, Mom. And you had school, and ☐ Watch the throne, Chrome … well … I didn't know how you'd react."

"What do you mean?"

Lisa popped the piece of pizza in her mouth and chewed. Then she shrugged. "I don't know," she finally said. "I'm just not sure computer science is what I want to do for the rest of my life. I mean, I started there because Dad encouraged me. He said it would be a good field because I was good at logic. But it's just numbers and letters. If this happens, do that. I'd hoped that being an intern would bring some life to the career, but…" She shrugged again.

"But it hasn't," Kelly prodded.

"Not really. I mean, Andrew is in the same field, but he loves it. He gets all excited when he figures something out. He's a year ahead of me, so maybe it gets better."

"Who are you doing your career for?" Kelly asked. "Your father?

Andrew? You?"

Her daughter sawed off another piece from her slice. "It's a good question, Mom. I don't really have the answer."

"Well, it's obviously something for you to think about." Kelly attacked her own slice with a knife and fork. It had taken her a while to convert from the East Coast habit of grabbing a piece of pizza and taking a bite off the end to the knife and fork method of the West. The pizza was totally different here, too—laden with large chunks of veggies and meat. She'd tried eating it like an Easterner and found the pizza didn't bend right and the toppings slid right off.

"Think about it, and then we can discuss it. So the job's a question mark and Andrew's parents are a bit difficult. How's Andrew?"

"He's amazing!" Lisa's face lit up with joy. "We have so much fun together. He gives me little things for no reason and tells me how much he loves me. He's really smart, and I know he's going to do well in business. He's perfect for me."

It was how Kelly used to talk about John when she first met him. Lisa always was her daddy's girl.

A shadow of misgiving darkened Kelly's sunny soul. Would things work out for her daughter? Would she lose herself, as Kelly was beginning to suspect she herself might have, in the role of wife and mother?

If she had advice for her daughter, she'd give it. But right now, Kelly didn't have any answers, never mind the best ones.

The next morning, Kelly skipped her brand-new habit of a beach walk to make her daughter her favorite breakfast: homemade blueberry waffles with sausage links and real maple syrup. Growing up in New England, it was the only kind she served, and her kids had grown up knowing the imitation varieties didn't make the grade.

When she heard the shower go off, a signal she'd used since the kids were in elementary school, she began assembling the breakfast. Ironically, Peter's showers were always longer than Lisa's because he would start thinking about something and forget how long he'd been there.

"Good morning," she said with a smile when Lisa walked into the kitchen. "Everything should be ready in a few minutes."

"Oh, Mom, thanks. It looks great. Can I help?"

"No, just sit." Kelly took the glass pitcher full of orange juice from the refrigerator and put it next to the small blue vase of pink cosmos she'd gathered from the garden earlier that morning. "Since your flight doesn't leave until late afternoon, I was thinking we could go to Redondo Beach and walk the pier, stop in the shops, and have lunch. What do you think?"

"Sounds great, Mom. I just wanted to spend time with you, pretend I didn't have to be an adult for a while." Lisa gestured to the table. "It's good to be home. You make it seem so easy."

"It's taken a while." Kelly smiled. "But your grandmother had very strict rules about how things were to be done, so I was prepared on that front."

"Yeah, she is a bit formal."

"A bit?"

The laughed and chatted as Kelly prepared the plates and brought them to the table.

"You really need to think about going somewhere this summer," Lisa said. "Somewhere like Hawaii is probably redundant. I mean, you live at the beach."

"True. But I don't need to go anywhere. I have plenty of books. Maybe I'll take up something new—learn to knit or crochet."

Lisa cocked her head. "Somehow, I don't see that."

Kelly thought for a moment. "Actually, I don't either. But going somewhere seems like a massive project. I thought about Italy for a few moments."

"I know. I saw the brochures on the coffee table. You should totally go. You'd love it. Art, music, good food. Remember that time we all went to London? We had a blast! You and Dad were so happy. Without all of us, going to Italy should be a snap."

"They speak English in London," Kelly reminded her. "Well, some form of it anyway. My Italian is limited to *Arrivederci, Roma*. Now finish up, and let's get going."

The pier was as lovely as Kelly had hoped. It reminded her of the best parts of being in California. The skies were a cloudless blue, pierced only by the white flash of seagulls and the sharp lines of pelicans.

They strolled down the pier, their summer dresses swishing in the ocean breeze. Caramel, popcorn, and coffee aromas scented the air around them as they window-shopped.

"Oh, look." Lisa pointed at a small, "permanent" fairy-tale sand castle. "I've always loved those."

"You are a romantic," Kelly said.

"You say that like it's a bad thing."

"Not at all. People who are romantic are far more hopeful, I think. There are more than enough doomsayers around." Although Kelly vaguely remembered someone saying that romantics were likely to turn into cynics as they grew older and the fairy tale didn't materialize.

"Besides," Lisa said, "I'm not only a romantic, I'm a realist, too. I know everything isn't perfect."

"I see." Kelly used her best non-committal voice.

"It happens all the time," Lisa continued, her gaze more focused on the window display than Kelly. "People are exploring. My friends identify their gender on social media. We're all trying to figure things out. Part of that isn't being as faithful to one person as you guys were. I mean, my girlfriend's boyfriend, the one she thought would be forever? He left her for a ménage relationship."

It all sounded terribly confusing to Kelly. How did anyone navigate that kind of world?

"But after you make a commitment?" she asked, "do you keep the promises you make? When someone says they'll forsake all others, do they really mean it?"

Lisa shrugged and finally looked at her mother. "I guess. I don't know anyone who's gotten married. It will probably mean as much as it did to your generation."

Which wasn't really saying much, considering the high divorce rate.

"Oh, Lisa," she said, gathering her daughter close to her. If only this were as easy as a bandage on a scraped knee. But this was adult stuff, far more liable to cause lasting pain. "I hope," she said as she held her daughter, "that Andrew knows what he's got and will take good care of you."

"I know he will," Lisa said as she pulled away. "We'll be okay. He's just like Dad."

An ache formed in Kelly's stomach. She prayed her daughter was right, that her husband had been as deserving of their trust as they thought he was.

Lisa dropped Kelly off at the house on her way to the airport. As she walked up the steps, Kelly automatically deadheaded the flowers that lined the path. The gardening service they'd hired when they first bought the property had been skilled at choosing what to plant and diligent about maintaining it.

When she reached the top step, she noticed a large white envelope from one of the expedited mail services. How long had it been there? She always went in through the garage, so she wouldn't have seen it. And she hadn't received any messages telling her that something was on its way.

The return address was from Henderson Law Offices in Whitefish, Montana. Something about her grandmother?

She opened the bright red door and went to the kitchen to open the envelope and quickly scan the letter. She struggled to comprehend it.

Slowing down, she read it a second time.

It seemed her grandmother who had passed during the winter had left her an entire retreat center in Promise Cove, Montana.

But there were conditions.

Chapter Six

After tossing and turning most of the night, Kelly wearily gave in around six-thirty and stumbled into the bathroom. Bleary eyes looked back at her. If she ever got serious again about dating, she'd need to find a better morning face.

Or stop having bombshells dropped into her lap at the end of the day.

A retreat center. What was she going to do with a retreat center?

She turned on the water in the shower, waited until it was steaming, and stepped in. The water sluiced down her back, slowly awakening her skin to the day. She raised her face to the spray, and soon the cobwebs were washed from her mind.

She wouldn't do anything right now. Her list of things to do today included throwing Lisa's sheets into the laundry before taking a look at the garage to see what needed to be done there. There were a lot of boxes no one had looked at in years, as well as some tools and toys John had stored there. Cleaning out all that history wasn't going to happen overnight, but it would be a good summer project.

With breakfast over and dishes and laundry in their respective washers, she picked up a yellow legal pad and headed to the garage. Opening the first box almost did her in. It was material from their first few years in Boston: old dishes, Lisa's baby booties and a silver plated rattle, a Lladro anniversary sculpture, and a few pieces of a blue and white Canton collection Kelly had forgotten about, given to her by some never-married aunt from a distant branch of the family. A jumble of the past.

This was going to take a lot longer than she anticipated. It wasn't the physical but the emotional lifting that was going to be a problem.

She paused and looked around. She needed a system. Mentally, she laid out a grid. There was the easy stuff—tools she didn't know how to use, equipment John bought and never used, duplicates of garden equipment before they hired a service. Boxes of out-of-date clothes and appliances could be sorted through fairly quickly. The emotional bombshell boxes could be done slowly—one at a time.

Hopefully, she wouldn't find any other surprises John had hidden.

After making a list, she tackled the garden equipment. Almost all of it could go, but her tony neighborhood would frown on a garage

Return to Promise Cove

sale, and she didn't really need the money.

She started another list: What to do with …?

A few hours later she had a substantial pile sorted into what she would keep, what to give away, and what to try to sell. New homeowners could use garden equipment, and young people bought homes. She'd ask Lisa for best places to get rid of the items.

Satisfied with the day's work, she cleaned up, grabbed a book, and headed for the pool. It was blissful for about an hour.

Was this really what she was going to do with her summer?

She picked up her phone. Gail was in Japan, but texting was still an option.

> Kelly: Grandmother left me retreat center in MT. Any ideas what to do with it?

She wouldn't receive an answer until later in the day when Gail got up. Maybe they could schedule a time to have a video call. Kelly needed advice badly.

While she was at it, she texted Lisa about how best to unload the items in the garage.

Satisfied, she took a swim, dried off, then went to the store.

"Sell it" was Gail's advice when she responded around dinnertime.

> Kelly: I'm not sure I can. Attorney says there are conditions.
> Gail: Like what?
> Kelly: Don't know.
> Gail: Then I guess you'd better talk to the attorney.

Gail was right, but it was a call Kelly dreaded to make. It was like the extra phone; ignorance was bliss. What if she were forced to go to Montana to deal with it?

Would that be so bad? It wasn't Italy, but it was out of her backyard. Would there be anyone still there from her teenage years? Doubtful. That was a long time ago.

Maggie and Alex had adopted her the first summer she'd arrived, lonely and shy. The first few years they'd played hide-and-seek in the woods until she grew comfortable with the silent spaces between the trees. Later, they'd been the ones to take her to the town beach and teach her to canoe and kayak.

Then there was Ryan. He'd join the fun once or twice, but mostly he stood off to one side, observing or reading a book. He must have been very shy. But there was something about him that drew her attention even way back then. Every once in a while he'd hold out his hand, and she would follow him to some secret place where they observed the lake, the birds, and the boats.

She hadn't had such good friends since. Nor had she found anyone to truly replace her first teenage crush on Ryan. Or had he been more than that? She'd never had time to find out. Was he still there?

Promise Cove had been a different world from uptight Boston. There was something raw and untamed about the small town in the woods. The nearest place of any size, Whitefish, was an hour's drive. People planned ahead and brought things back for others when they made a trip.

She glanced at the time display on the phone. Montana was an hour ahead of California, which meant the law offices would be closed. She'd call first thing in the morning. For now, she'd open the bottle of expensive Sonoma rosé she'd picked up at the store. The sign had told her that it was perfect for sitting by the pool.

And who was she to ignore a recommendation from authority?

"Bruce Henderson speaking," the somewhat older male voice said when she called the attorney's number the next morning.

What kind of lawyer answered his own phone?

She introduced herself.

"Ah, Henrietta's granddaughter. How nice to hear from you at last."

"At last?"

"Yes, I've been trying to get in contact with you for a number of months. For some reason, your grandmother thought you lived in Boston."

"I haven't lived there in decades," Kelly said. "But my mother's still there. I'm sure she would have forwarded it to me."

"Yes, well, there were times I'm afraid Henrietta's memory wasn't what it once was. She never mentioned your mother, and since you have different last names, the address didn't come up correctly." He chuckled. "Henrietta could remember who was poet laureate of the country for any year, but other details often escaped her."

"My mother said she died of a heart attack."

"She did. Right there in the middle of wrestling the snow blower into submission. The teenager who usually did it was home sick with the flu. Henrietta was always convinced that if she didn't get to her chickens early in the day, they'd starve to death by afternoon."

"I'm sorry I didn't get there often over the last years." She felt worse than she let on. It had been closer to a few decades.

"Henrietta was a wonderful woman. She'll be missed. But she lived a good life, so no regrets there. So, when can you get up here to look over the property?"

"I'm not sure. I'm very busy. Do I need to come at all? Can't you simply dispose of the property and arrange for me to get whatever proceeds are left after you take out your fee?" Two lies in less than two minutes. She wasn't busy. Not at all.

The truth was, she didn't want to face the past. Whoever that young girl had been was long gone, buried in tulle and lace, baby showers and teacher meetings. The reality of her life now didn't match any of the dreams she'd had when she was young.

Kelly sent a guilty look to the baby grand she'd dusted that morning.

"I'm sorry," Bruce interrupted her reminiscences. "That's not possible. The terms of the will are difficult but entirely legal. In order to dispose of the property, you need to come up here for at least a week and find the message your grandmother left for you."

"A message? Didn't she just leave it with you?"

Bruce chuckled. "Nothing so simple. It wasn't Henrietta's way. It's somewhere in the house. And before you ask, she didn't tell me where it was."

It was totally ridiculous. What could her grandmother tell her that Kelly didn't already know?

"What if I don't go?"

"Then the entire estate goes to a Montana arts organization. You get nothing."

Well, she didn't really need anything, did she?

But a longing grew in her heart for the towering mountains, clear lakes, and deep evergreen forests. She wanted to reacquaint herself with old friends and sit on the shore of Whitefish Lake and rediscover its secrets.

But it was totally impractical. She needed to be here for her children, not gallivanting around the woods.

Don't be ridiculous.

Her kids were almost grown up. She'd thought about going to Italy, where she'd be even more out of touch.

Montana was a return to something she couldn't quite remember, a place where the past might overwhelm her with its memories of who she could have been.

"I need more time to decide."

"I'm afraid you don't have much," the attorney said. "Because it took so long for me to find you, you'll need to make a decision by the end of summer."

She should be able to handle that.

After promising to call him back in a few days, she sank into her favorite chair in the living room, a heavily upholstered armchair with a soft fabric covering instead of the hard leather John had preferred. It was one of the few pieces in their home she'd fought for and won.

Maybe it would simple. If her late grandmother had memory problems, she might have simply forgotten where she put the note. Likely it was hiding in plain sight. Kelly could take a week, go up there, find the note and a reputable estate agent, and put her past behind her.

Easy peasy.

Chapter Seven

"Why would you even consider going to Montana?" Cynthia Paulson Norcross asked in the tone she'd cultivated over decades as the wife of a Boston Brahmin.

"Because, Mother," Kelly patiently explained once again, "if I don't go, I can't get any money if I sell it."

"Did John leave you that poorly off?" Kelly could almost hear the slight arch of her mother's brow in her voice. "I had thought more highly of him than that. The Richards weren't quite upper crust, but they do seem to do the right thing."

For a woman raised in the backwoods of a rural state, Cynthia could be a terrible snob.

"No, but it's my inheritance from Grandma. I should at least go see what it is and to pay my respects."

"Pay your respects to what? The lake? I don't understand why people want to be scattered everywhere these days instead of being memorialized under a good solid headstone."

Kelly stifled a laugh.

"Don't you remember what it was like?" her mother continued. "There is absolutely nothing to do. Your grandmother always had these strange people milling about. They were either fixing things or attending some kind of art workshop—not that I ever saw them do anything. The only sign of civilization is an hour away. Thank goodness I got a car early and worked at that nice lodge. I learned so much there. That's when I decided to really apply myself to school. I got a full scholarship to Wellesley, and then I met your father, and it was perfect."

That was one thing about Cynthia: she had set her ambitions, achieved them, and was fully satisfied with the result.

"Why don't you forget all about it," her mother continued. "Let the place go and come home to Boston. It's time you left the actors and surf bums behind anyway. Peter's here. I'm sure Lisa could be persuaded to join us. You can get back into dating shape. There are plenty of widowers and divorced men out there who could provide you the life you deserve."

"I can't leave here, and Lisa has her own life."

"Why?"

"I have a job. And friends." Well, really only one friend, but her mother didn't need to know that.

"You'll make new friends here. You could look up some of the girls you knew in high school. I'm sure they'd find enough to keep you busy. There are things that need to be done, you know. You could apply for a seat on one of the musical advisory committees. With your background, they'd pick you up right away. Think of the people you'll meet and the events you'll be able to attend."

"I'm not coming back to Boston," Kelly said flatly.

"I'm sorry to hear that. I really do want the best for you, sweetheart."

The thing was, her mother did love her. It was just that Cynthia's version of "the best" came nowhere near Kelly's own.

"Love you, Mom," Kelly said.

"Love you too. If you change your mind, your room is ready."

"Thanks."

After a few more exchanges, Kelly disconnected the call, finished her breakfast, and went back to the garage. Her mother and in-laws were nice enough people, but she always had to watch everything she did or said lest she did or said it wrong.

But all that was in the past, along with the mountain of junk she was facing. That's where she should leave her grandmother's estate, too. In the past. What was the point of dredging up old memories that probably had no connection to the current reality?

By the end of the day, she'd made some good progress, although there wouldn't be space for the car for at least a month.

After she'd cleaned up, she poured herself a glass of wine, retreated to the pool area, and called her daughter.

"I just left," Lisa said with a chuckle. "You can't be lonely already."

"Anytime you want to come back is fine by me. How are things going?"

"As good as they can. I just got home from work, and it's an hour before Andrew gets home and cocktails are mandatory."

"Sounds like my mother's house."

"Oh dear," Lisa said. "Am I going backward?"

"No, honey. It's all about what you want." Kelly wished her daughter were within reach for a large hug. "So, I've been cleaning out the garage."

"That's crazy, Mom. You should wait until one of us is home to help!"

"I'm still capable of moving things," Kelly joshed. "You can cancel the room at assisted living."

Lisa laughed. "Mom, are you that bored?"

She was, but she wasn't about to admit that to her daughter.

"I've got lots to do. That's not why I'm calling you. You know about things like Craigslist and eBay, don't you?"

"Somewhat. I'm not an expert."

"If I sent you pictures, could you post some things so I can get rid of them?"

"As long as it's not something of mine."

"Nope. Most of this stuff is old," Kelly said.

"Then I definitely don't want it. Sure, send them along."

Good, one less thing for her to handle.

"Have you thought more about Italy?" Lisa asked.

"I'm not going to Italy," Kelly said firmly.

"Oh."

"I might go to Montana, though."

"Why?"

Kelly told her daughter the story about the letter and her grandmother's requirements.

"A treasure hunt!" her daughter exclaimed.

"It's a nightmare," Kelly said. "The property is big, and who knows what she has after all this time. The attorney said her memory was fading. Who knows—she may have left it in the freezer."

"You'll find it, Mom. I'm sure."

"Well, I haven't decided to go yet." Getting too warm, Kelly rose from the chair and sat on the top step of the pool. Better.

"Oh, you totally should. You need to get out of California. Shake it up. Get your mojo back!"

Kelly laughed. "Have you been talking to your grandmother? She said the same thing, only in a more gentrified Boston way."

"If the shoe fits..." Lisa answered, her tone too serious for Kelly's liking.

Was she really turning into an old maid at the age of forty-four? Her life had been rewarding so far; there was nothing that made her happier or more satisfied than seeing a smile on her child's face, feeling the loving touch of her husband, or seeing the eyes of a student light up when they finally nailed a difficult musical passage.

But what happened next?

"Earth to Mom. I've got to go. Seriously. Go to Montana. Find Nana's note. She must have wanted to say something important if she wanted you to read it."

"I'll think about it" was the best commitment Kelly could make.

Her conversation with Gail went in a similar direction. She, too, thought Kelly should head north. Right before they'd quit the call, Gail had added the final zinger: "What are you afraid of finding?"

Why was she dragging her feet? She had the time and the money. She was healthy with no major commitments. But still she hesitated. Was she ready to step out of the routine she'd established? The one that had kept her stable since John's unexpected death?

The questions were piling up, and she kept shoving them in a corner. Eventually, she'd have to face them. Denial, avoidance, or even a large bottle of wine wasn't going to make them go away. Although her grandmother's bequest was demanding the most attention right now, the second phone was developing a voice of its own, popping into her brain at odd times during the day, reminding her she needed to find out how to get into it.

Who would be the best person to help her with that? Did she need to take it to the store? Would they unlock it for her? Or would she need oodles of proof that John was dead, she was his widow, and she had every right to see what was on that phone?

Would she need to find someone who operated at the edges of legality to open it? And where would she ever find someone like that? Somehow, she doubted her teacher friends would have a resource handy.

Once she finished breakfast the next morning, she put her calendar in front of her and dialed the attorney and made one more attempt to avoid the trip.

"Is there really no way I can simply sell it unseen?"

"There is no way," he said, "but why would you want to do that?"

"I don't understand what you're asking," Kelly said.

"Your grandmother was a wonderful woman who made significant contributions to the arts and artists by providing a safe haven to make mistakes and improve their skills as well as their emotional well-being. Many well-known artists, musicians, playwrights, and more held themselves in her debt. Is a week or so too much to sacrifice from your busy life to pay last respects to a woman who cared a great deal for you?"

The words hit Kelly like a punch to the gut.

"Sorry," he said. "That was over the top and unfair. I don't even know you except as a person Henrietta described. I cared a great deal for her. A great deal."

He was right. Despite all her doubts and neurosis, she needed to get on that plane and pay her respects.

"Okay," she said, "I'll pay a last visit to my grandmother's retreat."

Chapter Eight

Kelly stood in the rental car lot of the Glacier Park International Airport and stared to the east. The granite mountains she'd vaguely remembered seemed much more imposing, solidly blocking the way to the rest of America. Only two roads went through, she remembered: the twisty scenic road through Glacier National Park and the only slightly less convoluted route to the south of it.

Somehow, she was going to have to carve out some time for the park during the week she was here. Who knew when she'd get back again?

With a sigh, she got into the Toyota pickup truck she'd rented and started it up. Cleaning out a house often involved moving things out. At least she was prepared.

Navigating from the airport, she headed toward the park and then north to Whitefish, where she had an appointment to meet Bruce Henderson.

The attorney's office was in a small house just off the town's main drag. Many of the houses in that area had been converted to small businesses, leaving the main downtown area to the tourist shops and restaurants. The door was open, only the screen door keeping the few bugs out.

She pulled open the door and stepped into a comfortable waiting room. As soon as she settled into one of the overstuffed armchairs, an inner door opened and Bruce—at least she assumed it was Bruce—emerged from a hallway. His thinning hair revealed his years, but his physical appearance and movements were of a much younger man.

"Hello, Kelly," he said as she rose. "I feel like I know you already. Henrietta told me so much about you."

"Nice to meet you."

He led her back to the office where he went over the documents she needed to sign, as well as gave her a copy of the will. "Henrietta insisted I use as simple language as possible. None of that legal speak," he added in a voice close to that of an older woman who suffered no nonsense. He smiled, his dark brown eyes losing focus for a moment. He must have enjoyed a memory.

She glanced through the papers he'd given her, paying special attention to the clause about selling. "So no matter how long it takes," she said, "I must find my grandmother's note and show it to you before I can list the property."

"That's right."

"What if I never find it? What if she forgot to write it?"

"Look," he said, a touch of irritation in his voice, "I'm quite sure that your grandmother wrote that note before she even changed her will. She was not a woman to leave things to chance. Everything she did had a purpose."

"She wanted me to come back to Montana," Kelly said.

"It seems that way."

"But for what purpose? My home is in California. There is nothing for me here."

"Your grandmother apparently thought differently. I understand you're a teacher. So I'll tell you what. If you can't find it by the time summer ends, we'll talk about what to do next. Okay?"

Summer ends? She had a whole list of things to accomplish in California. She couldn't stay here for the summer.

"Thank you," she said. But she was going to find that note and fast. Even if she had to tear the entire retreat center apart.

Her grandmother's place was at the end of the point by the small town of Promise Cove on Whitefish Lake. Kelly made a left by Culver's General Store, a place she remembered for its old-fashioned candy counter but little else. Threading through the pines, she stopped only to open the gate to the center.

Not bothering to bring anything with her except her purse and keys, she carefully locked the truck before taking the path to the front door. Weeds and brush crowded the walkway, and the logs that made up the side of the house were graying.

Her hand trembled a bit as she inserted the key in the lock. The door, stiff with disuse, protested as she opened it,

The first thing she saw was the baby grand coated with a good layer of dust. When had that appeared? It had never been here during visits with her mother, only an aging upright. Next to it, the large glass window, which also needed a good cleaning, looked out over the cove and beyond to the lake that extended all the way to the town of Whitefish. As a young girl, she could sit in her favorite armchair, staring out at the water while her grandmother's soft, classical music played in the background and savory aromas drifted in from the kitchen on the other side of the great room.

The fireplace on the wall shared with the kitchen looked as if it hadn't been used in a while. There were no ashes, but a few logs and kindling had been set up to start a fire whenever she wanted. Who had been so kind?

To the right of the great room, the large dining room table and its set of mismatched chairs was as she remembered it, although it was also dusty. The kitchen toward the back was neat, with dated appliances. The new owner could take care of that.

She peeked in the mudroom. Freezer, washer, and dryer. Good. She had no idea where the nearest laundromat was. Bruce had assured her that the electricity was on and the water operated from a pump that had been checked out recently by a local handyman.

Returning to the great room, she looked around again. There was peace here. Her grandmother had accepted much that had happened to her, including her husband's desertion when Cynthia was only a few months old.

"It wasn't to be," her grandmother had told Kelly when she'd asked. "There was no point in making a fuss about it. Begging wouldn't bring him back to me, not in a good way. The only thing was to figure out a way to make a living and get on with it. Fortunately, this property had belonged to my parents, and we hadn't gotten around to putting his name on it, so I had a place to begin."

Kelly climbed the stairs to the second floor. The bathroom was here, along with a large bed covered with quilts, the iron bedstead dark against the log walls. A second fireplace rose above the one on the ground floor, serving as an anchor point for the sitting area that had been created with a large, braided rug and a padded rocking chair. Books and papers lined one outside wall, while the opposite wall held another large-paned window.

She turned the rocker toward the window and sank down. The great expanse of the lake lay in front of her, graying in the dimming light of evening.

What if she turned everything on its head and stayed in Promise Cove for the summer? The garage could wait. Her children didn't need her now; they could call Montana as well as California. If she ever decided to play again, there was a piano ready and waiting.

Not that she could see the point.

She stood so abruptly the rocking chair took a couple of hard thumps before going still again.

It was all nonsense. She'd find the note, show it to Bruce, and then get back to where she belonged.

Decision made, she retrieved her things, freshened up in the bathroom, and went back to the truck to fetch her lone suitcase.

Once she'd hung up her clothes, she walked around the property. The note could be anywhere. How was she going to explore all of those buildings in a week? Her grandmother wouldn't have made it that difficult, would she?

The note had to be in the house. That was the only thing that made sense.

Kelly headed back to the kitchen, hoping there was something there she could cook for dinner. After a day of flying, driving, seeing an attorney, and dealing with the house and its memories, she was out of energy for the people who'd be shopping at Custer's.

The same person who had set up the fires—but not dusted— had apparently thought of other needs. There were towels in the upstairs bathroom, the sheets on the bed appeared clean, and best of all, there were several cans of soup in the cabinet and pre-packaged meals in the freezer.

A microwave stood in one corner, so she opted for a freezer meal. While it cooked, she looked at the book she grabbed from one of the upstairs bookcases: *Montana Sunrises, Poems from a Quiet Land*. To her surprise, the author was her grandmother, Henrietta R. Paulson. She leafed through the book and settled on one to read.

Silent footsteps remain where others walked,
Native, white, coyote, wolf.
The whispers of their passing still linger
In the soft pines of the earth.

The ding of the microwave brought her back to reality, even though she was tempted to stay in the world her grandmother had created. What had it been like to live in this beautiful place and create poems that resonated with such bliss?

Chapter Nine

Kelly headed to the general store the next morning. Her angel of mercy had left dinner but nothing for breakfast. She should have stocked up in Whitefish, but she hadn't thought about life without a grocery store within a few miles.

The large clapboard building was two stories high with a good-sized porch on the front. Adirondack chairs lined the wall, interspersed with barrels and potted plants, many bright with summer foliage. An older couple was sitting at the far end, their gray heads together while they chatted over coffee.

The scene was interrupted when the screen door was flung open. A thin, wiry young man, his face in a scowl, rushed down the three stairs that led to the store. He was followed shortly by a teenager with uncontrolled brown curls, who yelled, "Wait, Gregg, I didn't mean it that way!"

Misunderstandings started young.

Kelly shook her head and headed inside, aware that the girl had looked like someone she'd known a long time ago, someone like…

"Maggie!" she exclaimed.

The woman behind the counter had the same curly brown hair. She stared at Kelly with bright green eyes that held a hint of caution. After finishing up with the customer in front of her, she came out from behind the counter.

"Kelly?" she asked. "Kelly Norcross? It *is* you." She held out her arms for an embrace and without hesitation, Kelly stepped into it.

They hugged for a long minute.

"It's good to see you," Kelly said when Maggie finally released her. "It's Richards now."

"Oh, yes, you got married. I remember that. But I know why you're here." Maggie grinned widely, then her expression crashed and burned. "I'm sorry about Henrietta. She was a wonderful person and so important to Promise Cove. Will you be staying? Will you be taking over the retreat center? It would be so great to get that up and running again."

"I'm sorry, but no. I'm going through a few things my grandmother left, then I'll be putting it on the market."

"Oh." Maggie's shoulders drooped along with her smile.

"My life is in California," Kelly defended her actions. "I have a job and a family there. Montana doesn't fit into the picture."

"Oh yes. You're married. Maybe your husband wants to come here?" The hopeful expression was back.

"Um, no. He passed away a year ago."

"That's terrible. Your kids must be so upset. No wonder you need to get back." Maggie looked around. "Let me get you a cup of coffee. On the house. A welcome back."

"That would be great. I'll also need some staples, including some breakfast food, to take back to the house."

"We can whip you up some breakfast for this morning, too. My mom makes a mean omelet." Maggie frowned. "It may take her a bit because Gregg isn't here to help out."

"Was Gregg the young man who ran out the door?" Kelly guessed.

"Yes. He and my daughter, Teagan, are seeing each other, and the road has never been smooth. I think he's too old for her, but you can't tell teenagers anything or they'll do the opposite."

"That is for sure," Kelly said. Lisa had been a terror that peaked somewhere when she was sixteen, but Peter's teen years had been surprisingly mild.

"And here I am blathering about myself when I should be getting you coffee and starting your breakfast order." Maggie pointed to a group of four tables by a large, mullioned window. "Take a seat, and I'll get coffee for both of us. It should be quiet for the next hour or so before the lunch rush starts. We don't do a lot of food business, but there are a few regulars who stop in almost every weekday. Nice weekends can be a bit crazy because tourists wander up here and find themselves hungry in the middle of nowhere."

Kelly headed for the tables and checked her phone. No messages.

The screen door opened and a young woman, toddler in tow, came in. The toddler grabbed at a candy bar and, when the woman didn't stop, began to wail. The mother quickly retrieved the bar, placed it on the counter, and said something to Maggie.

As Maggie rang up the snack, she spoke to the woman, but from the way the visitor was shaking her head, Kelly could tell Maggie's answer wasn't making sense. The toddler began to wail again, and her mother unwrapped the candy and handed it to her.

Finally, Maggie took out a map and pointed as she talked. With a weary swipe across her brow, the woman handed Maggie some bills, took the map and her daughter's hand, and left.

Catching Kelly's eye, Maggie shook her head, and just like she had that long-ago summer, Kelly knew exactly what she was thinking: That mother was in for a whole lot of trouble when her daughter became a teenage.

Who gave a toddler a candy bar at nine o'clock in the morning?

Maggie put the coffees on the table. "What a mess," she said. "She took a wrong turn when she lost the GPS signal, and this is the first sign of civilization she's seen."

"Where's she headed?" "Big Mountain. She was supposed to pick up her sister there early this morning. She took a wrong turn at Columbia Falls, wound up in Glacier, and has been trying to get back ever since."

"That really *is* lost," Kelly said.

"Yep, so tell me all about your life. What was your husband like? You have kids? How old?" Maggie's grin lit her whole face, while the light from the nearby window highlighted the freckles across her nose. Her olive-green T-shirt and jeans fit well over her still-slim silhouette.

Kelly gave her the bare bones of her existence, but as she talked, some of the burden of John's death began to lift. Gail was a practical friend, always ready to give advice or create a fun time to make her forget about things. Maggie was offering something more, almost a true understanding of emotions Kelly couldn't even name.

"I'm so sorry to hear all that," Maggie said when she was finished. "It must be very difficult to stop being with someone suddenly. Your kids sound great though. It's too bad you're not planning on being here long. I'd love to meet them."

"They really have their own lives. I couldn't even keep Peter in California for the summer, he is so set on starting his own life. His grandparents provided the perfect opportunity."

"It may be his own way of dealing with the pain of his father's death. Sometimes boys have more trouble expressing their emotions than girls."

Peter certainly had inherited his father's stoicism.

"What about you?" Kelly asked, awkwardly trying to figure out how to ask the whereabouts of Teagan's father.

"Oh." Maggie waved her hand. "Nothing special. I didn't have talent. Not like you or Alex."

Alexandria Porter. The other close friend Kelly'd had all those years ago.

"Do you hear from Alex?" she asked.

"Several times a week," Maggie said with a grin. "She lives on the point on the opposite side of the retreat center. She's a member of the art cooperative across the street. You'll have to go see it. She's got all these beautifully carved mirrors, lamps, tables, and more. She charges high prices and gets them. Once a tourist sees them, they can't leave them behind.

"And ..." she continued with a grin. "You have another old friend who exhibits there: Ryan Svoboda."

Ryan. Kelly's senses went on full alert. He was still here. Or back. Whatever. It didn't matter. She'd get to see him, find out if he was the same person she'd cared for a long time ago.

"Ryan? I didn't know he did anything artistic." Kelly tried to keep her voice casual.

"He didn't. I don't know how he got into it, but he's a pretty well-known art quilter. His prices put Alex's to shame."

"Huh. I wouldn't have thought that."

The door squealed open again.

"Hi, Tom," Maggie said as she stood. "You here for the usual?"

"Yep." Based on the uniform, Tom was some kind of law enforcement. His gaze never left Maggie as she walked to the counter, but it wasn't the look of a man watching for a misstep. No, unless she missed her guess, Tom the cop had a bit of a crush on her old friend.

And based on Maggie's attitude, she was clueless about the whole thing.

When she'd finished Tom's transaction, Maggie went down a hallway, returning with a steaming plate of hot eggs.

"Sorry it took so long. Mom got distracted. She told me she was trying to figure out how to put the simplicity of an egg into her next watercolor."

"She still does that? Do people buy her work?"

"Sometimes. She's got stuff in ART as well."

"ART?" Kelly asked.

"The art gallery. Across the street. Most of the locals call it ART because those are the only letters you can see on the sign at the top."

Kelly smiled. Things were different up here. In California, there would be a committee to make sure the sign was immediately repainted and upgraded to the current town standard.

She was about to ask again about Maggie's history when her friend interrupted her.

"Your grandmother did a lot for this community," Maggie said, her tone serious. "That retreat center supported a lot of people, people who have been out of work since she started failing. All her help was local, and she paid a good wage for maids, gardeners, handy people. If she knew someone needed help, she invented something for them to do."

"I'm glad she was able to do that," Kelly said, hoping the conversation wasn't going where she feared it was.

"It's left a hole, not only in our community but in the art world. Do you know how many people she helped get their start? Or famous people she helped heal so they could get back to doing what they loved? People came here from all over the world to sit by our bay, eat good food, and listen to her wisdom. That's one of the reasons her poetry was so popular. She could say things in ten words that would take ten days to fully figure out."

"I hadn't realized any of that."

"I'm sure you'll see the records," Maggie said. "They're up in the house or in the office in the barn."

Kelly almost groaned. An office would contain nothing but paper.

Maggie leaned across the table. "You have to find a way of opening it up again. If you can't, I don't know what will happen to Promise Cove."

"Maybe I can find someone to buy it who wants to run a retreat center," Kelly said hopefully.

Maggie shook her head. "It's got to be you. Henrietta had faith in you. She often said you have skills that you don't even know you have, beyond playing the piano beautifully." She took Kelly's hand. "Remember when Alex was struggling with her parents? Her dad was drinking too much, and her mom was threatening to leave them both. Alex thought the turmoil was all her fault. But you told her that couldn't be possible because they were supposed to be the adults. You got your grandmother to ask her to stay at the retreat center—a long sleepover—until her dad got some help."

"I'm sure Grandma did more than wait."

"Probably." Maggie laughed. "She wouldn't let things go until they were set right. But that isn't the point. *You* knew what needed to happen. You just needed her to help it along." She let go of Kelly's hand. "You were only twelve then. Think of what you could do now."

She'd totally forgotten the incident. Maggie was right; she'd instinctively known what to do. It had come from the same place inside her that was tapped when she was connected to the music—a space "in the zone," so totally absorbed that she lost all sense of time and place.

But that wasn't where she lived. Reality was different. No one could stay in the zone for long. They wouldn't survive.

"I can't stay, Maggie. No matter how much the town may need me, my life is in California. I have a job and house. It's where my children expect me to be. When I put the center on the market, I'm returning home."

The conversation shifted to less intense topics. Someone had come into the store, and Kelly took her opportunity to finish her shopping and leave. Time to get going. The sooner she went back to California to resume her life, the better.

Chapter Ten

A blue Ford Explorer was parked next to the house. Good thing she had locked up. She pulled in next to it, grabbed her parcels, and headed around the building to the front door that looked out over the flower garden. While she couldn't see anyone, she could hear someone hammering out of sight.

Should she call 911? Was there anyone to help besides the man who'd been in the store?

She looked around for something solid. By the time someone got here, the person would be gone. This was rough-and-tough Montana. It was up to her to defend her property.

And she was so ill-suited to the task, she had to stifle a laugh as she searched through the kitchen drawers. Finally, armed with a rolling pin, she marched out the front door and stalked in the direction of the noise.

A tall, sturdily built man stood by one of the cabins, hammering a board beside a window. As she drew closer, walking as stealthily as she could, he seemed to tense slightly, then relax.

"I know you're there," he called out. "Wait a moment while I get this last nail in."

How did he know? She'd been quiet.

Finally, he turned, his hammer still in his hand. She'd last ten seconds in a good fight. But she gripped her rolling pin more firmly.

She immediately recognized his dark brown eyes. He'd always said more with them than with words.

The rolling pin dropped to the ground.

"Ryan."

"Hello, Kelly. I heard you were in town."

Her heart beat faster, and her breath seemed snatched away by the air. Ryan had aged well. His brown hair was shaggy, as if he cut it himself, and his face, while still mostly unlined, held decades of experience.

They stood there awkwardly for a moment, then he put down his hammer and held out his hand. "Good to see you again."

"You too," she said. "But *why* are you here? I don't remember hearing about anyone coming to do repairs."

"Henrietta asked me to do a few things around here."

"May I point out that my grandmother has been dead several months?"

"I do know that. You should have come to her service. It was a grand affair, just like she wanted. A huge party. Some of the most well-known musicians played for hours."

"I ... I didn't know about it," she said. The space between them that had seemed almost intimate a few seconds before widened into a deep crack.

"Ah. Your mother kept it from you."

"I suppose. If she even knew." Kelly and her mother might have their differences, but no one else was allowed to participate. "So how did this ghost get you to do her chores?"

Ryan laughed. "I could tell you she appeared to me in a dream, but the truth is, Bruce emailed me and sent me a list of things Henrietta had wanted done around the place. But she'd only wanted them done once you'd arrived to take over the property."

"I'm not staying," she said.

"Too bad," he said, his eyes almost changing color as he retreated without taking a step. "Okay then. I have my instructions and you're here, so if you don't mind, I'll get back to it and leave you be. Have a good day." He turned and retrieved his hammer before disappearing.

Come back, she wanted to scream. For some insane reason, she needed to know every last detail of his life. Why was he doing chores for Henrietta instead of working on quilts as Maggie had indicated? Had he been in love? Had a family?

She picked up the rolling pin and headed back to the house. *You set me up, Grandma. You set me up, and it didn't end well.*

What had he expected?

Ryan tapped in some nails and held the board in place. Taking a mighty swing, he cursed as the nail immediately bent.

What he hadn't expected was to have a fire set in his belly by the mere appearance of a girl he'd cared for a long time ago. He carefully avoided the word "love," although he'd used it to describe his feelings for Kelly when he was fourteen—at least to himself. "Love" was no longer in his vocabulary.

He'd known he hadn't truly been in love with his wife; his feelings for Lorelei didn't burn nearly as bright as they had for Kelly. But they'd seemed to love enough, at least for a while. No, it was while working as a New York City cop and watching what human beings did to each other that had eradicated the word.

He looked in the direction Kelly had gone. She'd been so sweet, so vulnerable as a young girl. All he'd wanted to do was protect her so she could make her beautiful music, the music that had set his soul free.

But she'd made it clear she wasn't here for long. Best keep to himself and avoid her.

Yanking out the bent nail, he picked up a new one and tapped it in.

Once she stowed her groceries, Kelly changed into work clothes. She searched through the CDs by the downstairs sound system and started a thundering Beethoven symphony to suit her mood. Then she returned to the papers upstairs. She tore through them, not stopping to give more than a cursory glance to their contents, although some seemed to beg her to linger.

At the end of an hour, she had nothing to show.

She repeated the exercise with all the drawers in the house. She had to get out of here before old memories and dreams ensnared her in their web. The past was exactly that, and it needed to stay where it was. Reality was another decade of teaching, supporting her children, and looking forward to grandchildren to pamper.

Grabbing her water bottle, she headed to the barn. If that is where her grandmother kept her office, it was the most likely place for the note to be. It was also where she'd find the instructions on running the place, documents she would dutifully pass along to whoever bought it. She'd find the note, set the sale in motion, ship back whatever she wanted to keep, and wipe her hands of this place and its ghosts.

Ryan was working outside the barn when she arrived.

"Door's open," he said when she started going through her key ring.

"How did you get in?" she asked.

"Henrietta gave me a set of keys ages ago."

She couldn't have him appearing whenever he wanted. "Yes, well, I'll need them back as soon as you're through today."

"Yes, ma'am." As she opened the door, he added, "Sounds like you're upset about something or other."

"What do you mean?"

"You'll see."

She stepped into the barn and was almost blown back by the

effect of Beethoven at full blast.

"How do you turn it down?" she yelled.

He pointed toward a room at the back of the barn. "It's in the office," he shouted.

She hesitated a nanosecond to see if he'd offer to handle it, but he went right back to work.

Ugh. She'd made him angry, and there was no use in trying to fix it. He'd be gone soon.

She raced to the back of the barn and realized the office door was locked. Frantically going through her keys as the music thumped, she finally located the right one. Once she found the sound system, she punched buttons until silence mercifully descended.

After a deep breath, she looked around the office. There was a lot of paper, but there was also a new laptop sitting in the middle of the desk. Bruce had given her the password in the documents he'd handed her.

Would her grandmother hide a note there?

Probably not. Her grandmother was very precise with words, and a note meant something written.

As Kelly started looking through things, her enthusiasm, as well as the embers of her anger, fell away. There wouldn't be anything here. This office was all about her grandmother's business and retreats. Only an aging photo showed anything personal.

Kelly picked it up. The intricate wooden frame held a photo of her at a young age, arms around two other girls. All were smiling. In the edge of the background, a boy lingered. From the angle of his head, it appeared he was staring intently at the three of them.

Their lives were beginning back then. Heartache and happiness lay before them. There had been a feeling of expectancy in their lives, a possibility for greatness.

Had she given it all away for routine and security?

"Mind if I come in?" Ryan called from the doorway. "Henrietta wanted me to take a look at some of the cupboard doors that are sagging."

"Sure," she said, giving the office one more look. The note wasn't going to be in any of the usual places paper might be. She was sure of that now.

She walked into the larger space. With her rush to the office, she hadn't really had time to take it in. The back wall across from the main door, where Ryan was working, consisted of cabinets and cupboards that ran all the way across. She walked to one close to her and discovered a treasure of art supplies. Opposite the cabinets was a round table with chairs. The remaining wall, opposite Henrietta's office, had a small kitchen area with microwave, coffeepot, electric water heater, and refrigerator as well as kitchen supplies.

She went to Ryan. "Sorry," she began. "I've been nothing but rude. The only excuse is that this is all so unexpected, and I'm a bit thrown by it."

"Apology accepted. I have only a few more things to do before I get out of your hair. Then you can do whatever you have to and move on."

She clasped her hands together, trying to figure out how to smooth things over. Glancing at the kitchen area, she asked, "Do you want a cup of coffee? I'm sure I can figure out how to make it."

He finally looked at her. Close up, she could see more detail in the fine lines that defined his face. Some of them seemed etched there by worry and grief. Her first assumption of a happy life, hadn't been correct. What had happened to him? But the smile he gave her was genuine, an echo of the boy she'd known.

"That would be nice."

She readied the coffee, sneaking glances at him as she worked. Whatever had attracted her physically as a teen, when she had no idea what that was all about, was still there. Ryan wasn't classically handsome, but he had the rugged angles of a man used to being active.

He was just finishing up when the coffee was ready. She poured it into one of the handmade mugs that hung on a rack and brought it to him.

"So what have you been doing for the last few decades?" she asked.

"This and that," he said. "And you?"

"The same."

He grinned at the standoff. "What are you looking for?"

"How do you know I'm looking for something?"

"I heard rumors. Small town, you know. Tale is that Henrietta left you a puzzle to solve."

"Nothing so Gothic," she said. "I just have to find the note she left me, read it, then I can list the place and head back to my real life."

"Too bad. Summer's the best time around here. You should really think about staying for a while. I might be persuaded to take you hiking. There are some great views of the lake and mountains that are easy trails." The smile blossomed into the expression that had always made her feel like she was someone special.

"I ... that would be ... interesting," she stammered out.

He roared with laughter.

Return to Promise Cove

"You have been a long time away. You'd take any chance to get into the mountains when you were younger. Said they sang to you." He shook his head. "Who have you become, Kelly Richards? And what's it going to take to bring you home to yourself?" He slugged down his coffee and picked up his tools. "Think about it. What do you have in your life right now that's more important than being in the last remaining best place in the country?"

"I have kids, things to do, school to prepare for," she said rapidly.

"No husband?"

"He died."

"Oh, I'm sorry."

"Thank you."

"And your kids. What are they up to?"

She gave him a brief sketch of Lisa and Peter.

"So your kids aren't even at home," he said. "School doesn't start for another few months. Do it, Kelly. You owe it to the kid you used to be. One more summer fling."

"I'll think about it."

"That's good. I need to get some supplies to fix the cabinets." He pulled out his phone. "Give me your number, and I'll give you a call before I come back. That way I won't startle you."

She recited the digits. He entered them and then headed for the door. Pausing, he said, "Henrietta always knew us better than we knew ourselves. If I were you, I'd look for that note where you are most yourself." He waved and disappeared ... without returning the keys.

Where she was most herself.

Suddenly, she knew exactly where to find that note.

She dashed to the front door, ready to put her plan in action, then she stopped.

Ryan stood under the same tree he had in the photo in Henrietta's office. When Kelly appeared, he studied her, his expression serious, before a slow, bittersweet smile developed.

"Stay," he said, barely loud enough for her to hear.

Then he waved and headed to his vehicle.

She watched him get in and head out of sight, a small hollow in her chest echoing the emptiness. Her gaze moved away from the empty spot and panned the scene before her: a riot of bright flowers segued into tall grass, with cabins of various shapes and sizes dotting the space between her and the sparkling waters of the lake.

Her grandmother had named the cabins after Greek goddesses and muses. Athena was the first for the goddess of art, Terpsichore the second for poetry and dancing, Melpomene for tragic drama, the

Euterpe for music. She could almost feel Grandma's arms enclosing her, making her feel safe no matter what storms went on around her. It had been a time when she didn't need to be in charge, a time to play, to dream. She turned toward the spot where Ryan had lingered.

Maybe to love.

There was no real purpose to returning to California. Here, she might have a chance to remember who she was before claiming the roles of wife and mother. It was only a summer.

She'd stay.

Chapter Eleven

Kelly opened the lid to the keyboard. A pale blue envelope sat on the ivories and ebonies. She picked up the envelope, and a trace of spiciness she couldn't identify drifted toward her. Her fingers caressed the paper, searching for an echo of her grandmother's hands. Finally, she slid her finger under the flap.

Dearest Kelly,

I'm so glad you have opened the keyboard. Keep it open. I bought this for you after that last summer, hoping it would lure you back. I loved to hear you play, your soul guiding your fingers to just the right tone.

I wish I were here to listen again, but fate hasn't given me that time. Be sure I will be listening in the whispers of the wind through the pines and spying on you from the clouds drifting overhead. We have a connection that death cannot break.

When you married John, I was sad because I knew you were giving up a large piece of yourself to conform to your mother's view of the right way to live. She had always been in rebellion against how she was raised—an only child of a hippie poet who lived in the woods. I suppose I can't blame her, but I wish she hadn't put you in the same box. You didn't belong there.

Think of this as a second chance to be who you really are.

You have all you need in Promise Cove: friends, fresh air, and the possibility of true love if you are brave enough to take it. John was a good husband and father, but never the right man for you. Forgive me for being blunt, but it's the privilege of those who have passed on.

I hope you find it in your heart to continue my work, but if not, at least give yourself a chance to live and love fully. It's what makes a good life.

Love you forever,
Grandma

Kelly reread the letter several times before placing it on the black surface of the piano.

Then she lifted the top to the piano bench and found the faded yellow cover of Chopin's études. Another blue note read "the rest are in the bookcase."

After pulling out the music, she laid the note with the other and sat down. The piano was magnificent, a high-level Yamaha that must have cost several thousands of dollars. Poetry had never seemed that lucrative an occupation.

She began at the beginning. Her hands, used to the narrow range and easy rhythm of middle school songs, stretched to adjust to the simple but more demanding pieces. It was going to take a while to get back into practice. She went on to the second piece before stopping, her hands starting to protest with the unfamiliar movements.

That would be first thing to do. She had the summer to practice. If she did it right after breakfast was cleaned up, she'd develop a routine.

Something that no one else would interrupt or complain about.

But what to do about the property?

Grabbing paper and pen, she headed back outside, the ring of keys that had been hanging on a kitchen hook by her side.

The floral garden needed tending. *Hire someone for garden*, she wrote. Although her grandmother had been an avid gardener, that particular bug had never bitten Kelly. Some volunteer lettuce in the vegetable garden looked ready. She'd have to pick a few leaves to go with the sandwich fixings she'd picked up at the store for lunch.

The first cabin—Athena's—seemed to be in good shape. Kelly smiled as she saw the boards Ryan had put up yesterday, each board fitting perfectly. As she inspected the rest of the outside, she had no idea what to look for. She'd need a professional opinion. He might be able to help her. It would be nice to have him around, see if she could pry his story out of him.

The inside of the cabin would need cleaning, but it seemed intact. A trim, single bed, desk, armchair, and small microwave made up most of the furniture, with lamps at the desk and armchair. From there, someone could see a glimpse of the lake through a small window.

A hallway led past a compact bathroom to a large space with a greater view of the lake and skylights currently covered with pine needles and leaves. An easel and cupboard made up the furniture. Drop cloths lay in the corner.

Athena would be proud.

Kelly made some notes and closed the cabin back up. The building was restorative, the perfect place for someone to create or rest.

Terpsichore's abode was similar, except the back room had a dance floor, barre, and sound system, as well as a bank of mirrors against one wall. Melpomene had a bookcase full of scripts and recording and video equipment.

Euterpe's domain beckoned her, with its spinet piano and chairs for cellists and other performers. Cupboards contained a variety of music, plenty of rosin for bows, and reeds for wind instruments.

With a page full of notes, Kelly continued around the path that led to the firepit and chairs. She sank into one and took in the view to the mountains beyond. Sunsets must be spectacular from this spot. It looked like the chairs had been recently stained, and the firepit had new brass fittings. A sweep and it would be fine.

The outbuildings yielded garden equipment, a tractor fitted with a snow blade and a relatively new RAV4 with the keys in it. She'd have to call Bruce and ask him about it. If she could convince someone to take her back to the airport, she might be able to save on rental fees.

Ryan would be able to let her know what was going on with the barn. She couldn't see anything obvious, other than a cleaning. With some simple cleanup and the right marketing, she could find a buyer who would keep this property as a retreat center and keep the townspeople employed.

All in good time. For now, it was time to celebrate her decision to run away from home for the summer.

Pulling her phone from her pocket, she found the number for Culver's and punched it in. She was in luck. Maggie answered.

"Do you have wine?" she asked after she'd announced herself.

"Of course we have wine. Why?"

"What are you doing tonight?"

"Why?" Maggie repeated.

"Do you think Alex is busy tonight?"

"Why?" Maggie asked for the third time.

"Because we need to get together. I'm staying for the summer." Kelly took a deep breath. It was a pretty big ask. Why should the women invest in a short friendship with her? "You two were my best friends once. I want to get to know you again. Could you come over? Tonight? Please?"

She hadn't seen them in decades. What if they said no?

Silence stretched out. Then she heard the register ring and Maggie thanking someone.

"Sorry," Maggie said. "A customer came up right as I was about to answer."

Kelly waited.

"I'll check with Alex, but I can come tonight. Or tomorrow night. Or the next one. It's not like I have a full social calendar."

"Great. I'll be there this afternoon to pick up what I need."

"I'll let you know then what Alex says." Before Maggie could hang up the phone, Kelly heard her yell, "Boys! Either pay for those or put them back. I'll call your mothers if you don't!"

Kelly chuckled. It was going to be a great summer!

♡♡

When Alex and Maggie arrived around seven, there were awkward hugs before Kelly led them to the firepit. She'd found an old gardening table in one of the sheds, brushed it off, and repurposed it as a drinks and snack table. As she'd often done for impromptu parties for her husband, she'd decorated the table with a few cloth napkins she'd found, along with vases of fresh-cut flowers. A small battery-powered lamp was at the ready, but she seemed to remember from her summers that it stayed light until close to ten, if not longer, in June.

She'd prepared a basket of bags of chips and jars of dips, along with serving dishes and small paper plates. Wineglasses and corkscrews were tucked into the basket. The wine was already waiting by the pit.

Her two once-friends surveyed the goodies.

"She's learned how to plan a party," Alex said.

"That's true," Maggie replied.

"It came with the territory," Kelly said, leading them down the path.

"And present it nicely," Alex added when she saw the setup.

"It's easy," Kelly said, beginning to feel anything but easy.

"For some people," Maggie said.

"I can teach you," Kelly said.

"That's one possibility," Alex replied, grabbing a wine opener and swiftly undoing the cork of the Merlot Kelly had picked up along with the chardonnay.

"What do you mean?" Kelly asked, assembling the snacks and the bowls.

"We can talk about it later," Maggie said, tackling the other bottle of wine. "For now, tell us all the details about what you've been up to over the last few decades."

"Only if you do the same," Kelly said as she lit the fire.

When they were settled, she gave them her brief history, glossing over any sadness she'd felt with Peter's sudden decision to go to Boston early and the discovery of the second phone in John's office—a phone she'd inexplicably thrown into her bag at the last minute when she left.

"Very traditional," was Alex's only comment.

Her old friend was a bit taller than she'd been when they were young, and of a lean build. Her hands were strong and calloused, but her most obvious feature was a pale shroud of sorrow that seemed to invisibly wrap her in its folds.

What was the story there?

"How satisfyingly normal," Maggie said. "I'm very jealous."

"Any refills?" Kelly asked, standing rather than asking the others about their lives. Her mother's training had kicked in. One didn't pry. At least one didn't do so obviously.

"I'm also jealous that you've already gotten Ryan's attention," Maggie continued.

"What do you mean?" Kelly asked, raising her empty glass to see if again she could get any takers.

Alex handed her hers, but Maggie kept talking.

"He came into the store today to get some supplies, and he had a smile on his face."

"So?" Kelly asked.

"He never smiles," Alex filled in.

"Never?" Kelly asked.

"Nope," Maggie said. "At least not since he got home from New York. He was a cop there." She shuddered. "He probably had a lot of stress with that job. But he was smiling today. I asked him what he'd been up to, and he told me he'd been here, helping you with some repairs."

"Henrietta left him a list." Kelly refilled the glass and handed it to Alex.

"I don't think it was Henrietta making him smile," Alex said.

"It's nothing at all," Kelly said, grasping for a new topic. "The man simply had a good day. No need to make anything out of it. But let's plan some fun things for the summer. I'll be here until the end of August."

"Hurray!" Maggie said, raising her glass. Alex joined her, and they leaned toward each other and clinked. "You're staying for the summer. Montana will work its magic on you, and you won't have any choice but live here forever."

"I was wondering," Kelly said when she'd settled back in her chair, "how Teagan got here."

"The usual way," Maggie replied. "I gave birth." A sense of barely suppressed laughter punctuated the sentence.

"After high school," Maggie began softly, "I started at the

community college in Kalispell. I rented a room from an old friend of my mother during the week and came home to help out here on weekends. By that time, my parents had bought the store and were trying to make it work."

"I thought your mother was an artist," Kelly said.

"She is." Maggie smiled. "And she was totally in love with my father. It was his dream to own the store. He remembered it from when he was younger; it was a place where the owner always had time and candy for the summer kids."

Kelly vaguely recalled Maggie's dad as a short, slightly overweight man with thin, dark hair. He'd always had a smile and time to listen to her. As briefly as she'd known him, he was special to her.

Maggie got up to refill her glass and brought back a bag of chips and a jar of dip.

"There are serving bowls," Kelly said automatically, just as she had to her kids.

"It's Montana," Alex said. "We don't dirty bowls unnecessarily." Like her body, her voice was all angles. She'd become a little bitter in the intervening years. If they ever got past Maggie's story, Kelly wanted to know what had happened to defeat someone who'd never stopped smiling as a kid.

"Be nice," Maggie said. "Kelly's been away for a long time. She's forgotten, that's all. We need to give her a little time."

"Sorry," Alex said, somewhat automatically.

It sounded like it hadn't been the first time Maggie had swept up after her friend's words.

"I remember your dad," Kelly said. "He was a nice man."

"Yes. He doted on Mom. I guess it was what I was looking for when I hooked up with Paul."

"I think you're still looking for it," Alex said.

"Probably." Maggie looked at Kelly. "You'd think I could tell this story easily after all these years. Teagan's seventeen now. One more year of high school and she's gone."

"Unless Gregg convinces her otherwise," Alex said.

"Over my dead body. My daughter has potential. She's going to get the chance I never had. Anyway, to finish this up, I did one year, came back here that summer to work. Unfortunately, my dad died that summer. Mom was hopeless at running the store, but she wouldn't sell it. So I stepped in. It satisfied me. I didn't really have ambitions or talents."

"And then Paul came along," Alex said.

"Yes. He was perfect. He played all the right notes, reminding me

58

of Dad, bringing me flowers he picked or a special heart-shaped rock he'd found. I was head over heels almost instantly. Even though I knew he was on the lawyer track, just here for a long summer holiday before grad school, I totally believed what he told me, that he was going to give it all up and become a fishing guide."

Kelly knew where this was going to go.

"Some men have no character," she said.

"And most of them are lawyers." Alex grinned from the other side of the fire.

"Ain't that the truth," Maggie said. With unspoken agreement they all rose and clinked their glasses.

"To good women and friends," Maggie said.

"Indeed," Alex said.

"Yes," Kelly agreed, her heart filling with the memories of whispered nighttime confidences and hope for the future.

Chapter Twelve

As she'd promised herself, Kelly dutifully sat at the piano the next morning and practiced. Along with the études, she dredged up memories of old scales and finger exercises. After a half hour, her fingers ached. Fifteen minutes later, her hands and wrists screamed.

She stopped. It was so little. She used to practice for hours in the day, in the morning for exercises and in the afternoon for practice pieces. She'd have to try harder.

Gathering some cleaning supplies, she stalked off to the Athena cabin and began to clean. It didn't take much, but it worked off the excess energy from the truncated practice.

Maggie's story from the night before had gone down predictable lines. Paul had gotten her to have sex by telling her he was in love with her, promising to stay in Montana and give up his plans to be an attorney. But he was gone by early September, leaving her a cell phone number and a broken heart.

At least that's all she thought he'd left until her period failed to appear. When she told him she was pregnant, he'd told her it wasn't his and refused to get a paternity test. She'd reluctantly told her mother.

Maggie's mother, Elaine, told her daughter there was more than enough love in Promise Cove to welcome a new family member.

What would it have been like to have unconditional love like that? Oh, Kelly's mother did love her daughter, but the emotion came with so many rules, it was difficult at times to distinguish between Cynthia's approval of Kelly's actions and her unbiased approval of who Kelly was as a human being.

When she finished, she gathered up the linens but left the cleaning supplies. She'd tackle the next cabin tomorrow. It was time to head to town. Alex had let her know ART would be open that afternoon and seemed particularly eager for Kelly to see some of her pieces.

Before heading out, she cleaned up and debated her clothing choices. It was almost an outing, and surely that demanded more than jeans and a T-shirt. Pulling a comfortable teal cotton blouse from the closet, she paired it with some simple khaki capris.

She pulled into the lot of the log building and parked next to a newer model Subaru with Idaho plates. It was a good size for an art place in the middle of nowhere, but apparently it had a reputation as a destination place, which would explain the relatively new sweets shop up the main road. She needed to stop in there to see if they had any salted caramel.

When she opened the wooden door, she immediately saw Alex's urging had nothing to do with her artwork. Ryan was behind the counter, chatting to an older couple who must belong to the other car in the lot. She hesitated for a moment.

He spotted her, and his gaze pinned her in place for a few seconds before he returned his attention to the couple before him. Released from his inspection, she drifted to the far end of the gallery and started looking. Soon she was entranced by unique pottery, colorful woven table runners, and warm, exquisitely knit shawls in earthy tones. Mixed in with the clothing were racks of earrings and necklaces, perfect to pick up for Christmas gifts. Gail would love the graceful silver spirals, and even her mother would be pleased with an etched bracelet. A colorful stone necklace would be stunning on Lisa.

It was only when she turned around that she saw it.

The mammoth quilt dominated the far wall. A forest scene composed of thin strips of blues, silvers, and grays highlighted by spheres of brown and evergreen. She walked toward it just as the background music switched to "Afternoon of a Faun," one of her favorite pieces of music. She'd seen the ballet only once, but it had been as complex and engaging as the original symphonic poem.

As she drew closer, her eyes began to pick out something else hidden in the forest. At first she thought her imagination was playing tricks. Were those hands holding a pipe? And a ram's horns at the edge of a tree trunk? A cloven foot was hidden in the bushes at the bottom of the same tree.

"Very good," Ryan said behind her. "Most people don't spot it right away."

Her heart jumped. "The music was a hint," she said. "You did that on purpose."

"Could be. I thought you might recognize it."

She felt the faint breeze of his breath on her neck and stepped away. They weren't kids anymore. She had no interest in anything brief but intense, as she expected anything with him might be. It wasn't fair to even give him the perception of leading him on.

On that rule, she agreed with her mother 100 percent.

She stepped to one side.

"You did this?" she asked, still absorbing the details. Up close, she could see how the quilting emphasized certain lines while leaving the fabric to take up the design in others.

"Yes."

"It's amazing," she said. "Do people actually buy things like this?"

He laughed. "Museums, corporate offices, cultural centers, you'd be surprised. I know I was."

"How did you get started? I don't mean to sound sexist, but ..."

"I know. Quilting is usually thought of as a woman's occupation. There are a good number of us men, particularly in the art quilt world."

Stepping back far enough to take in the whole piece again, she let herself feel the emotions coming from the design, just as she would while listening to a piece of music. She also became aware that the sound system had continued to play Debussy, soft notes woven together in a tapestry. She lost herself in enchantment.

She was vaguely aware of a customer coming in, browsing, and leaving. But Ryan let her be until, with a sigh, she let go of the dream and walked to the counter where he was sitting.

"It's amazing," she said.

"What was it like?" she asked softly. "Being a cop in New York?"

"Ah, well." He moved a small carved bear an inch farther away from the counter edge. "Probably as bad as you think, but not without its good times."

"Were you hurt?" Somehow she had to know.

"Depends on your definition," he said with a sad smile. "But that's a story for another time. Let's talk about happier things. Rumor has it you found the note, but you're still staying for a while."

"Only for the summer."

"It's a beginning."

"No." She needed to be quite firm on that. "What you said about the summer was true, but I need to be back in California by late August. And even before that, I need to go to Boston to make sure my son is settled in school."

"We'll need to make sure you fit everything in before you go, then," he said.

"What do you mean?"

"You have to have the full Montana experience: hiking, kayaking, zip-lining, driving the Going to the Sun Road. All of it. Let's start with hiking."

"I don't hike anymore," she said.

"Everybody hikes. It's just like walking, only longer."

"And over rocks and logs and stuff. And mostly uphill."

"What goes up must come down," he quipped.

Return to Promise Cove

"No thank you."

"There's an easy hike with a view at the end that will take your breath away." He leaned closer. "And you'll be with me. I'll make sure the bears don't get you."

"See? Bears. Another reason to stay in town."

"Are you always so closed-minded?" he asked.

"It's not that. It's simply knowing what I can and can't do. Being practical."

"And you know you can't hike because ...?"

There was no reason. No reason whatsoever. Other than she didn't want to be alone in the woods with him. Even standing in the normalcy of a store, with a counter between them, emotions were bubbling somewhere around her middle.

"Where are Alex's pieces?" she asked instead of answering his question.

"Let me show you. She's a celebrated artist these days. Much the rage in Hollywood. I'm surprised you don't know about her, living nearby and all."

"How do you know where I live?"

"I was a cop. We were friends once. I wanted to know you were okay."

"Oh." She followed him to a corner of the store she'd missed. "Wow."

Contrary to the woman, Alex's work was swirls and curves instead of sharp angles. Flowing hair from a woman's face descended, circling the lower half of a variegated wood mirror. Tree limbs curved to support a small lamp. Even tables had a sense of flow about them.

"Doesn't seem like Alex, does it?" Ryan said.

"Not at all." She ran her fingers over the lamp. It would be perfect in the sitting nook her grandmother had created upstairs. Perfect until she looked at the price tag.

Alex must be doing very well, indeed.

"How do people even find this place? It's in the middle of nowhere."

"That's as much your grandmother's doing as anything else," Ryan said, caressing a whimsical rocking chair. "When she was starting her retreat center, she quickly realized she needed some kind of web presence. She found someone in Bozeman to pull a website together for her, but she wasn't happy with what it looked like. Searching for a while brought her to Makalia. Makalia is a very unique young woman. Her grandparents came here at the end of the Vietnam War, part of the group Jerry Daniels settled near Missoula. She went to the university, then left to work in California." Ryan grimaced. "Montana was a bit slow catching up to the rest of the world in technology."

He picked up a pair of drop earrings with polished brown stones. "These would look great on you. Almost the color of your eyes." He held them next to her face.

Her heart doubled its pace.

"So my grandmother hired Makalia?" she asked, taking a step away from the jewelry.

He put the earrings back.

"More than that. She encouraged her to expand her horizons and create her own company instead of working for others. Eventually, Makalia returned here and built a house and workplace up the mountain."

"I think I've caught a glimpse of that place or at least the sun glinting off the windows. It's pretty big. And she lives up there all by herself?"

"Kind of. There are relatives constantly coming and going. Some stay for a long time; others are gone the next day. She seems happy, but we all keep hoping there's someone for her someday."

Another of his quilts hung nearby. This one was smaller: a tree with a snarl of branches. Mischievous eyes below conical caps peeked out from the foliage.

"So your website does all the work?"

"Pretty much," he said. "Makalia's a genius. The presentation of our work is beautiful and clear, the shopping cart intuitive and easy. She's even found a local shipping company to take care of that end."

"All you need to do is create," Kelly said with a grin.

"Yep." He laughed. "If only it were that easy."

"I know," she surprised herself by saying. "I tried playing a piece on the piano today. I'm out of shape."

"Well, good for you," he said, his voice soft.

They gazed at each other for a long second, then she pulled herself back from the brink of whatever there was between them. "Thanks for giving me the tour," she said, "but that's the only reason I came in here."

"Okay. What else do you need?" His smile seemed to say he'd give her whatever he was able.

"Can you please help me out by doing an inspection of the retreat center? I need to know if there are any major repairs lurking before I put it on the market."

"Sure enough. Only one condition."

"What's that?" she asked.

"You go hiking with me on Friday."

She debated for a few moments. In spite of what she'd told him, there had been a time when she enjoyed getting off into the woods with a group of friends, tackling some impossible hike, and enjoying the view and the accomplishment at the top. But she was too out of shape to start again.

"You're not," he said with a grin.

"I'm not what?"

"Too old."

"How did you know?" she asked.

"Intuition." He tapped his index finger on his temple. "An artist's birthright. It's an easy walk. You'll do fine. Do we have a deal?"

"I guess."

"Less than enthusiastic, but it will do. I'll text you with the details. See you soon."

Ryan stared at the door long after it was closed. What was that line from *Casablanca*? "Of all of the gin joints …"

Why did she have to come back? She'd be here a few short weeks, then turn her back on the community, on him, a second time. While she didn't have any say in her first disappearance, this time she'd be leaving all on her own.

And more fool him, he was voluntarily going to spend time with her, give his heart a chance to break into pieces a second time.

He was an idiot.

Chapter Thirteen

Kelly stuck to her commitment. Up in the morning to practice, then off to clean at least one cabin. As she worked, she kept track of the little things she noticed, like a dripping sink faucet or a loose hinge on a cabinet door. Most of these things she'd take care of herself. Years of waiting for plumbers, electricians, and handymen to arrive had forced her to learn simple repairs or go mad with frustration.

She'd just finished her work in the Euterpe cabin, where she'd spent a few extra minutes checking out the piano, when her phone rang.

"Hi, honey," she said, recognizing the number as her daughter's. "What's up?"

"Where are you?" Lisa asked. "When I talked to Grandma Norcross last week, she said you'd been forced to go to Montana to clean up some mess. What's going on?"

Kelly laughed at Cynthia's characterization.

"I'm in a small—no, make that tiny— town in the northwest corner. Your great-grandmother had a retreat center here. She'd invite artists, musicians, dancers, even theater people to spend time here to recover their creative juices."

"Really? That's so cool!"

She should have brought her children to Montana, but her mother had always insisted on her time. John's parents were no better. Striving to be the perfect wife, mother, and daughter, Kelly had put away her desires and went along with everyone else.

"I spent a lot of time here as a child," she said. "Grandma left it all to me when she died last winter, but I found out about it only recently. In fact, I got the letter the weekend you came to visit me."

A picture of the envelope on her porch flashed through her mind. California seemed so far away right now.

"What are you going to do?" Lisa asked.

"Oh, fix it up and sell it. My life's in California with you and Peter, to give you a place you can call home."

"Thanks, Mom."

"How are you doing?" Kelly asked. "Work any better? Are you tolerating Andrew's parents any better?"

"Everything's okay. Andrew and I went to Napa last weekend.

It's so beautiful. We stayed at a beautiful inn near St. Helena, drank fabulous wine, and had great meals."

"Sounds wonderful. Relaxing."

"Yes. Andrew even ordered me a massage. I loved it! I love him. He's so good to me."

"He sounds like a nice young man with a good future. You can't ask for anything better."

"Is that why you picked Dad?" Lisa asked.

"I'm sure it was part of the reason. We loved each other, of course." Why *had* she picked John? And had they ever really been in love?

After a few more minutes of chatter, they disconnected.

Kelly had no sooner put her cleaning supplies away when her phone dinged. It was a message from Maggie: Come for lunch at the store. Alex is here, too.

"On my way," she texted back.

After a quick change into a new T-shirt and shorts, she headed to town. She immediately spotted Maggie and Kelly at one of the tables in the store. A couple of cans of soda and bags of chips lay next to them, along with what looked like a stack of papers.

"Hi," Kelly said and sat down. "I'm starved—cleaned Euterpe this morning."

"What?" Maggie asked.

"A cabin," Alex said. "Henrietta named them after Greek gods or something. Remember?"

"Muses and one goddess," Kelly corrected. "Should I go up to order? Who's manning the counter?" she asked, her questions covering her sudden nervousness. She was an outsider again, although she wasn't sure why.

"Teagan's got it. My mother is whipping up one of her special sandwiches for us. No idea what will appear."

"But it will be good," Alex said.

"What are those?" Kelly pointed to the papers.

"Notes for the Promise Cove Summertime celebration," Maggie said. "Somehow I got roped into being in charge again this year."

"You volunteered," Alex said.

"Yeah, well, there is that. Everything's right on target—"

"Which means it's only a week behind," Alex commented.

"Oh stop," Maggie said. "It'll come together. It always does."

"I remember the celebration," Kelly said. "It was our favorite thing all summer. Lots of tourists and hikers from faraway places like Germany. Cotton candy."

"The great caramel popcorn the Boy Scouts always made," Maggie said.

"You were more interested in the Eagle Scouts," Alex said.

"Was not," Maggie countered.

"I think Alex is right," Kelly said softly with a smile. "Once we hit junior high, you were always mooning about one boy or another. It's all you wrote in your letters to me."

"Why did we stop writing letters?" Maggie asked.

"High school, college, the internet," Kelly replied.

"Boys," Alex said.

"Boys," Maggie and Kelly agreed.

"Hello, Kelly," a warm voice said. "It's so wonderful to see you." Elaine Marston leaned down to kiss her on the cheek, a citrus aroma perfuming the air around her. Her wild red hair—probably kept that way by a hairdresser—was pulled back into a ponytail, although a number of curls refused the restriction. Her face was almost unlined, and her hazel eyes sparkled.

Maggie's mom had always loved life in a big way.

"My daughter tells me you're going to help with the celebration this year," Elaine said as she deposited three plates of amazing-looking sandwiches on the table.

"I am?" Kelly asked.

"Mother. We hadn't told her yet."

"Oops." Elaine raised her eyebrows and covered her lips with her fingertips in mock horror.

"Thanks, Elaine," Alex said, pulling a plate toward her.

Kelly grabbed the second plate. She could always say no to whatever they were plotting, but first she was going to eat. Once she bit into the grilled eggplant and mozzarella panini, she decided not to entertain any other idea until it was finished.

Maggie's mother was as gifted in the kitchen as she was on the easel.

"Tell me about what you have going so far," Kelly said once the rumbles in her stomach had died down. "It's only a few weeks away—there can't be much left to do besides enjoy it."

"That's what you think," Maggie said. "I thought you ran things for your kids when they were in school. PTA chair and all that."

"That was a while ago." But Maggie was right. The last few weeks before an event had always been chaos: people forgot or just ignored their commitments, promised supplies didn't show up, and some childhood disease always made the rounds at the last moment.

"Uh, yeah." Even though there was plenty to do at her

grandmother's place, she asked, "How can I help?"

Maggie grinned. "By finishing up the silent auction."

"I don't know a thing about auctions."

"All you have to do," Alex said, sliding a piece of paper from the pile on the table, "is see the people on this list and get them to donate something. The woman who was doing it had a family emergency and had to go to Des Moines or somewhere out there. So we're short. And luckily, you popped up to take her place."

"Convenient," Kelly said, her tone light with humor.

"Very," Alex agreed with more of a smile than Kelly had seen on her yet. It was clear it was going to take some doing to win her old friend back.

"But I don't know any of these people," she said.

"Then it's a great way to get to be part of the community again," Maggie said.

It seemed useless to protest. Maggie had always steamrolled them into some harebrained scheme or another.

"Remember when we decided to borrow my grandmother's canoe and paddle into the lake to spy on some guys who were fishing?" she asked.

"Kinda," Maggie said. "Why?"

"Because it was your idea, and I was the one in the most trouble. My mother was here that weekend, and she didn't want me having anything to do with Montana boys." Kelly could almost hear her mother's voice. Montana boys were only after one thing, she'd said, and then declared Kelly too young to know what that one thing was.

"And?" Maggie asked.

"I have a feeling the same thing's going to happen now. These people don't know me, Maggie. They're not going to give me anything for an auction."

"I think you underestimate your powers of persuasion. You can start tomorrow. If you haven't rustled up anything by Monday, we'll figure something out."

"I can't do it tomorrow," Kelly said. "I'm going hiking with Ryan." She clasped her hand over her mouth. She hadn't meant to let that slip.

"Well, you work fast," Alex said, the distance back in her voice.

"It's a hike," she said defensively, tensing up. Alex always had baited her. With three girls in a friendship, sometimes things could become unbalanced, with one or the other unintentionally excluded from the inner circle.

These days, it was Kelly herself.

"I've got to go," she said. "I'll see what I can do." She picked up the list and put it in her bag.

"Now you've done it," Maggie said to Alex. She placed her hand on top of Kelly's purse. "Stay. Finish your sandwich. My mother would be horrified if you left any food. She'd ban herself from my kitchen for a month. And I need her in my kitchen." She withdrew her hand. "Alex gets grumpy sometimes. Ignore her."

"Sorry," Alex added in a voice that didn't indicate any such thing. "I didn't mean anything by it."

"You'll do fine," Maggie said. "Start with Betsy. She runs the post office."

"Didn't she work there when we were kids?" Kelly asked.

"I think so. She's kind of a fixture. She'll give you something for sure."

"Tell me about the rest of the folks on this list," she said, pulling it back out. "That will make it easier."

And make it less likely her friends would talk about Ryan.

Chapter Fourteen

"I had Maggie put together a picnic for us," Kelly told Ryan when he picked her up at nine Friday morning. She had changed her clothes three times, finally settling on a coral T-shirt, jeans, and the sturdiest shoes she owned. She'd also placed a pair of stud floral earrings—a pair she'd had for years—in her ears. A light jacket completed the outfit.

"That's very thoughtful," he said. "Thank you." He took the small cooler from her. "We can eat it by the creek after we're done hiking."

"Is it a long hike?" she asked. "I'm not sure I can do a long hike."

"You'll be fine. It's about a mile and a half, slight uphill. We'll take it easy." He put his Ford Explorer into gear and headed out the driveway. "The trailhead isn't too far from Whitefish, and I'd planned to take you there for lunch, but a picnic is even better."

"Great." A mile and a half? One way? Uphill? He had more confidence in her than she did.

Ryan drove easily on the curving road that headed south around the lake. Glimpses of blue intermingled with summer houses on the right, while pines and firs trudged off to the east toward the Continental Divide. The sunlight played with the shadows, adding a sense of unreality to the excursion.

"How did all the artists end up in Promise Cove?" she asked.

"Word of mouth, mainly. And the interest heated up once Makalia built the website. Artists are an odd lot. We crave isolation for creation, but we still need community. Not any group of people will do, though. We need other creatives, as well as nurturers. If there weren't someone around to remind us, oftentimes we'd forget to eat or shave." He stroked his chin, which was bare of any stubble, and a faint hint of spruce reached her.

"And Promise Cove gives you both," she said.

"Yep. We've built a good community here. Montana is perfect for us. Individuality and self-determination runs strong through the population, but people who live here have always known they depend on each other. It can be as basic as huddling together around a fire in the dead of winter when the power has gone out. Or making sure Betsy's driveway gets cleared so the post office can open."

"Neighbors looking out for neighbors," she said. "We've got

some of that in California, but we depend a lot on services like paid firefighters. Things we buy with our tax dollars."

He nodded. "New York was like that, too. But it's a city made up of small villages, and when the services are stretched too thin for what's needed, we'd help each other out. It was a good combination for that many people."

"What was it like living in New York?" she asked. "How did you get there?"

"Different," he said, deftly maneuvering around a doe trying to determine the best place to get her fawn across the road to the lake for a drink. "Remember, we lived in Kalispell during the winter, so I was used to more people than the handful in Promise Cove. Still, I went from a town of about twenty-three thousand people to a place with about two and a half million in Brooklyn alone. That's a density of about thirty-seven thousand people per square mile. Montana has about seven."

"Intense," she said.

"Decidedly." He pulled into the trailhead and parked at the far end. "This way the car will stay in the shade. Help keep everything cool."

"Good idea."

He shouldered a light pack, attached a canister to his belt, and locked the car. "This way," he said, walking toward a dark brown bulletin board littered with flyers, tacks, and bits of paper.

A big sign was tacked to a post. "Grizzly mother and cub spotted in upper Haskill Basin. Exercise care."

"Maybe we shouldn't go," she said.

"That's beyond where we're stopping. We'll be fine." He pointed to the canister. "Bear spray. I always carry it when I'm hiking. As long as we don't get too close or between a mama and her baby, we'll be okay. And if it's a rogue bear, I'm prepared."

"You always were a Boy Scout," she said with a smile.

"Yes, ma'am." He grinned back, his face echoing the teen who'd captured her imagination so long ago.

As they walked, the creek flowed beside them, still heavy with water. Although it was late in June, snow still clung to the farthest reaches of the mountains. She remembered seeing it on the high peaks in Glacier as late as August. New growth edged the creek banks, and here and there pink and blue wildflowers peeked through the foliage.

She breathed in deeply, filling her lungs with mountain air. Ocean breezes may have invigorating ions, but here a gulp of air was like recharging with new energy after a cool shower.

The first part of the path provided enough room to walk almost side by side.

"So, New York?" she asked again. "Why there? I remember you swearing that nothing would ever get you to leave the state."

"Things change when you least expect it," he said. After another minute of walking he said, "A woman. That's how I wound up in New York."

That stung a little because Kelly remembered exactly how the comment about never leaving Montana had come about. She'd asked him to spend Christmas with her and her family in Boston. It had taken all summer to get her mother to agree to the plan, and Ryan had turned her down flat.

"Oh?"

"Yeah, well." He stopped and turned to her. "I'm sorry. I was an idiot when I refused your invitation. Teenagers can be very unbending and self-righteous."

He was right about that.

Starting to walk again, he continued, "My dad made detective during my high school freshman year. I was so proud of him. He worked hard to get it. All I wanted to do was be a cop like him. Two years later, cancer—mesothelioma—got him."

"I'm so sorry, Ryan. That's really young."

"Yeah. He'd been feeling off, but he was working so hard at the job, he didn't pay attention. He grew up in Libby; he should have known better."

"Why?" The connection didn't make sense to her.

"The vermiculite mines in Libby filled the air with asbestos dust. No one knew anything about asbestos at first, but by 1963, they knew. And they still kept working those mines." His voice was bitter.

"Are they still doing it?"

"Nope. They shut it down in 1999. EPA came in to clean it up, but by then it was too late for thousands of people."

"That's horrible."

"Yep."

They were quiet for a time as the trail narrowed. Ryan took the lead, and conversation was cut off. She had to watch her feet more, as the trail had spots where it was rutted or muddy. Large rocks required maneuvering, and a tree root tripped her up.

Next to them, the creek still gurgled. She stopped to take a picture of a pretty little waterfall and laughed. A chunky dark bird was flitting in and out of the water, sometimes dipping its head entirely in the creek and coming up with a squirming bug in its mouth.

Ryan turned, and she pointed. He laughed as well. "A water ouzel. They are funny to watch. Some people call them dippers."

"I've never seen one before."

"I'm glad you found it on our hike."

"Me too." They stood close and watched the small creature dip and eat, occasionally stopping on a nearby rock to stare at them. Finally, Ryan headed back up the trail, and she followed.

About ten minutes later, they reached an overlook. A log bench had been constructed, and Ryan indicated they should sit. Gratefully, she eased herself down, fully aware of the steps she'd walked. She must have moaned a bit.

"Here," he said, pulling a bottle from his pack. "Have a couple of aspirin." He also handed her a small water bottle. "I have my own, so you're safe to drink this," he said with a grin.

After taking the pills, she sipped her water and gazed at the scene below her. At the southern end of the view she could see a large mountain with ski trails carved in its side. To the west, Whitefish Lake sparkled before them.

"It's beautiful," she said.

"Yes, it is."

It was nice to sit with him without feeling like she needed to fill the void with chatter. When she'd been with John, she suddenly realized, if they weren't talking about something, it was as if she didn't exist. He would abruptly get up and leave. It was particularly disturbing when they'd be having a glass of wine together after the kids had gone to bed.

Or had he been leaving for another reason?

She shoved that disturbing thought aside, only to have it replaced by another.

"Maggie and Alex have roped me into helping with the Promise Cove Summertime celebration," she said. "They want me to ask for the remainder of donations to the silent auction."

"That sounds easy," he said.

"If I knew these people, what made them tick, it might be. But I don't. I know I'm going to mess it up, and everyone will be mad at me."

"You're not going to mess it up. You're better than that. It's a good way to get to know your neighbors. And I'm sure your friends didn't give you any impossible people."

"I wouldn't be too sure of that," Kelly said.

"You'll be fine."

He touched her hand but didn't linger. Her body still reacted with attention. Nothing more. Only a realization that something had shifted.

"Remember when we used to go?" he asked. "I won you that big teddy bear one year."

It was the first time she'd realized that he was as aware of her as she was of him. She'd been standing half behind a tree, watching him pitch a baseball at the fireman's booth, and he'd nailed every throw. When it came time to choose a prize, he'd gotten the large stuffed animal and walked it directly to her.

"Yes," she said. "I made my mother bring it back to Boston with us. I still have it somewhere." She relaxed, still staring at the water, a time of innocence settling on her shoulders.

"I got you those earrings, too," he said, touching the stud in her lobe.

"You did? I'd forgotten that."

"Probably because you never opened the box with me. I'd picked them up at that silversmith who was here one year. I'd only worked up the courage to give them to you right before your mother yanked you back East."

"Oh, yes. She and my grandmother had a big fight, and off we went." Her fingers traced the flower of the earring. "They're one of my favorites. I guess I never had a chance to thank you, so thank you. They were ... are ... a nice gift." She shifted her gaze from the lake to his eyes.

What would have happened if her mother hadn't interfered that summer?

Probably nothing. They were too young and their lives too different.

But what about now?

Now they were too old, and their lives were still opposites.

But how she wished it were different. What if there were second chances?

Chapter Fifteen

Betsy Wiznowski's home was a well-maintained one-story painted red. Two massive pines guarded the gate, and bright flowers lined the sidewalk to the house.

Tentatively, Kelly knocked on the door. Betsy had graciously accepted an appointment time, but things changed.

"Hello, Kelly," Betsy said warmly. "Come in. I've set up a table with coffee and buns on the back porch. We can talk there. It's so lovely this time of year."

Mutely, Kelly followed her hostess to the back, the aromas of rich coffee and sugar awakening her taste buds as she walked through the kitchen. The screened-in porch overlooked a generous backyard with a glimpse of the bay. Goldfinches and chickadees fought for position on one feeder, and hummingbirds buzzed around another. A black woodpecker with a deep red chest beat his beak against a suet block.

"They're hungry this morning," Betsy said. "I have to take the feeders in at night. Bears, you know."

People did seem to take the presence of the large predators for granted in Promise Cove. Ryan had mentioned a few wolves had been spotted at the far side of the lake.

"It's good to have you back," Betsy said, pouring coffee from a carafe. A mound of scones crested a cobalt Fiesta plate in the center of the table. "You were such a quiet child. I'd wondered how you turned out."

Kelly wasn't sure how to respond. There didn't seem to be a question.

"You've been postmistress a long time," she said.

"Yes. I never dreamed of becoming one." She grinned. "My heart was set on Hollywood. I had planned to be a star. Unfortunately, I found I wasn't the type they were looking for back then. Directors wanted waifish women, not tall, husky Hepburn types like me. But I was very organized and became an assistant to a producer. I suited me fine. And then I met my Harold." Betsy's expression became soft. "We honeymooned up here. It was so beautiful. I feel like he's with me even now."

"And you stayed in Hollywood?"

"Up until Harold passed away. Then, well, Hollywood didn't

sparkle for me anymore. So I moved up here. They needed a postmistress, so I took the test and here I am."

"No children?"

"Just one son. He stayed with a friend in LA and finished school. He came up here during summers. He was a good boy." Betsy's expression was vague, like she was existing in a time separate from the present. Suddenly, she straightened. "But you're not here to listen to an old woman reminisce. No doubt Maggie has sent you for the auction."

"Um, well…" All the awkwardness of her teenage years flooded back. It was one thing asking well-heeled California society women for donations, but this was a widow approaching retirement with not much more than memories to sustain her.

Betsy held up a finger. "But not yet. First, I need you to tell me everything that's happened from the time you left us until now." She held out the plate with the scones. "Have one. I made them fresh this morning."

Almost in desperation, she took one and immediately bit into it. The surprisingly moist and sweet confection vied with the almost bitter note of currants. Perfection.

Letting herself relax a bit, she gave Betsy the sanitized version of her life in between sips of deep roasted coffee and sweet scones. As she spoke, the postmistress nodded and said soothing words. She was the most attentive listener Kelly had encountered in a long time. So much so that she wound up revealing more than she'd intended.

"I remember hearing you play," Betsy said. "Your grandmother's door was always open, and it was a safe and tranquil place to spend some time. I was there with a group of knitters once, and your grandmother urged you to play a new piece you'd learned. It was lovely." The postmistress hummed a few bars of a Brahms melody Kelly barely remembered.

She'd missed so much. She skittered away from the regrets.

"What was Hollywood like?" she asked.

Betsy laughed. "That is always the first thing people want to know. What was it like? Pretty much like you'd imagine. All the big studios got a jolt when *Easy Rider* came out. That small independent film grossed an incredible amount of money for the investors. Peter Fonda came from a family with a name, but the rest were upstarts. Films no longer followed a tried-and-true path but were created by talented people determined to turn a mirror on tradition."

"It must have been a crazy time," Kelly said.

"It was. Lots of energy and social upheaval, much of it good." Betsy picked up her mug, a white cup with Screen Actors Guild in black script, and took a slow sip. "Sometimes, though, I wonder if we didn't help create a divide in America that has only gotten worse." She was silent for a few moments, then shook herself out of it like a dog shedding water.

"Like I said, interesting times." She put down her mug. "Am I the first person you've come to see?" Betsy asked.

"Yes."

"That's because I'm such an easy touch." Betsy smiled. "Let's go see what I have."

Once again, Kelly followed Betsy. This time she had a chance to look around. Portraits of famous movie stars of years ago, most of them signed personally to Betsy and her husband, were interspersed with large reproductions of movie posters. Tucked in a corner was a golden statue with a globe on top. Below that was a black-and-white still of a handsome man with the longish hair popular in the 1970s.

"My husband won that for best screenplay the year before he died. He was really on his way, but his heart failed him." She touched the photo lightly with the tip of her index finger. "Our time was short, but it was magical." She turned to Kelly. "You'd be lucky to find a love like that."

"I did. I married John."

Betsy shook her head. "Just the way you put that lets me know I'm right. Your husband didn't fly you to the moon and back just by being next to you. Maybe you'll find the right man here. You were interested in Ryan a long time ago."

The postmistress saw and remembered too much.

"That was a *long* time ago."

"And yet you went hiking with him on Sunday."

Small towns held no secrets.

"We're just friends."

Betsy nodded and opened a drawer. "This will do. It's a replica of Nurse Ratched's cap from *One Flew Over the Cuckoo's Nest*. My husband worked on the screenplay, although he didn't get top billing. It's signed by the cast, even Jack Nicholson." She held it out to Kelly.

"Oh, I couldn't take that. Surely, your son wants it."

"Take it," Betsy said, her voice flattening from the enthusiasm she'd shown all morning.

Kelly held the cap delicately.

"My son doesn't need it." A sadness passed over her face. "He doesn't need much of anything."

An awkward silence ensued.

"I should go," Kelly said.

"Come back any time," Betsy said as she walked her to the front.

"I will. And thanks again for the donation," Kelly said to the slowly closing door.

What an amazing life Betsy had led. So different from the wife-mother route Kelly had traveled. As she settled into the driver's seat, her phone buzzed.

"What are you doing?" the text from Ryan asked.

"My duty for the town." Her excitement wasn't containable. "She gave me a nurse's cap from *One Flew Over the Cuckoo's Nest*! Signed by everyone in the cast!" She followed the message with every excited emoji she could dredge up.

"Love to see it. Stop by ART."

Ryan was alone when she arrived. "Amazing," he said when he looked at the cap. "You can almost still feel the energy of all those people in this. It's going to fetch a pretty penny for our town. Good job!" He high-fived her, then his fingers flew over his keyboard. "I'm letting Maggie know so she can get it up on the website. It will be quite a draw."

When he'd finished, he patted her hand, but let his fingers linger a few seconds longer than necessary before pulling them away. "Thank you."

"It was fun. Well, up until the time I asked her if she didn't want to give the cap to her son."

"Ouch."

"What do you mean?"

"Not my story to tell. Let's just say it's difficult. He was a kid with a lot of promise, then 9/11 happened, and the course of his life changed."

"How?"

He shook his head. "If you stay past the summer, really become one of us, then Betsy may tell you."

"Oh." Well, that wasn't going to happen.

"Betsy's reaction to her son's problems was to double down on her community involvement, especially with the kids. She and your grandmother were a formidable pair. I think Betsy feels a little lost without her."

Kelly nodded. Everywhere she looked in this small town, her grandmother had left her mark. At some level, she felt incredibly guilty for selling the retreat center to a stranger. But what else could she do?

"Are you free in the next couple of days?" she asked.

"Up for another hike?" he asked with a grin.

"Not for a while! I'm still recovering from the last one."

"We need to get you in shape. No self-respecting Montanan is out of shape."

"Well, I doubt that," she said. "I want to return my rental car to the airport and use the RAV4 my grandmother left in the barn. I've talked to the attorney, and he said there's no problem. No use in paying for something I don't need."

"Sure, I'd be happy to take you. But let me come up to your place after I close down so I can check it out. I should be done by four."

"You know mechanics, too?"

"Whatever it takes to get by," Ryan said. "How about I bring a couple of venison steaks, and we can grill."

"I haven't seen a grill."

"I know where it is."

Of course he did.

"Sure." She'd have to pick up some things from the store. "I'll see you around four." She waved and walked out the door, butterflies flapping away inside her. She couldn't make up her mind whether she was nervous about more time with Ryan or excited to have dinner with someone other than herself or her kids.

Whichever it was, dinner with Ryan was a big change.

Chapter Sixteen

Kelly placed the grocery bags on the counter in her grandmother's kitchen. Thankfully, Teagan had been the cashier so she hadn't had to deal with the inevitable questions from Megan as to why she was purchasing so much for dinner. Sometimes she missed the anonymity of California.

Fresh corn had started to arrive, and while salad was the pre-packaged variety, it would do in a pinch. And for dessert? A sweet, locally baked blueberry pie and whipped cream.

She'd also picked up a bottle of cabernet from a winery she knew in Napa.

Where should they eat? Was she presentable? Should she throw the salad together first and then change? What was the best way to prep the corn?

This was a total mistake. She didn't know how to entertain someone out of her comfort zone. She didn't know how to entertain a man, period.

Her life with John had become rote pleasures. Prepping for this dinner showed her just how much.

She shucked the corn, prepped the salad, and went to her room to change.

The weather was warm, but the night would turn cold. They should probably eat outside—more like two friends getting together than anything else.

So, jeans then.

Silk tees were out. Too good a chance for a stain. But her striped blue-and-white button-down would work. She could roll up the sleeves to start with, then go full length as the night cooled. A few pieces of jewelry.

She stared at the image in the bathroom mirror. Too Californian? Then she spotted the time on the old-fashioned clock on the bedroom wall.

It would have to do.

She trotted down the stairs to the kitchen and outside just as she heard the hum of Ryan's engine by the side of the house.

"Hello," she said when he made it to the porch.

"Hi there."

"Let me take that." She reached for the bag in his hands.

"I've got it. I know my way around Henrietta's kitchen." He walked inside the house, then poked his head back outside. "Coming?" His gaze looked her up and down. "You look nice, by the way." Then the screen door closed.

She followed him inside.

He pulled two plastic storage containers from the bag and laid them on the counter, each dark with meat and marinade. A second bottle of deep red cabernet stood next to the one she'd purchased. He followed her gaze.

"Like minds," he said with a grin.

"Where's the grill?" she asked as he grabbed a few grilling utensils along with salt and pepper shakers.

He piled all of it on a tray, then picked it up. "If you could get the door, I'll show you."

She followed him down an arbor-covered path she'd noticed at the back of the house. It led to the back of the barn, where a cement patio was set up for outdoor dining. Her grandmother had thought of everything, including wicker furniture, a fireplace, a pizza oven, and a grill.

"It looks like something out of a California lifestyle magazine," Kelly said.

"I think that's where she got the idea. Henrietta had well-known clients, and she wanted them to feel at home."

Her grandmother had been a far more savvy businesswoman than either Kelly or her mother had given her credit for being.

"I'll get this heating, then take a look at the car." Ryan went about opening the grill and getting set up. He looked in his element, while she just stood there, feeling like she was on her first date at fourteen again.

He looked over at her, and their gazes connected. Desire flooded her, not only physical desire, but a longing for companionship, friendship ... for someone to love.

She turned away. "I'll get the dishes."

Slowly walking through the arbor, she savored the feeling of having a man around. Ryan was capable in a very masculine way. Not that she couldn't do what he did, but it was nice to have him take over a grill. Call her old-fashioned, but it was the way she was wired.

In the kitchen, she collected dishes, the prepared salad, and napkins, as well as the bottle of wine and a corkscrew. As the corn heated in the microwave, she slipped out to the garden and gathered a few pink blossoms. With a small arrangement in a vase, the tray was complete, and she walked it back to the patio.

"Perfect timing," Ryan said.

"Smells good," she replied as he deftly pulled the steaks from the grill and put them on the platter he'd brought out.

In between the time she'd left and now, a bright yellow oil cloth had appeared on the table. "Henrietta stored them in the barn," he said. He opened the wine and poured them each a glass. They clinked, their gazes once again catching over the rims.

"To renewed friendships," he said.

"Friendships," she replied.

"Let's dig in before it's cold," he said.

As they settled in for dinner, they talked easily about their lives. She told amusing stories about her kids, and he had her laughing about the ineptness of some criminals. Soon the plates were empty and the last glass of wine had been poured.

"I've got dessert," she said. "Coffee?"

He nodded. "Good idea."

She started the coffee, then rinsed off the plates to put in the dishwasher, giving herself space before she returned. The dinner had been far more relaxing and fun than she'd had since she and John were first married.

When had their marriage slipped away from them?

Returning with the pie and coffee, she found Ryan in one of the Adirondack chairs, the glass at his hand. He leaned back and stared at sky as it slowly filled with the pastel colors of a summer evening in north country.

She set the slices of pie and coffee mugs on the table between his chair and hers. Taking a deep breath, she sat down.

"Lovely, isn't it?" he said.

"Yes."

"One of my favorite times of day."

"You must have missed it in New York City."

He nodded.

"How did you ever wind up there?"

"Ah, well, that's a story." He finished his wine and set the glass on the table. Then he tented his fingers and stared at the side of the barn in front of him.

"You know my dad was a cop, right?"

"I vaguely remember that."

"In my family, there was an expectation that I'd 'man up' and become a cop like my dad and brother. I didn't really have a passion one way or the other, but I knew I wanted some time for myself—some time to see this country before deciding Montana really was the last best place. I promised when I came back I'd join the academy. In return, my parents gave me a year to travel with their blessing."

Kelly made the same murmuring noise she'd perfected when listening to her children tell a story that was more long-winded than it needed to be.

"It really is an amazing country," he said. "I started with the West Coast, worked my way through canyon country, even worked the cornfields of the Midwest. I made some friends along the way, and we'd travel for a while. But there wasn't anyone permanent."

There was another pause. "Until Lorelei. Her name alone should have made me hesitate." He picked up his mug of coffee and sipped, staring at the aged wood siding once again.

As much as Kelly wanted to rush the story along, stories in the mountains weren't rushed. They unfolded over time, like a glacier lily slowly unbending from the earth in the spring.

"She was a bit of a vagabond like me," Ryan said, "but she knew she eventually wanted to return to New York City, to the art scene. She was a watercolor artist. She was good. Still is."

"So you had art in common."

Ryan shook his head. "Art of any kind wasn't on my radar. I'd do a little writing in a journal or take some pictures while she painted. Mainly, I was taking it all in. Have you ever read Edward Abbey?"

Kelly shook her head. She hadn't even heard of the man.

"In one of his essays, he writes about a juniper tree, says that someone could write a book just on one tree if he took the time and had the language. I guess I spent a lot of time staring at juniper trees, trying to figure out what he was talking about." Ryan's rich laughter burst out, echoing off the rocks in the small canyon. "Probably how I wound up in that disaster of a marriage. Too much time looking at a tree and not enough minutes learning about the woman I was falling in love with."

How could someone laugh about a tragedy like that? Because that's what a failed marriage was, a tragedy. One did everything one could to keep it together, to fight against the trend of "starter marriages" and the normalcy of broken homes. It's what she would have done if she'd known John had someone on the side.

Or did he? Was that only her imagination?

She had to get that phone unlocked.

"So you went to the city with her," she said to push aside her inner demons.

"I did."

"But why a cop? Seems to me that away from your parents, you could have done what you wanted."

He shrugged. "I didn't have to think too much about it. I knew the drill. And I wanted to do something that mattered to other people. I got my training, got assigned to Brooklyn, and there I stayed. It was convenient. Lorelei wanted to live there. Back then, it was pleasant. A little run-down, but people could still afford a place to be."

"And so you stayed."

"For a while."

She wanted to ask what had happened, but his open look was gone, shut down behind a stony face.

He picked up his plate and dug into the pie. "This is good. Must be Charlene's." He pointed to an area closer to the crook of the cove. "She lives down there. Bakes out of her kitchen."

Kelly took a bite. It was indeed amazing.

"She supplies preserves and pies all summer long, a one-woman berry machine, although her husband and son help a lot with the picking. Wait until you taste her huckleberry pies."

"As long as they're here by the end of the summer."

He didn't reply.

"Ryan, I have a favor to ask."

"Oh," he said, waving his fork in the air. "Car's fine. Could use a tune-up, but the local mechanic can do that fast enough."

"Let me guess, he works out of his garage."

"Yep. No need to go erecting extra buildings out here. I'll take you to Kalispell next week. I need a few supplies at those big box stores on 93."

"Thank you, but that's not the favor."

"Another one?" The grin was back. "I'm going to have to think of some good repayment." Then he must have caught a glimpse of her expression. He leaned forward. "What do you need?"

"Do you know someone who can hack into a phone?"

"Why?"

She told him about finding the second phone and why she wanted to see what was on it.

"Are you sure you want to know?" he asked. "Sometimes secrets are better left that way."

"Or it could be nothing," she said. "I need to know that, too."

He nodded. "I might know someone."

"Good. Thank you."

"No promises. He might not be able to get into it."

"I'll deal with that when it happens." She had to learn the truth. If she didn't, she'd never be able to move forward with her life.

He was getting in too deep.

Ryan navigated his Explorer up the curvy dirt road to his cabin. Kelly had been too easy to be with. And when they exchanged glances too reminiscent of the ones they'd shared long ago, it took all his willpower not to lean in and kiss her.

But he couldn't do that. Not yet. Probably never.

She is leaving. She is leaving. If he told himself that enough times, it had to sink into his head.

He pulled to a stop and got out. Trudging up the steps to the patio, he leaned against the railing and hungrily drank in the sight of the stars above, a glittering mass gliding over trees to hover over the lake before disappearing into the light pollution of Whitefish and Kalispell. Why was it human beings needed to light up everything in sight?

He walked through the sliding door and poured himself a glass of brandy before returning to sit and stare at the universe. Perhaps it would have more answers than he did. Why was he setting himself up for a fall?

What kind of man had Kelly married? Based on what little she'd told him, it sounded as if John had been made from the same mold as Kelly's mother. There were rigid rules, and a free spirit needed to be contained. He barely remembered Cynthia. She'd only appear momentarily and then would be gone, much to Henrietta's relief. And, he suspected, Kelly's as well.

Life had well and effectively caged Kelly. Would she ever be able to free herself from the past? Could he help her? Oh, he wanted to, very badly. He wanted her to regain the spirit that had fluttered around him those summers she'd been here. But would it be a good thing? Or a disservice that would make her life more painful that it was right now?

Kelly had asked him to get the phone unlocked. He would do that for her. She may not like the answers she found, but he would be there to support her through it.

He could be there for the girl he'd once loved.

Chapter Seventeen

Ryan had left shortly after they'd finished their pie, returning to his own life. How nice it must be for him to know who he was and what he needed to do.

This morning, she grabbed one of her grandmother's shawls, taking it and her coffee to the front porch. Her shoulders were tense, the result of a dream of a thief stealing the Nurse Ratched cap. She'd chased the thief until she'd caught him. When he turned around, his face became her husband's and the cap a mangled heart.

No need to go to a dream specialist to interpret that one.

She stared at the mist rising from the lake. The morning chill was welcome, shrouding everything in pretense, hiding the rot underneath. Melancholy had taken too much of a hold. The antidote was work, and there was plenty of that around here.

But still she sat, letting the mystery drift over her. What if it could wash away all the years since she'd last been here, allowing her to return to the innocence she'd once known? But that wouldn't do either. She loved her children and her job. What she needed to do was convince her friends to stop interfering with what she had to do and get the place ready to sell.

Resolute, she stood, determined to start her morning.

But the garden called. She needed to get someone in to give it curb appeal, even though there were no curbs for hundreds of miles. Wandering the rows of volunteer vegetables and flowers, she automatically deadheaded the few that needed it, just as she'd always done at home. She ambled to the firepit and noted the spots where the fog was releasing its hold. Settling into a chair, she gazed at the world around her until her coffee was finished. She'd never known that simply staring at nature could be so fulfilling.

After her shower, she opted for jeans, an older button-down shirt, and a kerchief to keep her hair back. The earrings were studs, simple turquoise chips her kids had given her one year for Mother's Day. Gathering a dust rag, furniture spray, and several boxes she'd gotten from Maggie, she headed to the bookshelves in her grandmother's sitting room. These were going to be the most difficult to sort, so she'd tackle them first.

Poetry books and journals made up the first small bookcase. Mary

Oliver, Maya Angelou, Rupi Kaur, Marge Piercy, Adrienne Rich, and more lined the shelves. Kelly only recognized a few. What should she keep? Would she ever have the time or desire to read them?

She dumped all the books into a box, then plucked one out again. Rupi Kaur. Kelly had never heard of her. Opening the book randomly, she read, then gasped. "Celebration" touched something deep in her soul. Was the world really waiting for her? Waiting for her to do what?

Closing the book, she put it back in the box, more reverently this time.

Her grandmother's slim volumes went into the box next. Kelly fingered each one, trying to stir memories of the woman she'd once known and loved deeply. How much she'd missed of her grandmother's life and work. How could her mother have kept all of this from her?

The final unpublished book was less painful: *The Healing Art of Retreat*.

Crossing her legs, she opened the book and started reading. Before she knew it, a half hour had passed. Her grandmother had laid out the heart of her program. Not the nuts and bolts. They were probably in the office somewhere. But the purpose and the hopeful outcomes, the healing and re-energizing of creative artists were clearly articulated.

Henrietta had been one of the most amazing women of her generation. No wonder Maggie wanted to keep the center going. It wasn't only a cornerstone for the community of Promise Cove, but a light for the world.

Late that afternoon, Kelly put her car in the side lot of Culver's store and started walking to the porch. A movement toward the back of the building caught her eye. Teagan and Gregg stood almost in the shadows. It looked like they were arguing. Teagan was shaking her head and waving her arms in a way that was eerily similar to Maggie when she became excited. Gregg must have sensed Kelly's presence, because he looked over at her, then grabbed Teagan's upper arms. Whatever he said made her glance over as well.

They moved farther back into the shadows.

Should she intervene? But what, actually, had she seen? Maybe a word to Maggie? But again, there wasn't anything she could definitely say, just a vague uneasiness that something was wrong.

Return to Promise Cove

Continuing to the porch, she climbed the well-worn steps to the welcoming atmosphere of the old store. Even the moan of the screen door as she opened it was comforting. Rows and rows of all types of canned and boxed foods, often in ones and twos, lined the old white metal shelves. On a far wall were some inexpensive gardening and handyman tools, while another wall held kitchen gadgets and a shelf of bright enameled Lodge cast-iron pots.

She headed to the back tables, the nurse's cap in a brown bag, as well as a box containing a delicate lace shawl knit by the local school cafeteria lady that she'd picked up on her way to the meeting. They certainly were a talented lot in Promise Cove.

"Hey, girlfriend," Maggie called out. "Looks like you've had success. What is that?" She pointed to the brown bag.

"What's what?" Alex peered around from behind a row of shelves.

"It's from Betsy," Kelly said, a spirit of merriment filling her. She pulled the hat from the bag. "Ta-da!"

Maggie and Alex stared.

"It's a Nurse Ratched hat," Kelly said. "From *One Flew Over the Cuckoo's Nest*. Betsy said it was an award-winning film from 1975. Her husband worked on it."

"Did you hear that?" Maggie squealed to Alex. "That's going to fetch an absolute fortune!" She leapt up and wrapped her arms around Kelly. "You are amazing! I knew you were the right person for the job."

"I didn't do anything special," Kelly protested. "Betsy just offered it. I would think her son would want it, but she said he didn't." Maybe her friends would be more forthcoming than Ryan.

Alex and Maggie exchanged glances.

"What?" Kelly asked as she sat down. Alex and Maggie took their places as well.

"It's kind of a sad story," Alex said.

Maggie nodded.

"But it's not ours to tell," Alex said. "It's kind of an unwritten rule around here for most of the old-timers. Stories belong to the people they affected."

"The newcomers and younger kids, who seem to want their entire lives, including the color of their underwear, splashed across the internet, don't have the same idea," Maggie said.

"We don't tell them much," Alex added.

Which meant, in spite of the summers she'd spent here, Kelly was still an outsider. Even scoring the nurse's cap hadn't changed that.

Her spirit deflated.

"Oh, this is beautiful," Maggie said when she opened the box with the lace shawl. "Ruth's work?"

Kelly nodded. "And Charlene has promised three pies."

"Outstanding," Alex said. "I'll contribute a mirror, and I'm sure Ryan has a small quilt he can throw in. With what we have already and what you've gotten, it's going to be an amazing celebration."

"There's only one person we haven't tapped," Maggie said with a frown.

"Susan Thomas," Alex said.

Both of them stared at Kelly.

"Do you think she's up for that?" Alex asked.

"Well, she can't do any worse than the rest of us. Susan's never sent in anything."

"I'm right here," Kelly said. "Who is Susan Thomas?"

"She makes chain saw bears. She lives with her partner Gabriella at the B and B Gabriella owns," Maggie said.

"But not only bears," Alex said. "Horses, dolphins, all kinds of things. Her work goes for, far more than you'd pay for one of those bears you see all over Montana."

Maggie nodded.

"It can't be that hard, can it?" Kelly said.

Her friends exchanged glances again. "If anyone can do it, you can," Alex said.

Maggie pushed her clipboard to the side. "How about some wine while we brainstorm? White or red?"

"White," Alex immediately chimed in. "But only one glass. I've got a big order coming up, and I need to work on polishing the pieces."

"That's only an excuse," Maggie said. "I know you're binging on the latest streaming sensation." In an aside to Kelly she said, "That girl is seriously addicted."

"It's the beauty of living all by yourself," Alex said.

"Kelly?" Maggie asked.

"White's fine for me."

Maggie returned quickly with glasses and a bottle of supermarket chardonnay. After the wine was poured, the three clinked and Maggie announced, "Here's to the best Promise Cove Summertime celebration ever!"

"Yes," Kelly and Alex agreed and clinked their glasses.

"We've got the silent auction almost all wrapped up, thanks to Kelly," Maggie said. "The band is booked, and it's going to be fabulous! What I need to double-check is where all the booths should go." She pulled a paper from the clipboard and unfolded it. "What do you think?"

Kelly studied it. "You've got the kids' fishing pond next to the beer truck. That won't do."

"Ah, good point," Maggie said. She scribbled the change on the paper.

"Why are the pony rides so close to the food booths?" Alex asked.

"That's where there was room?" Maggie said.

Kelly and Alex shook their heads. Maggie wrote again.

"Got construction paper?" Kelly asked. "Let's cut up some and then we can move booths around and not make a mess of the paper."

"Oh, you are good at this," Maggie said.

For the next half hour, they moved booths around until all three of them were satisfied. Then Maggie glued them into place.

"So, dish, girl," Maggie said, leaning back in her chair. "Rumor has it a very eligible bachelor was grilling at your place last night."

"How did you hear that?" Kelly asked.

"Then it's true," Alex said.

"Well, yes, but ..."

"Told you Rose Doolittle never lies," Alex said to Maggie.

"Who's Rose Doolittle?"

"We're not entirely sure where she came from, but she's been here forever. She lives right there." Alex pointed to the few houses that lined the road heading up to the point that jutted out into the lake. "She spends hours watching who goes up and down the road. In between, she rides her bike around the point, taking note of cars that aren't in their own driveways."

"In other words," Maggie said, "she's the biggest gossip in Promise Cove."

"So no secrets?" Kelly asked.

"Nope," Maggie said. "As long as you're here, your life is an open book."

It was a good thing Kelly had no interest in being more than friends with Ryan Svoboda.

Chapter Eighteen

Kelly left Promise Cove in the rental car right after Ryan texted her that he was on his way to the airport. Not only had he agreed to drive her, but when she told him she needed to meet with the attorney about finances for repairing the retreat, he encouraged her to make the appointment for the same day.

"Anytime I'm near Whitefish," he'd told her, "I take care of everything I can. I even do doctors and dentists on the same day. Saves me lots of trips."

It made sense, and she was grateful for the idea.

The drive to the airport took her about an hour, and he was already waiting outside the rental car agency when she arrived.

"You must have flown down," she said.

"No, just took some back roads to avoid downtown Whitefish and the bulk of box store alley down 93."

"Who knew we needed so much stuff?" she asked with a smile.

"Indeed," he said.

She headed to the counter, where a lean young man with a bored smile waited for her. "I'm returning the rental car early," she said.

"We can't do that," he said.

"Of course you can," she replied. "I called yesterday and made all the arrangements. They even waived the fee. Look it up," she said, pointing to the monitor.

With a world-weary sigh, he looked at the screen and clicked a bunch of buttons. "Yes, here you are." He walked to the file cabinet, searched slowly, and finally retrieved a long sheet of paper.

If everything was computerized, why did everyone still need so much paper?

"Did you fill the tank?" he asked.

"Yes, just outside the airport." John had always told her to get a rental car filled before its return. Otherwise, the price for a gallon of gas was double the going rate.

"We'll have to have someone check on that, and if it's not full to the top, we're going to charge you for the remaining."

"Fine." She glanced at Ryan and rolled her eyes.

He grinned.

"Now it says here that there is a fee for returning the car early."

Return to Promise Cove

The clerk pointed to a line on the paper form.

"I told you they waived it."

"Let me see if the notation is there. Otherwise, I'll need to charge you."

"It's there."

"I have to check."

"Fine." These were the times she missed John the most. He always handled overzealous paper pushers like this one. She looked over at Ryan again. Maybe he'd step in.

He stood there, patiently.

Why wasn't he helping her?

"Ah, yes, there it is. You are good to go." He picked up the paperwork and evened it with a sharp rap on the desk.

"Don't I need my copy?" she asked.

"Oh, yes." He ripped out the canary-yellow copy and slid it across the desk.

"My copy with *your* signature." She slid it back.

"Oh, yes." He signed with a flourish and pushed it back.

With deliberation, she printed his full name on the edge of the contract.

"What are you doing?" he asked.

"Reporting your attitude," she said and turned away.

When she reached Ryan, she asked, "Why didn't you come help me?"

He cocked his head. "Why would I? You're a grown woman. You don't need my help. Besides, it looks like you did just fine." He nodded toward the clerk, who clearly had a worried expression on his face.

"I suppose I did." She grinned, satisfaction adding strength to her bones as she stood a little taller.

"Well, then let's go to Whitefish."

It took only a few minutes to get there, and he dropped her off at the attorney's office before heading out to do some errands of his own.

After getting the preliminary chitchat required for any Montana meeting over with, Kelly asked about accessing the funds her grandmother had left her for repairs to the retreat center.

Bruce Henderson shook his head. "Henrietta was quite detailed in her instructions. If you decide to stay in Montana and reopen the retreat center, the funds become available as soon as I am assured your intentions are going to be realized. If you decide to sell, you need to foot whatever repairs there are and the sale price becomes your inheritance. The rest of the money goes to the town of Promise Cove."

"That can't be," Kelly said.

"It is." Bruce waited for her absorb the information, then added, "I'm sorry I didn't make that clear when you were here the first time, but I didn't think there would be much need for repairs. Henrietta was meticulous about the retreat center."

"Oh, it's just a few little things. Curb appeal, you know."

Bruce smiled. "I'm afraid we're not all that concerned about that here." He gestured toward the mountains that dominated the eastern edge of town. "We've got national park appeal."

He had a point. Someone might actually buy the place as it was, simply to be close to Glacier.

"Well," she said, gathering her things, "I guess that's the way it is. I'll figure it out." John had left her well secured, so there was money to handle what needed to be done. The retreat would fetch a good price.

Bruce stood. "Once again, I'm sorry for your loss. Henrietta was a great woman."

"Yes," Kelly said. They shook hands, and she went to the front porch to send Ryan a text and wait for him to pick her up.

Ryan insisted on buying lunch at a local restaurant featuring fresh vegetables and fish. "After a few months of beef, hamburger, venison, or elk, I'm ready for a change," he'd said.

The food was delicious and the company easy, which was really the best she could say about being with anyone. Both her parents and John's had the ability to bring on a migraine with their insistence of how things needed to be done. Fortunately, her husband had been more laid-back.

Somnolent with food and friendship, she broached the subject that had been aborted at their dinner the other night.

"What happened once you became a cop?" she asked as they left the tourist town behind.

He shrugged. "It was as good a job as any. I liked the comradery, hated the bureaucracy, and loathed the men and women who used their badges as some kind of shield from admitting they were human. I started like everyone else, on the beat. Petty crime, mostly, some drugs. Then I made detective, and it became less physical. I enjoyed ferreting out the criminals but hated what they did."

"Robbing and such?" She didn't want to think about dealing with murder.

"Not really. I mean, we had that kind of crime. A kid breaking into a store for some easy cash for drugs, purse snatching. Even looting after social protests—mostly opportunists, those guys. But I kind of understood it. There was a frustration in some neighborhoods. The system had been working so long to keep them a rung down on the ladder, they couldn't figure a legitimate way out."

"Are you excusing crime?" She couldn't keep the incredulity out of her voice.

"Not at all. They did the deed and needed to be punished or corrected or make restitution. Maybe all three. People were hurt by their actions. I understand it, but that doesn't mean I condone it."

"Oh." Relief relaxed her shoulders. It was one of the few things she agreed with her mother about: people weren't held to a basic standard these days. If he hadn't agreed, it would have put a serious dent in their friendship ... or whatever this was.

"The criminals I couldn't understand were those who did it for a lark or to prove they could. Scam artists who rip off the elderly. Men—and women—who use phishing scams on the lonely or vulnerable. Landlords who promise to take care of something, never do, and raise the rent anyway."

"That's not illegal."

"No, merely immoral. Just because something is legal doesn't mean it should be done. I mean, otherwise, we'd have to have laws about everything people could possibly think of doing, and that's just nonsense. Don't you agree?"

The conversation was making her head hurt. She didn't want a philosophical discussion. She wanted to know the important information: Why had he and his wife broken up?

"What made you stay in the city after ..." She waved her hand rather than say the words.

"Loyalty. I'd made a commitment. I said I'd serve twenty years, and I did. But that's not what you really want to know, is it?"

She felt the blush flame her face. "I ... uh ..."

Once again his laugh rang free.

"I'll make you a trade."

"What kind?" she asked warily.

"You tell me why you stayed married, and I'll tell you why we divorced."

Well, that was easy.

"There was no reason to divorce. We loved each other. There were no problems. We had a family, kids, a future together, a home."

"He *had* two phones."

"So? There could be a perfectly good reason. Besides, I didn't know that until recently." She ignored the hole opening in her gut, but the conversation reminded her to take the phone out of her purse. "Here it is. Once you get into it, I'm sure we'll find there's a good explanation for it."

"If you say so."

"There were *no* problems." Now, he was pissing her off.

"Got it, got it." He held up his palm but kept his eyes steady on the road. "The truth is that Lorelei was bisexual. I didn't know it until about a year into the marriage. I found her making out with one of her friends. She told me it was just an experiment, that it didn't mean anything. I let it pass."

Kelly couldn't conceive of such a thing. She knew it existed, but it hadn't existed in *her* world. Well, there were several gay parents in her kids' school, but they were normal people. They knew who they were. They didn't … float … from one gender to another.

Her expression must have revealed her feelings.

"It's not a big deal," he said. "It happens more than you think. I wasn't crazy about the idea, but not because she was doing it with another woman. It was that she was doing it at all. There was a crack in the trust I believe a person has to have in a marriage. I made a vow. Nothing—not experimenting, not the most beautiful actress in the world, not a friend in distress—nothing would make me break that vow."

The conviction in his voice told her that belief was solid. No matter what, if Ryan gave his word, he would stick by it.

"I understand," she said quietly, glad that her belief in Ryan's trustworthiness hadn't been misplaced all those years ago.

He leaned back and twisted the bottle again.

"In the end, Lorelei decided the friend was a better match. I let her go. It was easier that way. I have to admit, I felt relief. The game was over. I stayed a cop until it was time to retire. And here I am."

"Wait, wait. Where does the quilting come in?" she asked, like a child begging for another story.

"That will have to wait for another time." He drained his bottle. "I need to get you back to the center. I still haven't finished the commission I've been working on."

"Oh, okay."

Once they were in the car, he turned the knob on the sound system so the music came in at a soothing level. Clearly, the time to talk was over. That was fine; she needed time to process. She leaned back in the seat to let sounds and thoughts drift over her.

Ryan was a good man. The starry-eyed, urgent passion of youth faded over time, in spite of feeling like there'd never be enough time in the world to satisfy it. Her mother had drummed into her that contentment came next, and it was more than enough to sustain a woman for the rest of her life, particularly if the man was a good provider like John had been.

But Ryan's physical presence belied that voice of good sense. Something was stirring within her, a sensation that every ounce of passion within her had not yet died.

Chapter Nineteen

Kelly delayed the visit to Susan Thomas as long as she reasonably could. But now she had run out of excuses. Maggie and Alex were expecting results, and she'd never let anyone down before.

"How are you?" she asked Ryan when he answered. "What have you been up to?"

"I finished the commission I was working on. Remember, I told you about it."

"Uh-huh."

"It's *gone*. I stayed up late the night we dropped off your car. I seemed to have a lot of extra energy," he said, his voice containing added warmth.

"Oh?"

"Seems like the company I've been keeping lately has renewed my zest for life."

"I'm glad," she said. "I've enjoyed your company, too."

"Well, UPS has picked up the package, and it's on its way to Omaha. I'm free if you have more work that needs to be done at the retreat center."

"That's not why I'm calling."

"Uh-oh."

"It's nothing bad. Really. The only person I have left to contact for the auction is Susan Thomas. Maggie made me promise. I was wondering—would you come with me?"

"Can't."

"Why not?"

"The woman scares me to death," he said.

"Oh, surely not, a big New York City policeman like you."

"Trembling in my boots," he said. "If I go, you'll need to protect me."

A memory surfaced. One summer, Henrietta had them all selling raffle tickets for a weekend at the retreat center. Kelly had been afraid to go by herself, and her friends weren't available. She'd asked Ryan, and he'd given her the same line: she'd need to be the one to protect him.

The strategy had worked then. They'd had an amazingly wonderful time, stopping at the general store where he'd gotten them

Return to Promise Cove

both ice cream cones to celebrate.

He was always doing things like that, probably trying to shore up her self-confidence, which was woefully inadequate thanks to her mother's constant improvement schemes.

"All right," she said. "I'll bring my trusty dagger and slay the beast if she poses any threat."

"You might bring something bigger," he said. "She *does* have a chain saw."

"I hadn't thought about that."

"That's why you need me along," he said. "To point out the obvious."

He picked her up early that afternoon. They needed his truck on the off-chance that Susan actually donated something for the celebration.

They pulled up to a Victorian-style house that stretched across a small knoll with a view to the south of the lake. Painted a deep forest green with brown shutters, it blended well with the pine trees that surrounded it. Flower beds were interspersed with arrangements of colorful rocks, grasses, and shrubs. Attention to detail was evident in everything.

Kelly knocked, and a petite woman with dark hair, dressed in a flowery blouse and dark slacks, opened the door. "You must be Kelly," the woman said. "I'm Gabriella. Maggie said you'd be coming by. And you brought Ryan. How nice. Why don't you both come in?"

Gabriella led them through the foyer and dining room, both warm with wide-planked floors, throw rugs, and sturdy furniture. The kitchen was bright with light, stainless steel, and gleaming counters and cabinets.

"Coffee?"

"I'm good," Kelly said. "Thanks."

"None for me," Ryan added.

"Well then," Gabriella said with a smile. "Susan's in the back with her woodpile. Good luck!" She opened the back door and pointed to a path that ran into the woods at the right of the house.

They followed the worn trail to a small building and a large amount of noise.

Susan Thomas was a tall but lean woman with a ponytail of thick brown hair. A face mask hid her facial features, and clothes covered her body, but from the way she wielded her chain saw, her muscles were strong.

Ryan shifted a little so Susan would be able to see him. There was a barely perceptible nod while she continued the cut she was making into a good-sized hunk of pine. After a few moments, she stopped.

"Kelly," she said after flipping up the face mask. "Nice to meet you, but no."

"It's nice to meet you, too," Kelly said, walking over and extending her hand.

Susan held up her sawdust-covered gloves with a grin, and Kelly dropped her arm.

But she wouldn't give up. "What are you carving?"

"It's going to be a dolphin," Susan said. "Like that one." She pointed over to a collection of animals: plenty of carved wood bears but also horses, eagles, and sea creatures.

"Wow," Kelly said, examining the pieces. "These are amazing and unique." Each piece was sanded down and stained, not at all like the crude pieces she was used to seeing at most stands selling similar art. "You put a lot of work into these."

"I didn't before," Susan said. "But since Makalia came to town, we've gotten quite a presence. Some guy in Texas wanted one of an eagle, but only if I'd finish it off. I spent a lot of time polishing and adding detail, particularly to the feathers. He paid me a pretty penny. And that's why I simply can't give them away, no matter how noble the cause."

At least the "no" had been softened.

"Doesn't the celebration contribute to the website?" Kelly asked Ryan.

"A good portion, yes," he said. "The rest goes to ART, where there are also some of your pieces on display. We've already sold two this summer." He moved closer to Kelly but took obvious care not to crowd Susan.

"Maybe there's a piece that's not as polished you might be willing to part with." Kelly turned and pointed to a small sculpture she'd spotted in her initial perusal. "That's an owl, isn't it?"

Susan nodded slowly. "It was something I was trying for the first time. The proportions aren't quite right for me, and I don't have the desire to finish it off. But why would I send something that isn't my best to be auctioned off?"

Kelly walked to the piece sitting on top of a stump. It wasn't very big, but it had its own charm. The eyes, as crude as they were, seemed to gaze right into her soul to ask who she was. "It's different from what you usually make," she said. "But it's definitely good enough."

"It could really help us out," Ryan added.

Frowns and pursed lips appeared on Susan's face as she obviously warred with herself, her recalcitrant side fighting hard against this new altruistic idea.

"What the heck," she finally said. She looked over at Ryan. "Pick it up and take it now before I change my mind." She picked up her chain saw.

"Yes, ma'am," he said, moving away quickly. He groaned a bit when he picked up the owl, and Susan grinned.

Kelly gave her a smile. "Thank you."

"You're welcome. Just don't ask again next year," she said. "Stop by the house. I think Gabriella has a gift certificate for you. She's an easy touch. You remember that."

"I will."

The chain saw roared.

"You were amazing," Ryan said as they headed away from the inn.

"I've been doing this awhile," she said.

"After we drop these things into the storeroom at ART, we're going for ice cream," he declared. "You've earned it."

She laughed. "Why do you think you've earned the right to boss me around?"

"Since I carried that owl away under threat of chain saw." He grinned.

"Hmmm. What am I going to use to get you to carry it into ART?"

"Your good looks and sweet personality?" He pulled behind the ART building. He looked over at her, and time seemed to pause.

Breath left her.

He reached over and touched her face. "Ah, Kelly." Dropping his hand with a sigh, he opened the door and got out.

What was she doing with him? In spite of decades of separation and lives lived with other people, it was as if they'd never parted. Every feeling she'd had as a young girl resurfaced, but the emotions were older, not giddy daydreams. She was seeing the man he'd become, and she was falling for him all the same.

Something that absolutely could not happen. Their lives were different. She'd freeze in Montana's cold winters and go out of her mind with nothing to do.

No, it would never work. She shouldn't even consider it. Why was she?

Pushing open her door, she walked over to the building. "Need any help?" she called into the space.

"Nope, all good. It's a great piece. I certainly can't see what problem Susan had with it."

"Maybe she said what she did to save face. She heard our arguments but didn't want to be seen as giving in."

"Could be. You are a very astute judge of people, Kelly Paulson. Now, let's see how good you are at analyzing ice cream." He headed to the car.

"Shouldn't we walk?" she asked. "It's almost across the street."

"We're not going to the general store."

"We aren't?"

"Nope," he said and sat in the driver's seat. "You coming?"

She hurried around and got into the passenger side.

He drove out of the parking lot and headed north. About a mile later, he turned into the parking lot of Promise Cove Sweets, a shop she hadn't known existed. It was a clever location. Across the street was a parking lot for one of the few free beaches on the lake. Locals and regular summer tourists knew about it, and what went better with a day of swimming than an ice cream cone?

While there was a window that faced the lake side, there was also an enclosed area with a counter and seating. Ryan led her there and took a seat on one of the red upholstered swivel stools bolted in front of the counter.

"Hi, Amanda," he said to a young woman with curly dark brown hair held back by a pink scarf. Her long dark eyelashes framed equally dark eyes. She had on an old-fashioned ice-cream waitress uniform: a pink shirtwaist dress with a perky white apron.

"Hi there, Ryan." Her gaze shifted to Kelly.

"This is an old friend, Kelly Paulson," he said. "I expect you to treat her just as well as you treat me."

"Nice to meet you, Amanda. But it's Richards now."

"Ah, yes," Ryan said, leaning toward Amanda. "She's the one who got away."

"I see," Amanda said.

"Amanda is the owner of this lovely shop."

"What should I get you?" Amanda asked.

"I'll take my usual. Kelly?" Ryan asked. "I suggest something rich and gooey. She's marvelous at that."

"Um … okay. Hot fudge sundae with chocolate chip ice cream."

"I have salted caramel," Amanda said, almost in a whisper.

"I'll take that."

Amanda slid two dishes dripping with chocolate syrup and mounds of whipped cream in front of them.

"I'll never finish this."

"Oh, but you will," Ryan said, picking up his spoon. "They're magic."

She dug in.

He was right. The combination of flavors was sweet perfection but somehow lacked the heaviness of a regular ice cream sundae. She was halfway through before she looked up.

"Why isn't this place mobbed?"

"She just opened this spring," he said. "The traffic improves every week. Makalia is doing a big push for the shop on the website and social media in August. Things will explode then."

Someday, Kelly would have to meet this miracle worker.

"Thank you," she said to Ryan. "This is wonderful. And thank you again for coming with me to Susan's. The help was appreciated."

"I enjoy helping you."

"Uh ... yes." She took another scoop of ice cream and stuffed it into her mouth while she studied the decorations in the shop. The pink-and-white theme repeated itself in pink plaster bows on white walls, shelves of pink bears, and candy jars full of pink candies. Somehow, the effect wasn't as overbearing as it could have been.

"You wanted to know how I got into quilting," Ryan said, his spoon clinking against the glass as he scraped up every last bit of the treat. He twirled his stool to face her.

"Yes, I'm curious."

"Most people are. The sanitized version is that I happened to see an exhibit at a museum one day. The artistic expression and creation was as impressive as any painting or sculpture I'd ever seen, only it was done with fabric. It challenged something within me, so I gave it a try."

She nodded, lingering over a particularly buttery chunk of ice cream. Would he give her the real story?

"Anything else?" Amanda asked as she stopped in front of them.

"A cup of coffee would be nice," Ryan said. He looked at Kelly, and she shook her head. It had been a while since she'd enjoyed flavors quite so much, and she didn't want to disturb them.

"The truth is," he said after Amanda delivered his mug, "I was going through a particularly bad patch." His gaze was straight on; he appeared to be looking at a memory and not what was in front of him.

103

"Lorelei had left, and, if I'm honest with you, I deflected whatever I was feeling. I threw myself into the job and was a bear to everyone on the force in the process. It was so bad, my captain called me in and said he couldn't get anyone to work with me and to tone it down or get counseling. Can you imagine a *cop* being told to get counseling?" He shook his head and chuckled.

After another sip of coffee, he continued. "I was hyperfocused on the job at hand, but the problem with being too focused on one objective is that you miss the other stuff that may be happening—little clues that might lead to danger." He stopped talking and stared intently at the back wall.

Whatever had happened had been bad; she could feel it in her bones. The desire to comfort him rose strongly within her, but she pushed it aside. He was too enshrouded in his memories to reach.

"Anyway," he said to the empty space in front of him, "I'd cornered a young man at the end of an alley. He was drug-crazed, pushing and shoving people, taking things for no apparent reason and tossing them a few blocks later. All I wanted to do was get him into custody and take him someplace safe. The alley had no spots for him to escape. My team was protecting my back." Ryan swallowed. "I forgot to look up."

Carefully, she put her spoon on the counter, not making a sound.

"Someone decided I was just another white cop going after a Black man and took a shot at me." Ryan touched his left shoulder. "I returned fire without hesitation." His voice choked. "I'm a good shot." Then he stopped talking and went back to drinking his coffee.

Should she speak? Stay silent?

This time, she placed her hand on his arm, remembering how sensitive her old friend had been. How could he have survived as a cop?

Her touch woke him, and he patted her hand as he turned to her with a smile. "The guy, a middle-aged man who'd seen too much in war—he survived. I testified for leniency at his trial, and he got a minimal sentence. I had to go through the police review board and was cleared. But I finally got that counseling my captain had recommended.

"I started taking long walks, looking for the good things around me, at the great portion of Americans who are doing the right thing. I went to gallery openings and museum shows. One of those was the exhibit I mentioned earlier. Something about the attention to detail and the imagination it took to build a quilt that told a story using only fabric and thread captured my attention. So I bought myself a sewing machine, took some online classes, and began."

Something beautiful from so much pain.

They were quiet for a few moments.

"Thank you for telling me," she said.

"You're the first person I've told the entire story." He grasped her hand which was still on his arm. "I feel safe with you, Kelly. You're the only one I was ever at peace with. I'm glad to know that hasn't changed."

"Me too." In spite of being married to John for a long time, she'd never had the absolute trust she had with Ryan.

But what difference did that make in her life?

Chapter Twenty

Kelly walked around the silent auction tent, straightening the clipboards with the bid sheets, reclipping papers, double checking that the case holding the nurse's cap was secure. She kept an eye on the people strolling through and examining the offerings. Many stood in front of Ryan's contribution, a small quilt of a river scene with small animals hidden in the rocks, water, and trees. All of the items had several bids, but the ones for the nurse's cap had already gone through three pages, and the sizes of the bids were increasing dramatically. There were still hours to go before the auction ended. There would be a substantial amount of money for the small town.

"How's it going?" Maggie asked as she arrived for her shift in the tent.

"Really well." Kelly followed Maggie to the main sale item.

"Wow. It's never been so good this early in the day. Betsy will be pleased."

Kelly smiled. The postmistress was a strong support to the town. Over the last few weeks, she'd learned how much the woman did behind the scenes.

"Go out and enjoy yourself," Maggie said with a big grin on her face. "Spend some of the California money. And I know a certain man has been asking for you."

"We're just friends," Kelly said.

"Says every woman about every relationship that is so 'not friends,'" Maggie said. "We may keep you here yet."

Not likely.

Kelly stepped out of the tent and was almost run over by a group of boys hurtling toward one of the booths, one of them clutching a small neon football in his hand. Squeals came from the bouncy house at the far end of the field, and in the field behind her, patient ponies walked around in circles. The cotton candy smell from the booth next door tickled her stomach.

Time to eat.

Drawn by the sweet smell of barbequed chicken, she headed for the Whitefish Rotary stand. Tables and chairs had been set up in a space between it and a beer truck. Groups, clustered around the tables, smiled and laughed as they ate through their meals. A group of men at the edge was having an animated discussion. Ryan sat in the middle, gesturing with a chicken leg. He waved it at her when she went by.

"Come join us."

She shook her head and got into line. Whatever they were discussing seemed far too intense. Instead, she took her plate to a table where Alex was sitting next to the sweet shop owner. Amanda? Yes, that was her name. As she sat down next to them, two other women sat in the remaining chairs.

"I'm getting some good bids on the owl," Susan Thomas said with a grin. "I stuck a stack of my cards next to the sheet. Hope you don't mind."

"Not at all," Kelly said. "This whole event is for the town, and if it weren't for people like you, the town wouldn't even be on the map."

"Oh, she's good," Gabriella, Susan's partner, said. "No wonder she got that owl away from you." She smiled at Kelly. "I'm impressed. You're a real asset to the town. How long are you staying?"

"I have to be back in California for my teaching job the last week of August."

"We're trying to get her to give up all that foolishness and stay here," Alex said. "But so far it isn't working. Maybe a weekend at your inn?"

"I have an entire retreat center," Kelly reminded her friend.

"Yes," Gabriella asked. "What are you going to do with it?"

Kelly's Boston not-your-business attitude wrestled with Montanan openness.

"The plan is to sell it." As Susan sputtered, she raised her hand. "I really have no choice. I don't live here. My children, even though they're almost grown, know California as their home, someplace to go when everything else goes wrong. I have a job that I love." Kelly shook her head. "It makes no sense to stay here. I will do my utmost to find someone who will keep it as my grandmother did, but you know there are no guarantees in life."

"She wanted *you* to run it," Gabriella said softly.

"My grandmother didn't really know me anymore. We didn't see each other and rarely talked or exchanged notes."

"I think she knew you better than you think," Alex said, her words landing with a thud.

The resulting silence was uncomfortable, and Kelly busied herself slicing off juicy bits of chicken.

"Sorry," Alex said. "Sometimes I speak before my brain catches up with my mouth."

"No problem," Kelly said automatically, but the atmosphere had shifted.

"The band they got for the evening entertainment is really good," Gabriella said, rescuing the conversation. "Susan and I heard them at the KettleHouse Amphitheater in Missoula last summer. Great dance band."

"I'll save one for you," Susan said, giving Gabriella an exaggerated wink. "Even though I'm sure my dance card will be full."

"You have two left feet," Gabriella responded with a grin. "I'm sure I'll be the only one to take a chance."

"We'll see about that," Susan said.

"You're on." The women clicked their red cups, sloshing a bit of beer over the rims. But the lightness had returned to the table, and Kelly let Alex's comment go. The rest of the meal focused on quirky customers who'd shown up at the inn over the last year.

On her way back to the auction tent, Ryan caught up with her. "Hey, you," he said. "Enjoying yourself?"

"Yes," she said. "Quite a lot. It's a lot less structured than a fair like this would be in California."

"Too many rules and regulations down there."

She shrugged. "Could be. So what were you and the other guys talking about during lunch? Seemed like an intense discussion."

"It was. Probably because we've been having the same argument for the past five years. Some of them believe we can't do anything about the increase in fires; some of us believe that no matter what, there is always something that can be done to make it better."

"Is it that big a problem here, too?" Devastating California fires were becoming almost constant.

"Unfortunately. The season starts earlier and earlier. In fact, the first one of the season popped up in the Cabinet Mountains last week. Someone let a burn pile get away from them. They got it out quickly. It's a sad truth that about 60 percent of Montana fires are caused by humans. We've got to be more careful."

She looked around her. Trees were everywhere, with houses and cabins nestled into every conceivable spot. The glint from Makalia's house high on a cliff caught her eye. It was so vulnerable.

"Think you can handle the summer?" Ryan asked. "Fire season can get intense."

"I'm good," she said. "It's not much different from California."

"Actually, it's a lot different." He scanned the mountains. "When I lived in the city, crime was impersonal. Someone else was a criminal, never someone you knew. Here? Here it's always personal. If you don't know the perpetrator, talk to a few of your friends and someone will know them. Fires don't happen to strangers; you and your family are staring down the same threat that someone down the Bitterroot is seeing."

His words made her an outsider, someone who'd never understand the ways of true Montanans. She didn't belong here.

The auction went off at five-thirty without a hitch. Every item brought in more than anticipated, but the nurse's cap topped any past bid, according to Maggie. People had come from as far away as Spokane and Billings to make their bids. Some people had even tried to bid via email or phone, but Maggie drew the line at that. People had to show up—and spend money at the fair—to be able to bid.

Kelly's old friend had turned into a savvy businesswoman.

All the booths put out their best food for dinner. The barbeque pit switched to ribs, and hamburgers, corndogs, and plain old hotdogs were plentiful. The church ladies had a huge batch of chili going, and that is where Maggie, Alex, and Kelly headed after their duties at the auction booth were complete and the money was stowed in the safe in the general store.

News of the income from the auction had made the rounds, and the women were given high fives wherever they went.

"Music's starting up," Maggie said, her hips already twitching to the heavy beat of the drum. "Got your dancing shoes on?"

Kelly had brought a pair of flats with her, but she noticed her friends both wore cowboy boots that worked with their outfits: Maggie in a long, flared skirt and Alex in tight jeans. Kelly had decided on jeans as well, but they weren't quite as form-fitting as her friend's. Childbirth had left her with a slight tummy that no amount of exercise could change. After numerous attempts, she'd finally decided it was a badge of honor and stopped worrying about it.

Maggie was immediately snatched up by a partner, and Alex soon followed. Kelly watched them spin to the music, trying not to feel left out. On the far side of the dance floor, Sheriff Tom Gerard watched as well, but his gaze was focused on only one woman: Maggie.

When was her friend going to see what was right in front of her?

What about you? a voice eerily like her grandmother's whispered in her mind.

"Dance?" Ryan asked, appearing beside her, his hand held out.

"Sure." He took her hand, and suddenly they were in the middle of a whirling sea of bodies. The floor shook with the beat of a few dozen feet, most shod in boots. Laughter and talk swirled around them, but all she could focus on was Ryan, mostly to keep from stepping on his toes.

After a few dances, someone else claimed her, and then a third person. It went on that way until the music slowed a half hour later. She found herself paired with one of the artists she'd met while soliciting donations. A nice man, just very ... young.

"I think this is my dance," Ryan said, once again holding out his hand. "You promised, remember?"

Even though she'd made no such promise, Kelly shifted to his arms and let him wrap them around her. She put her head on his shoulder, the movement as natural as making a cup of coffee in the morning.

As the dance went on, she was aware he was moving them to the edge of the platform. When the last note paused, he led her back behind the now-empty auction tent.

She knew what he wanted.

She leaned closer, giving silent permission, and he lowered his head to envelop her lips in a kiss. He was the first man she'd kissed since her husband died.

Should she feel guilty? She didn't.

All she felt was the sweetness of his closeness and the promise of possibilities.

For now, she'd take the gift and worry about the rest tomorrow.

Chapter Twenty-One

Kelly struggled out of bed at eight the next morning. With a groan, she stepped into the shower and turned the hot water up to stir her body into awareness. She had an hour to eat breakfast and get back down to the celebration site. It was all hands on deck to clean up the field and finish striking the booths and tents. The out-of-towners had left the night before, but locals had stayed to the bitter end, deferring duty for pleasure.

As the water slid over her face, Kelly touched her lips where Ryan had kissed her not once but twice, stealing a few moments when he walked her to her car. Her lips felt the same to her fingers, but life had irrevocably changed. She'd been loyal to John their entire marriage. He'd been gone almost a year. It was okay to kiss another man, wasn't it?

Life went on. At least that's what she'd always been told.

She still didn't feel guilty, but it was hard to describe exactly what she *did* feel.

When she toweled off, she rubbed extra hard, wanting her skin to share the same vitality yesterday had given her. It wasn't only the dancing and the kiss. Seeing the looks on the faces of the community when they'd realized how much money this year's celebration had brought in had made her feel on top of the moon. Even though she'd brought in more funds for the auctions she'd chaired for California events, this success was more personal and enjoyable.

Quickly dressing in an old T-shirt and jeans, she headed to the kitchen. With her cup of coffee in hand, she went out to the front porch and greeted the day.

The sun had dried the dew and warmed the air. Peace surrounded her, and there was no more important thing to do than take in the scenery around her. While she couldn't see the lake from where she was, the greenery, flowers, and aged wood of the cabins were a feast for her soul. What had it been like with retreat attendees?

She could almost imagine women emerging from their artistic cocoons, coffee in hand, maybe still in their pajamas, walking barefoot through the grass to turn their faces to the morning sun. Would there have been a morning gathering at the easternmost part of the property, a variety of female figures performing the sun salutation to greet the dawn?

No rushing to be any particular place at a set time but a slow emergence as the artist integrated with the soul of the human in a fresh pattern, and the whole became visible.

Kelly breathed deeply, invigorating her lungs with the mountain air, and smiled. This was what it was like to be totally present in one's body. She stretched her fingers, almost feeling the ivory keys beneath them. There was just enough time to practice before she left for the field. Her friends would understand.

Maggie and Alex, and Teagan were already at the field, along with a group of volunteer firemen who were assisting with booth takedown and loading pickup trucks. A group of teenage boys and girls, shepherded by Teagan, were scooping up piles of horse droppings and loading them into a wheelbarrow.

"Want to join them?" Susan said as she handed Kelly a plastic bag and gloves.

"I'll pass, thanks. What are they going to do with all that?"

Susan pointed to an old Willy's truck at the far side of the field. "Once that's full, David will run it back to his farm. He grows organic produce—supplies many of the fancy restaurants in Whitefish."

"That's cool," Kelly said.

"Why don't you start over there," Susan said, once again pointing. "That's the next area that needs picking up."

"Sure."

"Hey," Susan called as Kelly started to walk away. "Thanks."

"For what?"

"For convincing me to get involved. It's been hard for me to feel part of the community." She hesitated and glanced toward where Gabriella was working. "I'm a bit different, and you know, well … not everyone is tolerant. Plus there's Gabriella's past. But … anyway … thanks. It feels good to be part of all this." Susan waved at the part of the field she'd designated for Kelly. "Have fun," she said and walked away.

How could sweet Gabriella have any kind of past that needed to be hidden?

None of her business.

But as she began her chores of digging out random wrappers, paper plates and cups that had gotten away from their owners as the night had worn on, and various other debris, she thought about the other part of Susan's statement.

She'd felt accepted by the community. And Kelly had helped make that happen.

It was a good feeling, even if Kelly herself really wasn't part of the town.

But could she be?

Her life was in California.

Was it? What was to keep her there? She'd barely heard from Peter since he'd been gone. His grandparents let her know he was doing well, and when she texted her son, he responded within a few days. Lisa had been more forthcoming. Since their weekend together, her daughter had made more of an effort to check in and see how her mother was doing.

Reading between the lines, Kelly sensed things weren't as good as they could be with Lisa's boyfriend and parents. But Lisa would need to handle that problem on her own. Kelly's own mother had interfered too much. She hoped she wasn't interfering too little, but it was something she'd realized the more she taught. Guiding a person was one thing. Demanding they adhere to the advice given crossed a line that didn't allow a child or adult to grow.

She loved her teaching job, but she'd been doing it for a while. She had enough time in for a small sum from the teacher's retirement fund, and with John's life insurance, she had no need for worries, particularly if she sold the house. Maybe restarting the retreat center made sense.

Who was she kidding? It was the kiss that was tempting her to stay, but that was ridiculous. It was merely a gesture. True, they had had some moments that reminded her of being young again, but that time had passed. She was an adult, and adults—real adults—didn't build their lives on romantic flings or what might have been.

Placing her hands on her hips, she leaned back, stretching out the kinks in her back. All around her, people worked at a steady pace. Some had taken a water break or were chatting with each other. There wasn't a sense of obligation but more a pulling together to do something that benefited all of them. Yet the people she'd come to know were as individualistic as any she'd met in her life, maybe more so. They just knew when to tone it down to achieve something they all needed.

She was an outsider looking in, and she wanted to be more.

"So did you have fun with Ryan last night?" Maggie's saucy voice whispered in her ear.

"Of course. I see you finally broke down and gave poor Tom

Gerard a dance," she teased back.

"There's nothing there," Maggie protested. "He needs to find someone more suited to be a sheriff's wife than a woman tied up by a teenage daughter, an artsy mother, and trying to keep a general store afloat."

"Right."

"But what about you and Ryan? There's a rumor you were kissing behind the tent like two teenagers trying to escape the parents."

Darn small towns.

"It was nothing of the sort," Kelly said, plucking a Coke can from the grass and stuffing it in the bag.

"Hey! Recycle that," Maggie said. "Didn't Susan give you a recycle bag?"

"She must have forgotten."

"Give it to me."

Kelly dug the can out and handed it over.

"We've both got children," Maggie said. "Let's try to give them the planet in better shape than it looks like we're going to do."

"Okay," Kelly said, feeling a bit like a chastened schoolgirl.

"Sorry," Maggie said. "It's a bit of a hot button for me. Fire season brings it all home. I just heard there's new one over by St. Regis. They start earlier and earlier every year. There are times it feels like we are using teaspoons of water to keep it all under control—and we're running out of water as well."

"It's bad in California, too." Kelly touched Maggie's arm. "All we can do is our best and pray that we can all work together to find a solution soon."

"Yeah." There was still doubt in Maggie's voice. "On another note, you did a great job on the auction. Everyone's raving about it. We all want you to stay, to open the retreat center again. Everyone's willing to pitch in and help."

Kelly took a deep breath. "Selling still feels like the right decision for me."

Maggie put her hands on her hips and studied her. "There sounds like there might be a 'but' in there."

"I've enjoyed being part of this. My life is in California, but the kids are growing up—grown up, really. It's just going to be me rattling around that house with John's ghost."

"Sounds like a change is due," Maggie said softly.

"But I wouldn't even know where to begin."

"I'm sure we could help with that. My mom and Betsy were close friends with your grandmother. I'm sure they know things they even don't know they know. And you said Henrietta left you manuals and a computer drive full of stuff. Alex would be a great help. She worked in an events company before ... well, before."

There were too many secrets in this town, but she'd never find them out if she left.

"Okay," she said with a nod. "Let's get together and look things over."

Maggie started to babble, and Kelly held up her finger. "No promises."

"You got it."

Kelly hoped she knew what she was getting into, but deep inside her she knew she'd always regret the decision to sell if she didn't look at the whole picture herself. It was time to let go of other people's opinions of what she should do. John, her mother, even Henrietta didn't matter. Nor did possibilities with Ryan, although he certainly weighted staying.

No, it was time to figure out her own life.

Chapter Twenty-Two

"Hey," Ryan called as he opened the screen door to the kitchen. "Mind if I come in?"

"It seems like you're already here," Kelly said with a smile. Happiness glowed inside her. "Coffee?"

"Great. I can get it." He went to the correct cupboard for the mugs, then poured himself a cup of coffee. Leaning back on the counter, he asked, "What are you doing?"

"Making up some coffee cake for this afternoon. Maggie and Alex are coming over."

"You have more talents than I could ever imagine. Baking eludes me. I've learned to cook a decent meal, but I have to rely on others for my sweet tooth."

"Kids forced me to learn. It was one of the ways I could get them to sit down long enough to tell me about their day. But I'll never be as good as Charlene. That woman is a goddess."

"I think you are probably a great mom," he said softly.

"I try." She finally looked at him again. It was as if she'd never seen him before, and yet he was as familiar to her as her own hands. Grabbing the prepared baking pan, she poured the batter into it, then popped it into the oven.

"How are you doing?" he asked after she refilled her cup.

"I'm okay." She wasn't going to talk about the kiss. Kisses. She hadn't made up her mind what she thought about them, so how could she?

"That's good."

The air crackled like dry heat before a thunderstorm.

"Do you want to go to dinner some night? There's an off-beat place north of Kalispell I've wanted to try."

"That would be nice. Thank you. I'd like that," she said.

"Just like that? I don't even have to work at it?" he said with a grin.

She gestured to the screen door. "Let's sit outside."

"Sure."

She led him to the chairs, and they settled in to watch the bees buzz around the flowers.

"I really do need to get someone in to clean that up, maybe plant something a little more ornamental."

"Oh, don't do that," Ryan said. "Yes, get someone to clean it up, but Henrietta was very deliberate in her plantings. She created a pollinator-friendly garden of perennials that attract bees, butterflies, and hummingbirds. You need to add some annuals, like petunias and such, but be careful to avoid hybrids."

Kelly nodded. She could see it in her mind's eye. Bees buzzing through the flowers, hummingbirds lingering in purple and pink petunia baskets hung on the porch. How like her grandmother. She never did anything that she didn't think through and align with her values. She didn't simply go along with anything that was trendy unless it served her purpose.

How often had Kelly gone along with what someone else said without thinking it through? Her mother's training, no matter how good-intentioned, had led her to put more weight onto what other people said she should do than she did on her own thoughts. In fact, there were times she'd adopted what other people wanted for themselves until it became a driving need for her.

She remembered begging John for some very expensive jewelry that she'd seen on a woman, someone everyone looked up to and respected. However, when her husband had finally given in, she'd realized it didn't suit her, and after a few times, she let it languish in her jewelry box.

Maybe that's why she had to explore all her possibilities in Montana. She simply had no idea what she wanted to do, if she was truthful with herself. Who was she? Was the life she'd built with John a good representation? Or was the wide-eyed child with concert dreams the true spirit of herself?

She had absolutely no idea. For now, she was keeping an open mind.

"Do you have any idea how the electronics work in the barn?" she asked Ryan. "Maggie and Alex are coming over to discuss what would need to happen for the retreat center to open again."

"You're thinking of staying?" There was hope in his voice.

"I'm exploring. I still believe I'll sell the center and go back." And even if she did try to give it a go, that was a separate decision from whatever happened between her and Ryan. "My grandmother had a great deal of information on the computer. There are lots of wires and a console in her office, and it looks like a screen can be lowered on one of the barn walls. There had to be a way to project things so the three of us aren't crowded into her office."

He nodded. "Yep. Henrietta had a guy from LA—someone Betsy

knew—come set it up. I'm pretty sure I know how it works." He rose. "Let me go over and see what I can do. I'll let you know when I'm ready to show you."

"Thanks," she said.

He waved and walked toward the barn with an easy gait.

She took a few deep breaths, rose, and went back into the house to continue her preparations for the day.

Ryan had easily hooked things up and showed her how they worked. Then, after extracting a date for their dinner, he went on his way. Alex and Maggie arrived shortly afterward.

"Wow, fancy," Alex said, sitting at the table where Kelly had laid out the binders she'd found, a few folders, and a pad for each of them to take notes, just like she would have done for any organizational meeting she'd ever run. She'd even supplied a pitcher of ice water and glasses. Coffee was perking in the small kitchen, and the coffee cake and plates sat nearby.

"Well," Kelly said, "I think we have a big job ahead of us."

"I don't know," Maggie said. "Henrietta made it look easy."

"That's when you know that someone has the details down pat. Besides"—Kelly pushed a folder to Maggie—"open that."

Maggie opened it, and Alex leaned in to see what was inside.

A heavy white cardstock with a brightly painted bird sat on top of what looked to be dozens of letters and cards. Maggie opened it and scanned it, her eyes widening as she looked at the signature.

"Oh, wow," she said. "Isn't this that actress that dropped out of sight for about a year?"

"You mean the one who was at the top of her game and then found out her husband had been cheating on her? The critics panned her movie. They said she cracked."

"But then," Kelly said, "she came back stronger than ever, but in totally different movies. She even began to direct and produce independent films. I don't know what miracle my grandmother performed, but I'm quite sure I'm not up to the task."

"Don't give up before you've even tried," Alex said, leafing through the rest of the letters.

Kelly had already been through them. Not only actors but musicians, famed artists, and writers were there, as well as many lesser-known talents. All had been grateful for what most called the sanctuary her grandmother had provided. Kelly had read through them all last night, becoming more and more overwhelmed by the project as she went on.

"Look," Alex said when she'd read through a few of the letters, "you don't have to be Henrietta. You just have to be *you*. Your grandmother believed that you had what it took to take over this place." She gestured to all the things Kelly had done before they'd arrived. "It's obvious you have a natural instinct for making people feel welcome and being ready for their arrival."

"I'm not worried about the mechanics," Kelly said. "I'm worried about the spirit."

"Let it flow naturally," Maggie said. "One thing I've learned from my airy-fairy mother is that things will come together in time. It's no use forcing them. Of course, I wish both my mother and the universe would be a little speedier about completing their work."

They chuckled. Maggie rose. "I'm getting coffee. Anyone else?"

The start of the meeting was delayed while her friends oohed and aahed over the cake and filled their coffee cups. But mindful of Maggie's advice, Kelly tried to let the beginning of the meeting play out like it was going to do rather than force everyone to move according to her time schedule. After all, her friends were doing her a favor.

Eventually, they got back to it, and Kelly screened the information she'd found on the computer, which included lists, marketing plans, and a project plan for running a retreat. Unfortunately, it was a plan with a lot of holes in it, as was the schedule for the actual retreat itself. "Depends on the participants" was written in many of these blank pages.

"What am I supposed to do during these times?" Kelly asked.

Alex was scanning through one of the binders. "I think some of the answers might be in here."

"I haven't had a real chance to look at those. I mean, who does binders anymore? We've got phones and computers for everything."

Alex shook her head. "Henrietta believed there was great value in putting pen to paper or paintbrush to canvas or fingers on strings and making a tune, even if there was nothing much to say. She told me once that it was the act of beginning that required great courage, and that performing the actions of your craft, even if you hated the result, was the way to get everything in concert to achieve magnificence."

Maggie looked at her. "You never told me she said that. And I have no idea how you remembered all of it. That sounds exactly like something she would say."

"It made a huge impact," Alex said.

"I see that," Maggie replied.

"But anyway," Alex said. "This binder is full of her notes. She apparently kept reams of loose-leaf paper around and wrote out whatever she was struggling with. See here,"—she turned the book so Kelly could view the page—"she's talking about two women who were coming to the retreat, women who had once been close friends but now hated each other. She'd invited them both deliberately."

"She must have been out of her mind," Maggie said.

"Maybe," Alex said, "but you can see her thought process laid out here. There were a lot of massages that week, as well as healing ceremonies. Daily written exercises followed by a nightly fire where they burned everything they'd written. Everything was focused on cleansing and rebuilding."

"I think I remember that week," Maggie said. "People said there was a lot of screaming and yelling, too."

What had she gotten herself into?

Well, she'd only promised to think about opening the retreat center, and it was clear she wouldn't have to think about it very long.

"I know what you need to do," Maggie said.

"What?" Kelly asked warily.

"You need to run a retreat."

"That's a great idea," Alex said.

"That's a horrible idea," Kelly countered.

"No, really, open it to a few of the local artists. We'll help you select a few who are struggling but genuinely nice people. Only do it for a few days. Then you'll really have a good idea of what it's like."

"We'll help you," Alex said. "It's the only way you'll be able to come to an honest conclusion."

Kelly looked at them. They were crazy. They were right, but they were crazy.

"You have to do it," Maggie said. "For Henrietta's sake."

Kelly's look turned into a glare. How dare her old friend play the sympathy card?

Alex smiled at her, an expression that said they had Kelly where they wanted her.

"Okay," she finally said. "I'll do it. And when I fall flat on my face, you'd better be there to pick up the pieces."

Chapter Twenty-Three

The next morning Kelly headed to the barn right after breakfast. She was eager to get started. Scared to death but excited. Alex and Maggie had brainstormed a list of likely candidates and reasons why they might need some time for renewal. Kelly had decided to spend the morning researching them to see where they were on their journey and whether there might be synergy between some of them.

As she sat behind her grandmother's desk, a new sense of purpose seem to fall over her. She knew what it was like to abandon a dream because of someone else's influence and a sense of duty. Too many lives, especially women's, were derailed by the twin pressures of expectation and obligation.

Ruth Anderson was the first on the list. Ruth, her friends had explained, was the chief cook at the elementary school. She was up at dawn, even in the coldest part of winter, and worked hard to bring nutritious lunches to children, a significant number of whom were members of a food-insecure household. When she wasn't doing that, she was watching reruns of old murder mystery shows and creating delicate lace scarves and shawls with her water-reddened hands.

Basically, the woman needed some good old-fashioned TLC.

Pamela Cuzins was a nature photographer specializing in birds. Her images were fun and colorful, but the Whitefish galleries always tried to get her to take less, saying everyone with a camera was a photographer these days. She needed encouragement but also some sound strategies that allowed her to look beyond the local.

Susan Thomas was an odd choice. Her own website was non-existent, but she still appeared to be doing well.

There were a few more ideas, and Alex had asked to be there as a participant to see it from that point of view. Maggie would be available for help. She said she'd press her mother and daughter into extra service.

All Kelly had to do was pick four participants.

Her phone rang.

"Hey, Lisa. Good to hear from you. What's up?"

"Oh, Mom," Lisa descended into tears.

"Baby, what's wrong?"

"It's ... over ... and it's all my fault." More crying, and Kelly couldn't make out the next bit of whatever her daughter was saying. Then she heard, "Andrew's parents … not good enough for him…"

Whatever was going on was very wrong. Someone was trying to make her child take the blame for something that happened, a criticism that would impact Lisa's sense of self-esteem. And that was not going to happen.

Not on Kelly's watch.

If she could be there to help Lisa in person, it would be so much easier. "Lisa, sweetie, take a deep breath."

A shuddering sigh came through the phone.

"Again." Kelly waited a few seconds. "Now, just tell me the facts of what happened."

"Andrew and I got into a big fight. He said things were moving too fast for him. He wanted a break. But … he was … I knew it, but I didn't want it to be true."

"Knew what, sweetheart?"

"He was working late … all these hours. But there was a woman there … with him. He says they haven't done anything. But he's attracted to her. And he wants to break up with me." The last was a long sound that once again dissolved into sobs.

What Andrew had done was hurtful, but it was at least honest. Kelly, too, had privately thought things were going too fast, but she'd known better than to say anything.

"Okay," she said, trying to find the right words that wouldn't make it worse. "That hurts. I'm so sorry."

"Why are you in Montana?" Lisa said. "You should be here. I need you."

"You were the one who told me to go somewhere. At least I'm not in Italy."

"Oh yeah." There was an attempt at a giggle. "Silly me. When are you coming home?"

"Not for a few weeks yet. There are things I need to do yet." *Like run a retreat.*

"What am I going to do?" Lisa asked.

"You could come here."

"Not possible. I have to finish this job. I leave and it looks bad."

At least her daughter was still thinking straight.

"But I can't stay here." Again the last word was long and drawn out, but Lisa held it together this time. "And I can't afford to live anywhere else because I'm doing this internship for minimum wage. San Francisco is sooo expensive!"

"I'll pay for it. You've only got another six weeks, right? How is the job going?"

"All right, I suppose. I'm just not sure this is what I want to do with the rest of my life."

"Well, you still have two more years before you graduate. As long as it's close to the same field, you should be able to transfer credits to a new major."

"Not if it's theater," Lisa said softly.

"Theater? You can't make a living in theater. It's a fine avocation but not something you can use to build a life."

"I knew that would be your reaction. You've never taken a risk. I think I'm good enough to make it. I want to take that risk. Even if it means dropping out of school. I hate computer science."

"You're upset," Kelly said, trying to ignore the hurt clawing at her insides. Her daughter was just transferring her own feelings. That was all.

"I don't know, Mom. I'm so mixed up. I thought I had it all figured out with Andrew, and now? He barely talks to me, and his parents have asked me to leave by the weekend."

Kelly had always thought Andrew was a cold fish. Apparently, he came by it naturally.

"It sounds like the first thing to do is get a place of your own. You've said you'll finish out the summer. That's a good plan. Then we can discuss everything else when I get home at the end of August."

"Thanks, Mom." Lisa hesitated. "And, Mom? I'm sorry about what I said. You're a great mom. You were always there for us. We were lucky." She gave a tentative laugh. "I could have wound up with Andrew's mother!"

Kelly smiled. Her life had been worthwhile, in spite of following the traditional path. Soon it would be time to go home, pick up the mantle of motherhood, and look forward to being a grandmother. There was no doubt Lisa would find the right man, someone who deserved her outgoing, loving daughter.

But it meant, no matter what, she was going to have to return to California. Running a retreat center in Montana was out of the question. She should end this now.

Then she looked at the names on the list again. These were good people, women struggling to make the world a more beautiful place. What if she did it anyway, even if it was a one-off? Everyone would benefit. She'd have a proof of concept that would help sell the property, the artists would get a week supporting each other, and Maggie? Well, maybe there would be time to push her old friend into at least talking to the poor sheriff.

"Hello!" Ryan's voice boomed in the empty barn space.

"Hey!" With a smile she left the small office. When she reached him, there was a moment of awkwardness. If their relationship were further along, a kiss might work, but now? She fluttered her fingers. "Coffee?"

"Love some." He smiled, looking relieved that she'd figured out what to do.

She already knew he liked it black. Milk was too difficult to get if he ran out in his cabin high in the mountains. And sugar without milk? That was simply wrong, according to Ryan.

"What brings you by?" she asked as she handed him the mug.

"I brought lunch," he said, holding up a tote bag that proudly proclaimed Culver's General Store. "Elaine made Reubens today. All I need to do is heat them up in Henrietta's panini pan, and they're ready to go."

"My grandmother had a panini pan?"

"She had everything. She loved to cook, you know. Before she married your grandfather, she'd spent a year at a culinary institute in California. But then she got pregnant with your mother, married, and they came to Montana in an effort to live off the land. A lot of young people wound up here on the same quest."

"I didn't know that." Maybe that's why her grandmother was so intent on her following her dream. Her stomach growled, and she realized how hungry she was. It must be later than she thought. There were no clocks in the large barn space. She suspected that was a deliberate oversight.

They went back to the kitchen in the house, where Ryan quickly found the pan. He certainly knew his way around this kitchen. He must have spent a lot of time with her grandmother.

Was Ryan the one her grandmother had meant when she talked about the possibility of true love?

She watched him prepare the sandwiches with practiced ease. He was comfortable to be around, and she didn't feel the need to take over that she'd often felt when John attempted to bungle around the kitchen. She trusted Ryan here.

What had that to do with love?

Probably everything.

"Any word on the phone?" she asked.

"He's got a major work project this week. He said he won't get to it until next week or the one after."

"Oh."

"Sometimes bad news can wait," Ryan said as he put the plated sandwiches on the table.

"It could be good news," she countered. "It's probably an extra work phone. I'm imagining things."

"I hope so. Dig in while they're hot."

She took a bite. The corned beef, sauerkraut, and dressing melded together perfectly with the marbled rye. Ryan was smiling.

"Told you," he said as he took a big bite of his own sandwich.

They ate in relative silence, mainly interrupted by moans of culinary ecstasy. There was even a kosher pickle to cleanse the richness of the dressing.

She leaned back and placed her hand on her stomach. "Oh my. I don't think I can do another thing today."

He laughed, stood, and picked up the plates.

"I'll do the dishes," she protested. "You cooked."

"It won't take long," he said. "That will give you a chance to look at this." He slid a folded piece of paper across the table.

"What is it?"

"It's a final list of repairs that need to be done. Some I can fix, but for a few of them you need specialists. Unfortunately, I noticed a new problem with the plumbing in the Athena cabin. I think it's been there for a long time. When I went back in to fix it, the whole thing fell apart in my hand. Then I traced the water line back to the main pump and discovered that was leaking as well. The whole thing needs replacing."

"And that means it needs to be dug up."

"And it means a real plumber," he said.

"It's going to be expensive."

"I'm afraid so."

She sighed and put her head in her hands. For a day that had started out so bright and shiny, it had sure turned cloudy fast. First Lisa's crisis, now this. Both things were going to take a chunk from her savings.

The sooner she got back home to her paycheck, the better.

Chapter Twenty-Four

Kelly chose a dark, flowing skirt and a blue button-down crepe silk shirt for dinner. He'd said it was casual, but it was still a date, and she was still her mother's daughter. She added a gold link necklace she'd purchased for herself during one holiday trip and a pair of matching earrings. Low black heels completed the outfit.

Her auburn hair was brushed and tied back neatly in a ribbon the same color as her blouse. Her makeup was light, just enough to brighten the tan she was beginning to get from spending time in the summer sun. She was never going to be a teenager again, but that was okay. She'd decided a long time ago she wasn't going to begrudge lost youth, but be happy with the age she was.

Grabbing one of her grandmother's shawls—had Ruth Anderson knit it?—she waited on the porch for Ryan. It was a peaceful place at the end of day, the chorus of birds becoming more pronounced, while the breeze from the lake kept everything fresh.

She'd bitten the bullet and called the plumber Ryan had recommended, as well as someone named Larry, who was a full-time handyman.

"He understands things about construction that it would take me a lifetime to learn. It's like he has an intuitive understanding of wood. It almost speaks to him."

She'd decided she wanted Ryan's input on her proposal for retreat participants. Because he'd spent so much time away, he looked at the community from a different perspective than either of her friends, and because he was a man, he might see things she couldn't.

The sound of the motor caused her to stand. She grabbed her purse and shawl and headed to the parking area on the side of the house. Ryan had gotten out of the car by the time she arrived. He'd also made an effort with his appearance. His khakis looked neatly pressed above his dark brown loafers, and the forest-green patterned shirt gave him the same whimsical look that had been reflected in the quilt she'd seen in the gallery.

"Wow," he said. "You look amazing." He kissed her quickly, then helped her into the passenger seat.

She didn't mind; it was nice to be treated to old-fashioned manners as long as the old-fashioned attitudes didn't come along with it.

"It's going to be a beautiful evening for a drive," he said as he started south.

The lake sparkled between the trees to her right, and the sun dappled everything around them.

"Yes," she said.

He tentatively took her hand, and she didn't pull away. She wouldn't think about what might or might not be in the future. She'd simply enjoy the moment.

They drove in amicable silence for a while.

"So, tell me about your retreat plans," he said.

"Maggie suggested I do a proof of concept. She said it might help a few of the women artists in town."

"So why are *you* doing it?" he asked.

"To make Maggie happy," she said. Even as she said it, she knew it was a lame reason.

"I see. Who are you thinking of having stay?"

"Alex, of course. She can be a sounding board for how the retreat went from a participant's point of view."

"Makes sense."

"Then I thought about Ruth Anderson, Pamela, and Susan Thomas, although Susan's an odd choice. I'm not sure how much she'd mesh with the others."

"Because she's gay?"

"No. Of course not." At least she hoped not.

"Susan's had a bit of a rough time. She was in the army for a while—combat in the Middle East. Plus, many women feel like you—a little uncomfortable around her. There's no shame in admitting that." He squeezed Kelly's hand gently. "Invite her. She might teach you more than you do her."

"Okay," Kelly said. "She's on the list. That would be four. That's all the place can hold. I wonder why my grandmother never put up more cabins."

"Henrietta thought the symmetry of the buildings was perfect the way it is."

"And the other problem I have is that these women are all artists. Promise Cove has lots of them. But my grandmother always had a mix."

"I have a suggestion. Leave Pamela out. She needs to get some business help more than emotional help. I'll try to get Makalia to talk to her. There's another woman. Just a second." Ryan pulled his hand away to put both hands on the wheel to navigate through the center of

Whitefish and continue south. Once they were headed toward Kalispell, he reached for her hand once again.

She was grateful to have him touching her again. It was good to be with someone who really listened. Was that she had been missing in her marriage with John? They'd functioned as a team, each knowing the role they were supposed to play. But if she strayed out of her assigned role, like the time she thought about joining the local orchestra to keep her skills alive, he'd quickly clipped her wings.

Had she done the same to him?

"You okay?" Ryan asked.

She shook the past away. "Yes. Just thinking. If I eliminate Pamela, who do you suggest to replace her?"

"There's a relatively new woman in town—new as in she's been here only a year. Her name is Julia Leonard. She's about your age, maybe a little younger. I don't know her story; she's close-mouthed. But there's something about her eyes." Ryan glanced at Kelly. "It's the same look I saw while I was a cop. The look of a woman who's been mentally and physically abused."

"I hope you're wrong," Kelly said.

"Me too." Ryan shrugged. "All I can tell you is my gut feel, a notion that served me well on the streets. Anyway, she's a singer-songwriter, so at least you'd have some variation. And since you're a musician as well, you may be able to reach her when others can't."

"I don't possess any magic powers," Kelly said. "My grandmother may have had them, but I'm just an ordinary woman."

"Oh, you're far from ordinary to me," Ryan said.

Contentment made her smile.

They began to enter the area that had been built up primarily by big box stores. Ryan pulled into one of the smaller areas with a grouping of storefronts. A number of cars were huddled in one corner.

"Good," he said. "They're getting more customers."

Glass windows allowed her to see tables lit with candlelight. Couples sat at about half of them. Over the windows, a brightly lit sign declared Two Continents Restaurant.

"What an odd name," she said.

"It's a unique situation," he said, getting out of the car.

She opened her door, and he was standing there to help her out with a big smile on his face. "May I say again how lovely you look? You are as I'd imagined you'd be when I was a teen. I was so hoping you'd come back that summer."

"My mother kept me away."

"That's what Henrietta said. I had finally worked up the courage to ask you out on a real date, and I never saw you again." There was a sad note in his voice.

"But I'm here now,"

"Yes, you are." He kissed her, lingering a little longer than he had when he'd picked her up.

Holding hands, they walked into the restaurant. A young woman in a sari greeted them and led them to their table. Shortly after they ordered, she came back to talk with them. "Do you know the story of our restaurant?" she asked in a musical voice.

Kelly shook her head.

"We are both refugees from different countries. We're here for different reasons. I am here because in India, some men make it hard for women to exist. My husband is here because in the Congo, it seems impossible for good men to find peace. We met here, in America, and fell in love."

"How wonderful," Kelly said.

The woman smiled. "My husband is an amazing cook. I like to create a place where people can enjoy their food. It works well for us. We hope you enjoy it too."

"We will," Kelly said.

The woman gave a slight bow and walked away.

"I'd heard a bit about them," he replied. "It was one of the reasons I wanted to come. The food should be interesting."

They chose several small dishes and tasted each other's orders. Kelly lost herself in pure enjoyment. The laughed as they tried to describe the flavors they were tasting. One dish was particularly hot, and Kelly fanned her mouth as Ryan quickly refilled her water glass.

They were almost finished when a slim Black man in a chef's outfit came to their table. "You like my cooking?" he said. "It's making you happy?"

"Yes," Ryan said. "Very happy. Thank you."

"That's good," the man said. "You should come back. Tell your friends. Okay?"

"Okay," Ryan said and put his hand out.

The other man shook it with a grin that took up the lower half of his face.

"Thank you. Enjoy," the chef said.

Once they finished their meal, they headed home, discussing the meal and the plight of refugees across the globe and how the couple from such warm climates would fare in the winter.

"I'm not sure how I'd do," Kelly said.

"You've become a California hothouse flower," Ryan said. "It would take you a while, but you'd get used to it."

"I'm not sure I want to."

"Oh," he said. Then the conversation lulled.

They had just gotten back to her grandmother's house when Ryan's phone dinged.

"Another fire," he said. "This one's closer to home. It's on the southeast side of Big Mountain. They're going to have big problems if it gets out of control. Too many houses up there." His voice was strained.

"How can you live this close to such danger?" she asked.

He shook his head. "I thought you were beginning to understand. Montana is my home. That means accepting what nature has to throw at you here—fire, wind, and winter."

He got out of the Explorer and walked to her side, opening the door for her. Leaning on the top, he looked down on her. "I was hoping you'd stay. Maybe I'm trying to recapture a dream that has no possibility of existing."

"I like you," she said. "I'm not sure I can always like Montana."

"But that's the problem. I left once, but I decided I'd never make my home anywhere else once I came back."

"I haven't decided totally," she said. "There's still the retreat to create."

"But you've got your suitcase packed," he said without emotion.

"Give me a break, Ryan," she said, her temper unexpectedly rising. "I've been here only a few weeks. You can't expect me to flip to a country girl overnight."

His smile slowly came back. "You're right. I'm being too tough on you."

"Thanks for dinner," she said. "It was lovely—and unexpected."

"You're welcome. I enjoyed it." He leaned in and kissed her cheek before waving and getting into his vehicle to leave.

Everything between them had shifted, and it wasn't for the good. Regret and sadness filled her heart.

Chapter Twenty-Five

Kelly went through the motions of the next few days. The recommended plumber came and handled the work, receiving a nice check in return. She transferred money to Lisa's account for her new apartment, shared with a few women looking for a temporary roommate. Larry, the other handyman, came over with a list Ryan had sent him.

From the man himself? She heard nothing.

She'd made her final pick of candidates: Alex, Susan, Julia, and Ruth. She'd laid out the broad brushes of a schedule, but there were big question marks on the spots for group activities. She wasn't a therapist or a spiritual adviser or any helpful occupation. She was a music teacher. Give her a handful of kids and she'd keep them occupied for an hour or so. Adults were a whole other breed.

"Hello!" Maggie called to Kelly, who was sitting at one of the portable tables in the middle of the barn. "Alex texted me. She's on her way." She held up a bag. "I've got bread and cheese and a good bottle of wine for later."

"Definitely later," Kelly said. "There's a whole lot of blank spaces we need to fill in first."

"Be right there." Maggie stowed her stuff in a small fridge and grabbed a cup of coffee. She'd just settled when Alex breezed in, travel mug in hand. Her hands were covered with stain.

"I had to finish a lamp before I came," she said. "I didn't get started soon enough on a commissioned piece, and the stain needs to be dry before the client comes on Saturday."

"Sounds like you could use a time management course," Maggie said.

"Pot and kettle," Alex shot back.

Kelly wished she had the ease the two of them shared with each other. They'd had it once, but then she'd gone away. Maybe if she moved up here permanently …

"How bad *are* the winters here?" she asked.

"Some are good; some feel like they will never end," Alex said.

"And it's not only snow," Maggie added. "Temperatures can go below freezing, even zero, and sit there for a couple of weeks. Nothing moves well."

"How do you stand it?" Kelly asked.

"I guess it's what we've always known," Maggie said. "Plus we're all in this together. It provides community."

"You'll get used to it," Alex said. "But first we need to get through fire season. It's looking like a bad one."

"Did you hear about the arsonist?" Maggie asked.

"No," Alex said.

"Apparently, some of the fires, like the one on Big Mountain, are suspicious. They haven't found evidence of anything nature caused, like a lightning strike, or an unintentional human event, like a campfire that wasn't properly doused."

"Why would someone do something like that?" Kelly asked. "It's so dry here, everything could go up quickly. People could die."

"Some people get off on it," Alex said. "They come back to the scene of the fire to watch things burn. And some people do it because they can't find a job and want to be hired to put it out."

"They don't think of the long-term effects," Maggie added.

"That's sad," Kelly said.

"Yes. And dangerous. I hope they catch him soon," Maggie said.

Alex and Kelly nodded.

"Rumor has it you went to dinner with Ryan," Maggie said.

"That rumor would be true," Kelly said without enthusiasm.

"Doesn't sound like happy times."

"Dinner was great. But I don't think my dinner dates should be the topic of this discussion," Kelly said as politely as possible. She got up to get the water pitcher and some glasses. "We've got work to do."

"Whatever you say, boss," Maggie said, but her tone indicated the subject wasn't closed for long.

Kelly ignored her and put three glasses and the pitcher of water on the table. "The primary question I have is, what do I do with the artists when I have them together in a group setting? What did my grandmother do?"

"There's nothing in her notes?"

"There's lots in her notes, just not anything that makes sense to me."

"Let me see," Alex said.

Kelly slid a second binder to her, and Alex started paging through it. Maggie leaned over to get a better look.

"It says here that Henrietta made them send in a self-portrait, both written and drawn, before they got to the retreat. The first evening they got in a group and discussed them. The rest of the program evolved from there, with plenty of time for self-reflection, taking walks, massages, and practicing their craft if they wanted, but only if they wanted."

"I saw that. It's how I came up with the schedule." Kelly turned her plan to them.

Maggie and Alex studied it. "Is there a journal somewhere?" Alex asked.

"I'm not sure. Let me look." Kelly went back into the office. All the binders she'd found were already on the table. Then she remembered the shelf in her grandmother's quarters. There had been several pretty journals she hadn't had time to look through stuffed in the bookshelf. Maybe there was something in there.

"Be right back," she said. She quickly returned to the house and raced up the stairs. Gathering all the volumes she could find, she headed back to the barn, where she dumped the books on the table. "Maybe in here?"

"Let's see," Maggie said, grabbing one and opening it. She read, "Journal Reflections" and the dates it covered.

Kelly and Alex grabbed the others. There were four journals, two that declared they were personal reflections. Kelly put those aside. "Let's each take a volume to skim and make notes," she said. "Then we can see what we found." Her pulse quickened. Maybe the answers would be in those pages.

And maybe the personal version would contain some advice as to what to do next with her own life.

A few hours and many cups of coffee later, they'd extracted all kinds of possibilities from the journals. Although her grandmother's notes about what had worked and what hadn't were informal and changed over the years, there was a clear picture of what she would have done if she'd lived to do another retreat.

The methodology didn't suit Kelly, who liked schedules and to-dos laid out neatly and clearly, but at least it was a plan.

"Thank you," she told them as they gathered the papers, books, binders, and laptop and put them back into the office. "I couldn't have done this without you."

"It's fun," Maggie said. "It's what I like best about the store—coming up with ideas of what I can add to entice people to come in and buy more, even if they're just passing through."

"Can you stay a little longer? I bought some wine and made up some snacks." She tried to keep the thin strand of desperation from her voice. She didn't want to be left alone with her thoughts. There were too many questions straining her mind.

"Sure," Maggie said without hesitation. "All that's waiting for me at home is a mother painting wild art while heavy rock and roll plays at full blast and a teenager I may strangle at any time. See, you're preventing a homicide!"

"And I'm celebrating being done with a commission, so let's party!" Alex said, raising her hand in the air and twirling around.

They laughed, and Kelly led them to where she'd stashed bottles of red and white, along with a number of savory dips and chips.

"This woman knows how to make us happy," Maggie said. "Are all California get-togethers this good?"

"I don't know," Kelly said. "There always seemed to be a certain standard that had to be met." Even the teacher gatherings had been more lavish than she imagined an everyday gathering was in this area.

"Stuffy," Alex said.

"I think it's delightful!" Maggie countered. "You are so minimalist these days. What's wrong with some pretty paper plates and a sprinkling of parsley on the dip?"

Alex shrugged. "Not my style."

"But," Kelly said, "you do those beautiful lamps, mirrors, and whatnot. Those aren't simply utilitarian."

Alex took a sip of her reddish-purple pinot noir as she took time to answer the question. "I guess it's because the things I create last. Paper plates clutter the environment. A potter's plates can be beautiful and last a long time. You don't even need a lot of them." She gestured to the array of dips. "This is pretty, but after an hour, it disappears."

"Less, if I have anything to say about it!" Maggie said, scooping a large amount with a sturdy tortilla chip.

"Not to say I don't appreciate all this," Alex said. "I do. I really love that you went to all this effort for us. It's amazing." Her eyes glistened with moisture as she looked at Kelly, a half attempt at a smile tugging at her lips. "There are just things ... stuff I don't want to talk about now ... that make me long for permanence in my life, not things that are here and gone too quickly."

Kelly took two steps and pulled her old friend into a hug. At first, Alex was resistant, but then she relaxed and put her arms around Kelly. They held each other for a long while, and Kelly could sense the deep sorrow centered in the other woman.

What had happened?

She'd have to let it come out in its own time.

"Oh, let me in," Maggie said and threw her arms around both of them.

They stood wrapped together for several minutes before they released each other. Kelly wiped her eyes, noticing the others did the same.

It was going to be really difficult to leave this blooming friendship behind.

Chapter Twenty-Six

Kelly's shoulders ached as she awaited the first person to arrive for the retreat. Alex had told her she'd be late because of a rush job for a valued customer. That meant Kelly was waiting for one of two strangers or Susan.

The sound of gravel crunching under a vehicle's tires made her stand up and walk toward the parking lot. A tall, robust woman with fine blond hair in a nondescript cut climbed out of the driver's side. Without noticing Kelly, she opened the back seat and yanked out a gray duffle bag with ease.

"Ruth?" Kelly asked.

"That'd be me," Ruth said with a generous smile. She held out the unencumbered hand. "I'm so glad you're doing this. I've wanted to be in one of Henrietta's retreats for years."

"Welcome. I've put you in the Terpsichore cabin. She was the goddess of poetry and dancing." Maggie and Alex had strategized with her to determine which guest to put in which cabin.

Ruth nodded. "I do love to kick up my heels, so that will be good."

"Feel free," Kelly said. "There's a great stereo system and a good-sized dance floor with that cabin."

"Cool!" Ruth looked around. "Am I the first?"

Gravel kicked up under a heavy vehicle rapidly coming down the drive.

"Not for long," Kelly said.

A black aging pickup roared into the lot and slammed to a stop.

Susan jumped down and strode in their direction. "Hi, Kelly, um …"

"I'm Ruth." The knitter held out her hand, which was rough from hours spent cleaning in the school kitchen.

Susan took it and shook it vigorously. "Good to meet you." Then she seemed to run out of words and dropped Ruth's hand.

"Let's get you settled," Kelly said. "I've laid out some snacks and towels in your rooms. We won't get started officially for another hour, so feel free to relax or take a walk around the grounds. The one thing I ask is that you don't get on your cell phones. This is a retreat, which means it's *your* time, not available for anyone else."

"Okay dokey," Susan said, then went back to her truck to pull out an old army bag.

Didn't anyone use proper luggage up here? Kelly led the pair to their respective cabins, grabbed a cup of coffee she didn't need, and waited for the next guest. As she waited, she watched Susan and Ruth emerge from their cabins, chat, and walk toward the firepit.

The sight lessened a bit of her anxiety.

Julia showed up minutes before the requested arrival. As soon as she emerged from her car, Kelly could see what Ryan had meant. From the way she held her body and the hypervigilance of her eyes darting around, it was clear that the woman's trust had been badly broken.

Kelly wished she were the miracle worker her grandmother had been.

"Hello, Julia," she said softly.

"Oh, hello. Am I too late?"

"No, you're right on time. Let me take you to your cabin. It's named after Euterpe, the goddess of music."

"I hope she provides inspiration," Julia said. "I haven't been able to write anything for months."

"That's why you're here," Kelly said. "It's a time to rest and recharge. Don't force anything to come."

"What happens first?" Julia asked.

"We'll have a meet and greet, a light supper, then an hour to ourselves before meeting in the barn for our first session."

"Are you doing this too?" Julia asked. "What do you do, I mean, besides this?"

Kelly hesitated for a moment. Her friends had encouraged her to go through the same exercises as the participants. It would be the best way for her to understand the guests' emotional toll. But she wasn't ready to declare herself an artist.

"I'm a middle school music teacher," she said. "I used to have dreams of being a concert pianist."

"Oh," Julia said, but her eyes lost a little of their scared rabbit look, replaced by compassion.

Kelly suddenly felt like she'd stepped on thin ice.

"Well, let's get you settled," she said, coming up with a professional smile.

Supper had been a pleasant affair, with everyone on their best behavior. She and Alex made sure they talked to everyone, although

Alex seemed to have more success with Julia than Kelly had.

"What am I supposed to do with myself all weekend?" Ruth asked as they were cleaning up from supper. "I'm used to sitting down with my murder mysteries and knitting for hours on end. But you don't have a television."

"No, but there is music, and each cabin has a screened-in porch so you can sit and let nature tell you its secrets," Kelly said with a smile.

"I'm no tree hugger," Ruth declared. She glanced over at Julia. "What's her story? She's like a shy mouse. She reminds me of one of my students." Ruth's brows furrowed. "This little boy, he's tough and fragile all wrapped into one. Rumor is, his parents drink a lot and the father is a mean drunk."

"She'll need to let us know what she wants to share," Kelly said. "But back to you. In the far corner of the barn, there's a small library of paperbacks—quite a varied selection. I think I've seen some mysteries in there. Several of them look like books you might like, where the detective is a knitter or a weaver or something like that."

"Hmm. I'll have to look into them. Thanks."

Kelly smiled. It was one of the techniques they'd found in her grandmother's journals. Almost everyone had a withdrawal from electronics. Books and music were a bridge to eventually developing the ability to be quiet. On longer retreats, her grandmother had had several sections of quiet time when the only activities were sitting or walking without conversation.

Kelly didn't think she'd be able to handle that herself.

After supper, she returned to the house, grateful for some time to herself. Beside the door was a cardboard box. "Do not open until after retreat, Ryan" was scrawled across the top.

She scooped it up on her way inside and dropped it on the table. Although she was curious, she didn't have the energy to deal with whatever was inside it. She went upstairs and sat in the rocking chair for a bit, staring out at the view.

Why was she doing this retreat at all? Her answer to Ryan was inadequate. No way should she be doing something this big because someone else wanted it. What she needed to do was prepare to go back to California. School started in less than a month, and there were required meetings, bulletin boards to create, and lesson plans to write. Even that wasn't giving the district much time.

But here she was, running a retreat and worrying about a relationship that had no future.

Had she totally messed things up with Ryan? Who was to say anything would even become of a relationship between them? She'd left him behind as a teen, but it had left an empty spot in her soft teenage heart. Would it become unbearable when she left again?

The ache inside her grew at the thought. Was she falling in love with him? Was that why returning to California was proving to be too difficult? But what were the alternatives? She could be a total failure at running her grandmother's business. What would she do with her life then?

Her wristwatch buzzed. She shook off her own problems. This time was about others. After washing up and running a brush through her hair, she headed to the firepit.

Ruth was the only one there. She was staring steadfastly at the lake, but the expression on her face was anything but peaceful.

"Oh, hi," she said when Kelly joined her.

"Beautiful, isn't it?" Kelly asked, gesturing to the lake.

"Boring. I've never understood what all the fuss is about scenery."

"But you live here."

Ruth's smile turned genuine. "Pure laziness. My husband and I moved up here when we were first married. He died in a logging accident about ten years after we got here. I'd already landed the job at the school and didn't want look anywhere else. It suits me. I like the kids—as long as they're not my own."

"I'm sorry about your husband."

"Don't be. It was a long time ago. We loved each other well enough, but I've never felt the need to find another one. I heard you were recently widowed. How are you doing with that?"

Rather than give a flip answer, Kelly checked in with herself. "Okay, I suppose. It's starting to feel more normal. But at the same time, I'm wondering if I even knew him at all."

"That's what makes people fascinating," Ruth said. "How well do you really know someone? Do they even know themselves?" She shrugged. "I'm not sure."

Susan strode into the space and plunked herself into the nearest chair. "I don't know what I'm going to do with all this time to myself. Lets me think too much."

"Why don't you want to think?" Kelly asked gently.

Susan shot her a glance. "You do know I served in the army, don't you?"

"Yes."

"The memories aren't always good ones."

Kelly felt like a jerk. Her sheltered life hadn't let in the horrors Susan must have dealt with.

"It must have been hard," Ruth said. "My late husband served a few years. He never talked about it, but there were many nights he couldn't sleep."

"What did he do?" Susan asked.

"He'd watch old episodes of *Perry Mason*. He told me they were great because there wasn't any real bloodshed and the bad guy always got his due. Everything was neatly tied up in a package."

"And war seems to go on and on," Susan said softly. "Old *Perry Masons*, huh?"

"Yeah. We started making it a habit before going to bed, and he slept better. After he died, I branched out to some of the others. *Murder She Wrote* puts me to sleep all the time."

Susan laughed. "I'll have to try them."

Trust the wisdom of the group. Her grandmother had written that several times in her journals.

As the evening wore on, Kelly saw more and more of that wisdom in action. Susan relaxed a bit as she found common ground with Ruth. Alex slowly coaxed Julia from her shell. And Julia tested Kelly as she probed into Kelly's past dreams. At the end, they all sounded tired but freer.

It was Ruth who suggested the group hug. As she slipped within the circle of women's arms, Kelly was aware of their spirits infusing her with newfound hope.

Chapter Twenty-Seven

Kelly glanced at the box the next morning. In spite of the instructions, she was tempted to open it.

But there was no time. Grabbing her mug of coffee, she headed to the barn where she'd asked the women to gather. She'd already started coffee in the small kitchenette and put out the pastries Charlene had delivered. Once they were all settled and the morning chatter subsided, she began.

"I'd like you to give us a brief sketch of the biggest thing that may be holding you back," she said. "It doesn't have to do with your art or music—it can be a place where you feel stagnant in your life. My grandmother believed human beings were a whole. Everything we think, feel, or do influences everything else."

As they'd planned, Alex volunteered to begin.

"Like Susan and Ruth's husband, my husband was in the war. We'd been married for only a few years. He couldn't find a job—there was a large recession then. I couldn't work at the time because … well, that's not important. He felt he had no choice. The only way he could figure out how to earn money was to enlist. I begged him not to, but …" She sniffled, and Ruth pushed over one of the tissue boxes Kelly had placed within reach.

"He wasn't even there a month before he was killed."

Silence took over the space.

Kelly's heart ached for Alex.

"But … I guess it's the thing that holds me back," Alex said. "When we had our quiet time yesterday, and even listening to everyone talk about their lives, it's all I could think about. I still have all his things. Sometimes I touch them and try to remember … but I can't. Creating my pieces allows me to focus, to push it all aside. But as soon as I put away my tools, it's there, like a splinter I just can't get out."

Susan touched her hand. "I'm sorry. That's very hard. Losing someone you love when you've barely begun to be together."

Alex nodded.

"I think we can all get stuck in the past," Ruth said.

"Yes," Kelly added. "There's a kind of false security in it." She suddenly made a connection. "Even if it's not as large as hanging on to someone's things, it can be doing something just because the person who is gone used to do it." She looked at Ruth.

"Like my television watching," Ruth said.

The other women nodded.

"And sometimes it's holding onto the illusion of the other person," Julia said quietly. "What you wanted him ... or her ... to be, in spite of being shown over and over again that your belief is false."

There was a thoughtful silence.

"How about you, Susan?" Kelly asked.

"Well, when you told us this morning that you wanted us to talk about something holding us back, I had to think long and hard about it. All my life I thought being gay was my biggest problem. I'd hoped if everyone would just get over it and let me live my life, everything would be okay."

She stopped, and they waited for her to gather her thoughts.

"Don't get me wrong," she said. "That's still part of it, but I think there's more. Like every other human being, I've got my own issues to sort out that have nothing to do with what anyone else thinks or does." She absently rubbed at a scar on the back of her hand. "In the military, there was a sense of a team. In the field, you didn't question a person's sexuality. What mattered was that they were on top of things and could shoot straight."

Staring at her fingers, Susan paused again before continuing. "I think the thing holding me back is that I don't feel part of this town. And that's my fault. I haven't given people a chance to know me." She finally looked at them all. There was a vulnerability Kelly hadn't seen before in her face.

"Thank you," Ruth said, touching Susan's hand.

Kelly hesitated. While she'd originally planned to leave Julia to last, she sensed that now might be a better time.

"Julia?" she asked softly.

"Well," Julia said and then stopped. "I'm not sure. I mean, there's lots." She looked up, her deep blue eyes wide. "I've been in therapy for a long time. I ... uh ... something happened ... traumatic."

"PTSD?" Alex asked.

Julia nodded.

"We're a safe space," Kelly said, "but only share what you want to share. This weekend is for you. You don't have to meet anyone else's expectations."

"Thanks. But I want to accomplish something for myself. I'm tired of spinning in the same old box. He still wins if I don't change." She took a deep breath. "Someone—an up-and-coming country singer—well, she heard a demo I put out before ... well, just before."

Julia took another breath, as if she were trying to breathe in courage. "She wants me to do a guest track on her next release. She'll provide studio time. No other singer will be there. Just me and the studio people. And her ... she says she'll be there to help me."

"Wow," Alex said. "That's big."

"It's huge," Julia said, losing some of her scared rabbit appearance for a few minutes. "But I'm afraid. What if I mess it up? What if there's someone there who makes me uncomfortable? I could lose it and not be able to perform. I'd never get a second chance."

Kelly nodded. "It's a big risk. I can see that."

"But I want to do it."

"I'd go with you," Alex said. "That might make you feel safer. Someone you know. We could meet now and again, get to know each other better."

"You would?" Julia said. "I couldn't ask that."

"You didn't. I offered. I'd be happy to do it. Gives me a chance to get out of here for a while. If I'm lucky, she wants you to record in Hawaii in February."

The group laughed, even Kelly. Though she hadn't been through a winter in Montana, cabin fever had to reach its height in February.

"I'll think about it," Julia said. "Thank you."

"I guess that leaves me," Ruth said. "After our discussion last night and this morning, it's pretty clear how I'm stuck. I need to leave Perry and Jessica behind. My life has revolved around school and old television shows. Like you, Susan, I need to become more of the community."

"That was inspiring," Kelly said. "We've got a lot to think about. To close—"

"Wait," Julia said with the loudest voice they'd heard yet. "What about you? It seems to me you need to move forward, too. What's holding you back?"

"Me?" Kelly hadn't prepared an answer. She hadn't even thought about it. Four pairs of eyes looked at her expectantly.

Her grandmother's journals had indicated that she had always participated and learned something new about herself at each retreat. Kelly glanced at Alex, who nodded.

"I guess ... right now I've been focused on what I'm going to do with this property," she said. "Whether I should stay or go back to California." Whether she should open herself up to the possibility of a new relationship or let the past be the past. "I don't think anything's holding me back." Her heart thudded as she realized how close the time was.

"Are you sure about that?" Alex asked her.

Kelly thought of the lovely, and tuned, baby grand in the house. She'd started her practice diligently but had let other things take over. There had really seemed no point to practice—what was she going to do with her talent other than teach?—so other than those first few sessions, the piano lid had stayed closed.

And Ryan? Her grandmother's dream? All of that belonged to other people, the people who could live with fires and months of freezing cold and snow.

"Yes," she said. "It's only the decision holding me back." She smiled brightly. "And you lovely ladies are helping me to make it. So, we're done with this session. Let's have lunch!"

As they rose, Alex stepped to her side. "You're lying to yourself," she said. "Isn't it time you took a good look at why you're having so much trouble making this decision?"

"I'm fine," Kelly said, taking shelter in the timeworn denial women had been using for years.

But she wasn't fine, not at all. The box Ryan had left sat on the kitchen table, his note, John's phone, and a glass of pinot noir were right in front of her. In spite of the instructions, she was going to open it early.

Kelly,
I didn't want to disturb your retreat. I'm glad you're taking that on. I hope it helps you make the right decision.
My friend got John's phone unlocked. Best of luck there.
Ryan

Tonight's assignment to everyone, the one she'd suggested all on her own, was to do something quiet and brave. And mindful of her grandmother's example and leery of what Alex would say, she'd decided to participate.

Now she was stuck with her decision.

She took another sip of the wine. She didn't *have* to turn it on.

If she didn't, it would nag at her all night.

She pressed the on button and waited for it to go through its succession of steps. The familiar icons appeared in front of her. With a deep breath, she checked the phone messages. Only one.

"John?" a female voice she didn't recognize asked. "John? What happened? We were talking and you were cut off. Are you okay?"

Kelly checked the contacts for the number. Lydia. Who was she, and what was her relationship to John?

Kelly grabbed a notepad from the counter and jotted down the name, phone number, and a big question mark.

The text messages were a little more revealing. Apparently, John had planned to meet Lydia on his next trip to New York—the unused ticket she'd found. They were both looking forward to seeing each other.

Other messages were chatty little notes—exhibits she'd seen in New York, a dinner he'd had with colleagues, an update on how well Peter was doing his senior year. There was nothing specific, but the correspondence was between two people who obviously knew each other well for a long time.

She carefully placed the phone on the table, her emotions moving from the mild disturbance of a spring storm to a full-blown hurricane of doubts, pain, and anger. How could he? He was married. He'd made vows. She'd stuck to hers. They'd discussed her kids!

She moaned out loud. She needed to talk to someone. There was no one she could talk to. How could she ever reveal what her husband had done? He'd betrayed her. What could she have done better? She'd given up everything to be the model wife and mother, and she'd even failed at that.

Ryan. He'd know what to say. Whenever she'd fought with her mom or had a falling out with Maggie or Alex when they were younger, he'd been the one she'd turned to. He'd offer comfort or humor, whichever would put the situation back into perspective as quickly as possible.

But she'd messed that up as well, all because she couldn't decide what to do with her life. Had her mother guided her so well that she was incapable of inventing her own future?

She stuffed everything back in the box. They were all supposed to meet back at the firepit for a final evening. It was time to put her game face on, the one every woman knew how to pull off, the one that showed the world she was in control, even if everything inside her was crumbling.

Chapter Twenty-Eight

"I'll go first," Susan said after they were all gathered at the firepit that evening. "This has been great. Thank you," she said to Kelly. "I wasn't sure I'd get anything. I mean, I thought not being accepted here was because of who I was. I didn't realize I wasn't really making an effort. You all have shown me that.

"Kelly asked us to write down one action we'd take toward becoming unstuck. We can share or not." Susan stood. "I'm going to share. I've decided to become a volunteer firefighter. I got some training when I was overseas. And they're always looking for people. With fires getting worse all the time, it's something I can do to help the community." She held up the index card Kelly had given her, then placed it in the fire.

They watched it burn, and when it was finished, Susan sat down.

Ruth got up.

"Mine's kind of easy, too. There's a group of women in town—knitters and crocheters—who've been trying to get me to join with them once a week to make blankets and hats and stuff for charity. I've been telling them I'm too busy. Hah! Too busy watching shows I've seen a hundred times before. So next Thursday, I'm joining them." She, too, tossed her paper in the flames.

They were quiet as they watched it burn.

No one else said anything for several minutes. They stared at the fire. Kelly didn't push. Would they expect her to say something?

Alex cleared her throat. "I'll go next." Quietly, she stood. "I've decided to remove my husband's clothes from my house," she said in a voice hoarse with emotion. "What's still good, I'll donate. What's not, I'll toss. I'm not ready to move beyond that right now." She threw her card in the fire.

Three women had taken significant steps forward and said their commitments out loud. And that was after only two full days of the retreat. What could be possible after more?

She and Julia stared at each other as if they were playing a game of blink. She could bluff it, pretend to have something and simply fold the card and toss it in the fire. Sharing wasn't obligatory. She even had a copy in her pocket ready for that purpose.

"You don't have to say anything," Alex said to Julia. "Just fold it and put it into the fire. What it said or didn't say is part of your journey and no one else's business."

"But I do want to say something," Julia said looking around at the other women. "That's a big step for me and part of what I need to do for myself. I need to speak up. I've been afraid to speak up for so long." She choked a little. "My husband ... ex ... well, let's just say he wasn't very nice."

The energy of the circle darkened. Whatever John had or hadn't done had been nothing compared to what this woman had experienced. And yet, there Julia stood, ready to face her demons.

An owl hooted in the distance as the night slowly darkened and a sliver of moon brightened over the lake.

"I'm going to contact the artist about doing the track," she said. "And I'm going to start writing a new song." Her voice grew stronger with each word. She crumpled the card and defiantly threw it into the fire.

Everyone's gaze turned to Kelly.

"Well, that was wonderful," she said.

"What about you?" Alex asked. "I seem to remember your grandmother always had something to say."

"It would be good for you," Julia said. "You seem a bit ... well ... tight."

Tight was an excellent word for how she felt. Every ounce of will she had was intent on keeping herself together.

"I'm going to make my decision by the end of next week," she said. In spite of Alex's challenge, it was the thing she had to do to determine the next part of her life. "That's a week earlier than I had planned. I know it doesn't seem like much, but it will determine the next part of my life." She stood and folded the blank card in half before she tossed it into the fire. There was no need to bring John into this conversation.

"You have all been wonderful," she said. "I'd like to read you the poem my grandmother always read at the close of the ceremony." With more confidence than she'd had describing her future actions, she read,

"The winds of change blow soft and hard,
Sometimes they may stall.
But if your sail is open to receive the smallest puff.
You will survive the squall."

Once all the guests except Alex had left, Maggie arrived carrying a bag of sandwich wraps and soda. "For our work session," she announced. "I'm sorry I couldn't be more help. Teagan was in crisis mode. All I can figure out is Gregg is up to something and she doesn't approve. But she doesn't want to get him in trouble. She l-o-o-ves him. Ugh. Was I ever that young?"

"In spades," Alex said. "You were in love every other week."

"Oh. You're right."

A stab of jealousy hit Kelly. She'd lost time with these friends. They could reunite now, but they'd never share the teenage years or young motherhood. But then, she'd never had to experience what Alex had, and she'd had a husband, no matter how flawed, to share the burden of parenting.

"How did it go?" Maggie asked as she handed them each a wrap and can of soda.

"Well, I think," Kelly said.

"It was intense. Well, for some of us it was." Alex glared at Kelly.

"Uh-oh. What happened?"

"She didn't go all in."

"I'm not required to go all in," Kelly shot back. "I'm running it. And I participated. I said something last night. Doesn't that count?" Alex was beginning to really annoy her. She felt sorry for her old friend, but Alex could be judgmental. It had rubbed her the wrong way when they were kids, and now it bothered her even more.

"Those were the same words you've been using all summer. 'I have to make a decision.' So make it already and move on with your life. Stop torturing the rest of us."

"Stop it!" Maggie said. "Both of you. Wow, this weekend must have been stressful. How did Henrietta manage to do it all the time?"

"Because my grandmother wanted to do this. I only did it for you." Kelly clapped her hand over her mouth as soon as the words were out.

"Wow," Maggie said.

"No one asked you," Alex said.

"Of course we did," Maggie said. "Kelly's right—we wanted her to do this retreat."

"You wanted her to do this retreat," Alex said.

"Okay. You're right. I think it's important for the town and for the people in it." She gazed at Kelly. "I'm sorry. I shouldn't have pushed so hard."

Kelly waved off her apology. "It's okay. It was an interesting experience. I was glad to do it for you. It will be a proof of concept when I sell the center, encourage the buyer to really consider the retreat. Besides, I like making people I care about happy."

"Thanks," Maggie said, but her eyes still looked troubled. She sat down. "Let's eat."

Pulled by Maggie's gaze, Kelly obediently sat, and Alex did the same.

Kelly undid the wrap and took a bite. "Ohh," she said and lost herself in the tastes of summer.

They kept the talk neutral during their meal. Maggie let them know about three new fires in the general vicinity. "Someone thought they found the arsonist because they've seen an old tan pickup driving near every fire. But they found that guy, and he was an auxiliary firefighter looking to pick up some extra work."

"Yes. We've got the same problem. And power lines are a big problem, too."

"Up here it's often lightning," Alex said, "especially if it's a dry thunderstorm where the moisture never meets the ground. But like California, most of them are somehow related to humans—a wind that picks up a spark from dragging metal, a controlled burn that got out of control, that kind of thing. With more people living so close to wilderness, there are more people who can accidently cause a burn. And because they suppressed fires for so long, there's a lot more undergrowth and downed trees to burn."

After they finished their meal, Maggie said, "Let's start with logistics. Did everything go smoothly, or were their bumps?"

Alex and Kelly agreed on a few things that could be improved, but as they went through the exercise, Kelly wondered if she would ever do another. Alex's words still stung, and she didn't see herself becoming more forthcoming in future retreats. She wasn't really an artist. How could she relate to problems they faced?

Part of her inexplicably yearned to stay in this land of danger and possibilities. There was something about the raw nature of it and the people who inhabited it that was more real than anything she'd ever dealt with in Southern California.

"Leaving Kelly's participation out of it," Maggie said firmly, "do you think the participants got something from the retreat, as short as it was?"

Kelly looked at Alex, waiting for her to answer.

"Yes," Alex finally said. "They did. *I* did." She looked at Maggie. "I'm going to get rid of Sean's old clothes."

"Really? Oh, that's wonderful!" Maggie pulled her friend to her feet and gave her a long hug. "I'm so glad for you." Over Alex's shoulder she mouthed, "thank you" to Kelly.

At that moment, all the stress and the emotional drain of the retreat became worth it.

Once Maggie and Alex helped her clean up from the retreat, they left. Alex had stopped a moment before she got in the car.

"I know I was hard on you, and I really do believe you're avoiding something major. But you're good at this. Better than you know. Think about staying. Please. The community needs you."

A lump formed in Kelly's throat as she watched them drive away. Were they right? Was this her calling?

What about her music? The grand piano in the living room had begun to feel like a great weight she was dragging around with her. Then there was the phone still on the kitchen table, another bomb ready to go off.

Unwilling to stay indoors with her thoughts, she grabbed a book of her grandmother's poems and a blank journal and headed to the firepit. There was no need for a fire, no ceremony, and the air was warm. She also took her water bottle.

For a while she simply sat there, letting the beauty of the water, the dense forest of lodgepole pines, and the dim mountains beyond wash over her. Montana was nature at her grandest. No subtlety. The stark contrast of mountains and sky, water, and parched prairie earth declared her power over anything as puny as a human being.

No wonder Kelly was so adrift here. It took strong people to view this world and still keep their feet under them.

She opened the journal and began to write.

Chapter Twenty-Nine

An hour or so later, Kelly was still sitting in the chair. She'd written pages and pages, unaware of the contents, only the need to put her thoughts and feelings down before they drifted away in the wind. When she'd finished, she'd closed the book and rested.

Footsteps crunched on the gravel.

"Who's there?" she called out.

"It's just me," Ryan said. "I looked for you up by the house but couldn't see you. This is where Henrietta always went after a retreat, so I figured you'd be here."

"I hate being predictable."

He chuckled. "It's a natural draw. Peaceful. May I join you? Or do you want to be alone?"

"Please, sit. I've had enough alone time for the moment."

"Good. I've brought an extra beer in case you might want one."

"That'd be nice." She took the opened bottle.

"Look," he began. "I was pretty rough on you the other night. You're right. You've only been back a few weeks. I should give you some time." He slid his fingers over the arm of the chair. "But I have a sense that time is running out. You have to make a decision soon, and there's a lot stacked against you staying here."

"That's true." It wasn't only the fires and the snow, although that was the easiest thing to tell everyone. Montana was an alien place to her, opposite from everything she'd grown up with in Boston and lived with in Southern California.

To top that off, she wasn't sure she had what it took to be a Montanan.

"I'm not good with talking about emotions and stuff like that. I never was. After Lorelei, I shut down what little emotion I did have." He took a deep breath, then reached over and took her hand. "But I've always had a soft spot for you. When we were kids, you were the only one who didn't push me to join up with others or explain what I was thinking. You let me be. That was a gift—to be accepted for who I was."

The warmth of his hand was natural, as if their connection had been there forever.

"I was only thirteen or fourteen," she said, leaving her hand where it was. "I didn't know any other way to be. I was a shy kid, too. Add to that being pulled between my mother and grandmother, and fading into the background seemed fine to me." She'd always let Alex and Maggie do the talking.

"I'd like you to stay," he said. "I feel something for you, although I can't really call it love or anything approaching that yet. I think you feel it too. Am I right?"

All she really knew was that he made her happy when he was around. He was comfortable, but at the same time, looking at him started a vibration she hadn't felt in a long time.

But was it love?

"There's something," she agreed. "But I don't—"

"That's enough," he said. "That's all we need to talk about right now. Thank you." He gave her hand a gentle squeeze. "You've had a long few days. How did the retreat go?"

She told him in vague terms what had happened, without discussing who had said what. As he listened, she began to think out loud about the lessons she'd learned, as well as the insights she'd gained by writing in her journal.

"Do you think Alex is right?" she asked. "Am I being less than honest with myself? It all seems a muddle. There are too many balls to juggle: the center, my kids, my teaching job, John's ... John's whatever ..." She stopped talking as her breath seemed to leave her.

"You opened the phone," he said.

"I had to. It was taunting me. Besides, I'd told everyone else to do something brave and quiet. I had to go along."

"I can see that," he said.

"It was horrible. But it wasn't clear. There was someone—Lydia. Nothing overt, but it seemed like they'd been friends for a long time. You can tell when two people are close by the way they talk and the shorthand they use."

Ryan nodded.

"He was going to meet her in New York. She left a voice message. I think that was the worst of all, that I had to hear her voice."

"What are you going to do?" he asked.

"I don't know." She pulled her hand from his, drew up her legs, and wrapped her arms around her knees. "I don't have to do anything. He's gone. What's the point in knowing? Would you want to know?"

He studied the darkening lake. "I think so," he said.

"Why?"

"Closure. I'd want to know where it went off the rails, if I could have done anything differently."

She wasn't sure she wanted to even think about her part in his infidelity.

Nope. She definitely didn't. She'd let sleeping dogs lie.

"On another note," he said, "how about you come to dinner on Thursday? I've got a piece I have to ship out on Wednesday, and I could use a little celebration before I start the next project. I'd like you to see where I live. Let you know me a little better—the man I've become."

"That would be nice," she said, warmth spreading through her chest.

They were quiet for a while longer. As they walked back to the house, he held her hand. Before he got into his car, he gave her a brief kiss.

"Hope that was okay," he said.

"It was perfect," she told him.

"Good. See you Thursday."

She watched him pull out the drive, a sense of peace and hope filling her heart.

Over the next few days, Kelly busied herself organizing the office and doing some investigation on selling a retreat center. Whether anyone liked it or not, she needed to make this decision, and she needed all the facts at her fingertips. When she saw the prices some centers were getting, she had to sit down. They ran into the millions of dollars.

Her grandmother had left her quite a gift. With that kind of money, there would be no need to do another lick of work for the rest of her life.

What would she do with herself?

She also dug up the teacher's handbook and researched how to take a sabbatical or another form of a year off. She'd left it to the last minute though, and it didn't seem that option would be open to her. If she wanted time off, she'd have to quit her job and try to find a new one if she decided to stay. Mid-forties was a tough time to find a new job, but there had been a teacher shortage for years, so that shouldn't be much of a problem. Besides, she could sell the house if need be.

Lisa rang in the middle of her musings.

"I've done it," she said without much of a preamble. "I know you're going to be disappointed, but I changed my major. I'm still keeping computer science as my minor so I can get a job if need be.

Better than waiting tables. I'm going to follow my dream, Mom. I'm going to be an actor."

Where Kelly's mother had succeeded in steering her to stability, Kelly had failed abjectly. At least her daughter would find out for herself whether her dream could stand the stress of reality.

"Okay," she said. "But try not to be all starry-eyed. Talk to actors and see what it's like out there."

"I will, Mom. I promise. I have to give this a try. It's important."

"I understand."

"I love you, Mom. So are you staying in Montana or what?"

"I'm afraid I really don't know."

"It's your turn," Lisa said. "Peter's off doing nerdy things, and I'm doing what I love. Don't worry about us. We've got our own lives to live. It's time for you to do your thing."

Kelly didn't have an answer for that, but she didn't need to. Lisa immediately launched off into other topics.

After they ended the call, Kelly stared at the phone. Gathering information like prices and options was the easy part.

She strode to the kitchen, opened John's phone, and dialed Lydia's number.

But when she heard the woman's voice, all she could do was give a sharp gasp and turn off the phone.

She simply didn't possess that much courage.

Kelly followed Ryan's directions easily and arrived at his house, a large log home with a view tucked into the forest. Steps led up to the front porch. Toward the back of the property, she spotted a large structure that looked like it could hold heavy equipment.

"Come up," Ryan said from the top of the stairs.

She climbed the flight. "Wow," she said, taking in the view of the lake and Black Mountain beyond it. From the front of the property, a rocky cliff dropped off, keeping the cabin above the trees. "This is amazing."

"I think so. Here, I've made us some snacks to munch so we can sit out here and enjoy the weather. It's about perfect."

"I brought wine," she said. Then she chuckled.

"What's so funny?" he asked.

"It's feeling very formal and awkward," she said.

He laughed. "You're right." He gestured to one of the outdoor chairs. "White, red, beer, or a cocktail?"

"A full-service bar," she said with a grin. "I'll have the white." She gestured to the wine she'd brought.

"White it is." He went inside, and she relaxed into the chair. When she first got to Montana, she'd wondered at the people who spent so much time on their porches, not doing much beyond looking around them. Now she understood. There was a lot to absorb.

He came out with her glass and a wooden board loaded with cheeses, meats, and an array of crackers.

"I'm not going to be able to eat dinner," she said.

"Oh, I think you will. Fresh caught trout, grilled to perfection, salad, and a side of homemade macaroni and cheese."

"Oh my."

He leaned down and kissed her. "Sorry I didn't do that when you first arrived. I think I was too overwhelmed that you were actually here."

She smiled at him. It was nice to be treated well.

They spent the next half hour catching up on their doings of the week, although she left out her attempt to call Lydia. Ryan was sympathetic about Lisa's decision and mentioned he'd seen Susan Thomas training at the fire station.

"I'm so glad!" Kelly said.

"Some of your doing?"

"No, she came up with that one on her own."

He froze for a moment and sniffed the air. "Do you smell smoke?"

His phone blared.

"Fire!" he yelled. "And it's headed right at us!"

Chapter Thirty

"It's above us," Ryan said. "They've built a fire line, and they're hoping it holds, but the wind is supposed to come up. I need to get ready."

"We need to leave," Kelly said. "Now! Nothing is worth our lives."

"This *is* my life," he said. "You can help or leave. Your choice."

"Of course I'll help. Tell me what to do."

"Follow me."

He led her into his house and to a large room at the back. Shelves of fabric in plastic boxes lined two of the walls. A large, flat table stood on one side, a sewing machine and cabinet on the other.

He pointed to the last wall. "Those boxes need to go into the Explorer. It's unlocked. There's a door over there that leads outside. Go as fast as you can, but don't hurt yourself."

"What are you going to do?"

"Wet things down—especially the roof. It's sparks that keep these monsters going, sparks and wind." He shook his head. "There are canyons up there. Depending on which one it picks to run down, we could be incinerated or the whole town could be in trouble."

"No other options?"

"They stop it," he said grimly. "But that's tough to do in this terrain."

She'd pray for that then.

He left, and she got to work. Who knew fabric and thread could be so heavy? She soon settled into a rhythm, her mind whirring over what-ifs and imagining the crackling of fire over her head.

Susan was being thrown right into it.

Her phone rang, and she set down the box she was carrying.

"It's Maggie," she said. "Have you heard?"

"I'm at Ryan's," Kelly replied. "I'm helping him move quilts."

"Be safe. From what I've heard, it's coming right at you."

"They're trying to stop it. Ryan's keeping an eye on it."

"Don't wait too long. These things move fast. Get back down here."

"Is the town safe?" Kelly asked, her pulse pounding hard.

Maggie was silent.

"Depends on a lot of things, but the state will throw everything on it. The forest service has sent in their crews, and the local departments are there to help do a lot of the grunt work. They're building a line to stop it."

"That's what Ryan said."

"Okay. Get to work. Call me if you need anything," Maggie said. "And get out of there, soon." She hung up.

Kelly went back to work. The smell of smoke was stronger now, and thick, unnaturally gray clouds menaced the blue sky. How long was it safe to stay? What if the line didn't hold?

The vehicle was about halfway full when she took a break. She needed something to drink. The heat and smoke were making her throat feel scratchy and tight. She went to the kitchen, rifled around for a glass, and drank some water greedily. A hunk of cheese lay on a cutting board, so she chopped off a slice and stuffed it in her mouth.

She had to find Ryan. This was insane. He should help her with the quilts, and then they needed to get out of here.

She went out to the porch and was immediately drenched.

"Oh, sorry about that," Ryan yelled from the roof. "How's it going?"

"I'm not sure it's all going to fit."

"Can you put some in your car?"

"Sure."

"Thanks."

"Look, Ryan, don't you think—?"

"No!" he shouted. "Not yet. If you want to go, I understand. But I'm not ready to give up yet. I've created defensible space around the cabin, and with a little help, I can save it. I know I can."

A loud noise, like an explosion, thundered in the mountain above them. The smoke cloud grew.

"I've got to keep at it," he said, then disappeared from sight.

After grabbing another hunk of cheese, she went back to work.

This was insane. Nothing was worth this. They could lose their lives.

She'd loaded both cars and the wall was empty when she went to find him again.

He was in the kitchen on the phone, a hunk of French bread and salami slices added to the cheese she'd already found. He pointed to it with the sharp knife he had in his hand as he talked.

Her stomach growled.

Hunger drove away any manners her mother had painstakingly instilled. Eagerly, she pulled together bread, meat, and cheese, scarfing it down as the world imploded above them.

"Yeah. Got it. Keep me posted. I need probably a fifteen-minute warning," Ryan said to whoever was at the other end of the phone. "You sure we can't take a stand here? I've pushed the trees back seventy-five feet all around the house. No, I'm not a trained firefighter, you know that!" Ryan's fist clenched as he spoke.

Was he really thinking of staying here to the bitter end? How could he be so foolish?

"Okay. Fifteen minutes. That's all I need. And good luck. Hope the line holds. And, thanks, man." Ryan put the phone down.

"How is it going?" she asked, trying to keep her fear at bay.

"They're still holding the line. It all depends on what happens overnight. If a wind comes through, we're sunk. Or if the fire gets hot enough to make its own weather, it becomes unpredictable. They'll let me know when I've got about fifteen minutes to get out."

"Isn't that cutting it close?"

"I can make it." He took her hand. "*We* can make it. Trust me. I won't let you burn."

She wanted to believe him. But did she know him? Did she know anyone?

She withdrew her hand.

"I can't do this. It's too close. I can't stand it!" She wanted to throw up everything she'd just eaten. "And how do you get out of here in the winter?"

"There's a plow in the shed," he said mildly.

"Well, I don't know how to plow. And I don't want to learn." She stood and paced. "I don't live in the woods in California. I live in a nice, civilized place without snow and without forest fires. I don't know the first thing about running retreats. Look—now there's Susan, putting her life in danger because of something I did."

"Susan's there because she wants to be there," he said.

"Then she's nuts. You're all nuts. I can't do this!" Hysteria rose within her. She felt trapped. She needed to get out of here.

He stood, his face a blank. "Then go," he said. "Go home. And while you're at it, why don't you keep going—all the way to California. Just close the door on the way out."

He headed to the porch.

Her stomach roiled as she watched him go.

The ladder thumped against the side of the house.

"I'm sorry," she whispered to the empty air. Then she ran down the stairs to her car.

Ryan watched the RAV4 hurry down the long, dirt road, his heart tearing in two. He'd hoped, prayed that she'd be okay in Montana. To lose her once had been torture; twice was unbearable.

He should go after her. The cabin wasn't worth her loss.

Then what?

Could he move to California? Give up the solitude for sunshine and surf?

New York had been gritty and real. Everything he knew about the West Coast was posturing and fluff.

It wasn't him. He'd die there.

He glanced down the road again as the RAV4 pulled around a corner and out of sight.

He wasn't going to survive here, either.

A white FedEx envelope glared from the bench on the front porch.

Now what? Her life had been turned upside down in the last few months, and all for what? She snatched up the package and went inside. The return address was New York. She threw it on a far counter.

Her heart ached. She'd gotten too close to Ryan. She'd known this was impossible from the beginning. Her mother was right. Montana was a place for uncivilized and uncultured people who were ready to survive anything. Well, maybe her mother had been wrong about the uncivilized and uncultured part. But she hadn't been wrong about the survival.

This part of the country asked too much from a person. Not only were there fires and snow, but animals—big animals—lurked in the shadows. On her way down from Ryan's, she'd spotted a bear in the woods not far from the road. She'd never seen one so close before.

She'd recover from Ryan.

And John.

Eventually.

What did she need right now? Her stomach was still unsettled. She was too keyed up to sleep.

Maybe she should pack.

She sank into a chair.

If only she were braver.

Her phone rang.

"Hello?"

"It's Maggie. You still up at Ryan's?"

"No, I'm back."

"Good. I need you."

"I'm not sure I—"

"You have to," Maggie said. "This is what we do. We all pitch in. If you aren't helping Ryan, then get down here and help make sandwiches. They'll figure out how to feed all those firefighters tomorrow, but for now we need food and we need it fast. Alex went down to Whitefish and got supplies. We've got an assembly line going."

"I'll be there." She could make sandwiches. "Is everyone okay?"

"Only one injury so far. A large tree branch fell on Susan Thomas."

"Oh, no!"

"It's okay. She only broke an arm. They took her down to Kalispell. She'll be fine."

It wasn't okay. Susan would have been fine if Kelly hadn't run that retreat. Somehow, she'd have to find a way to fix it.

"I'll be there in fifteen minutes," Kelly said and ended the call. She headed to her room to change her clothes. At least she could do something. And then she was going to pack up her things, put the retreat on the market, and go back where she belonged.

Chapter Thirty-One

In spite of a late night, Kelly woke early the next day. Maggie had said she wouldn't need her today. Catering for the fire crew had been finalized, and she'd be working with a couple from Kalispell that had a contract with the forest service.

Alex had headed to Oregon to pick up some special wood.

Everyone had their jobs, their places to be. In Promise Cove, everyone seemed to have a purpose, except her. Firetrucks still roared down the main road before turning up the mountain to the edges of the burn. The fire was still only 25 percent contained, but at least it was burning away from Promise Cove. Hopefully, Ryan's house had survived.

Her finger had hovered over his number a dozen times, but she'd always stuck her phone back in her pocket. He didn't need to hear from her right now.

Wandering into the kitchen, she went through the motions of making coffee. John's phone was sitting on the table, the FedEx envelope next to it. Two inanimate objects, their silent voices screaming her inadequacy.

She tossed the FedEx envelope on top of the washer in the mudroom and threw John's phone in the junk drawer. Out of sight, out of mind.

Leaving the coffee to drip, she walked to the great room and plopped in one of the chairs by the fireplace. The day was gloomy, but it wasn't rainclouds causing the haze. If she stepped outside, all she would be able to breathe was smoke. It would be best to stay inside.

She could start to pack up things she wanted to keep. Some of her teacher friends had part-time jobs as real estate agents, so she knew uncluttered spaces moved faster.

You could play me the piano mocked.

She went back into the kitchen, poured the coffee, then trudged upstairs, an area absent of any ticking time bombs.

Settling in the rocking chair, she picked up a novel she'd brought with her, a best-seller that couldn't seem to hold her interest. Her gaze lifted to the view from the window, the placid lake stretched out below her, the air hazy. A large bird, long legs floating behind it, swooped past her window and onto the water's edge.

The beauty of nature worked to calm her, but she knew better now. It was a beauty with an edge. Danger lurked beneath the waters and in the air she breathed. It was not the place for her.

If only it didn't work so hard to lure her to stay. The bait was tempting. A new life. One where John's secrets wouldn't haunt her every day. She wouldn't be able to stay in the house when she went back to California. It was their house, and his mark was everywhere.

Here, there was a possibility not only of a new life but a new love. Truthfully, it had never really died, but as she'd gone through high school, all the authorities—her mother, magazine writers, her friends—had convinced her what she'd felt for Ryan had only been a crush, a normal occurrence of life, one to be moved past.

She'd believed them.

Maybe they were right. Maybe people needed to be adults in order to have anything real blossom between them.

But what if they had been wrong? Could she and Ryan have grown together, making each other the best version of themselves they could be?

Without making an actual decision, she rose and returned downstairs. Pawing through the aging yellow sheet music books, she pulled out Chopin, sat at the piano and began to play. She didn't care about the wrong notes she hit, she only felt the emotion of sound as it traveled from her fingertips through her body, the sorrow that Chopin had infused into so many of his pieces. This was a man who'd known many highs and lows, including his love affair with the novelist Aurore Dudevant, leading to the happiest and saddest moments of his life.

As Kelly played, the notes grew into a movie score behind images of her life: meeting John, their wedding—as perfect a society affair as her mother could make it—Lisa's birth, Peter's constant crying, a second honeymoon with her husband. But then the little things intruded: a forgotten anniversary, sudden trips, a gift she'd discovered that wasn't for her.

The signs had been there all along.

She flung Chopin aside and found Beethoven.

Her mistakes with the extravagant flourishes and range changes of the symphony pieces were more frequent. No more lilting melodies. Here, she could throw her whole body into playing, her arms and shoulders relishing the remembered exercise. Up and down the keyboard, wrong notes and all, letting the music tear her heart's pain from her body, the deaf man's anguish wrung from her fingers.

A half hour later, pain radiated through her muscles and joints. Sweat, not the delicate perspiration of a Boston Brahmin, but the honest sweat of hard work, poured from her skin. She dragged her limp body from the piano and flung it on the bed, falling into a deep, dreamless sleep.

The shifting angle of the sun finally woke her. Disoriented for a few moments, she glanced at the old-fashioned clock on the wall, a delicate craft of workmanship that must have come from Alex's hands. It was late afternoon.

Thoughts and memories played along with the kaleidoscope of light sparkling on the bedroom wall.

The past couldn't be undone. She had the rest of her life in front of her to make her mark. When she went back to California, it didn't have to be the same, did it? She could find a bungalow with enough room to house the piano. She didn't need much room. Except there would need to be a guest room for the kids and a place to entertain. Maybe not a bungalow.

She hauled herself from the bed, shucked her clothes, and stepped into the shower. The water slid over her, wiping the grime and smoke from her skin. She let it cleanse her for a good long time. The light forest smell of her shampoo scented the room, and moisture dampened the air.

The air outside must still be smoky; the sky was hazy over the water, and the sun had a red cast to it. It wasn't quite time for dinner, but her stomach rumbled. She grabbed an apple from the bowl on the counter and walked to her grandmother's office in the barn.

She spent the next few hours going over her grandmother's retreat notes as well as her own and organizing them into some kind of system. Should she sell the business separately from the property? It made sense, although she had no idea how to go about doing it. But there would be someone who knew, someone at home who could help her. In the meantime, she'd streamline some of the information and store only the binders and notebooks it made sense to keep.

Glancing at the piles of journals and notebooks stacked in the small bookshelf, and thinking of all the supplies in the barn, she leaned back in the chair and wiped the palms of her hands over her face. She wouldn't be able to take the time that was needed. In fact, she'd have to hire a service or several people in town to get it boxed.

And then what would she do with it?

This was her grandmother's life work—this and the poems in the house. Kelly couldn't let it go until she'd given herself a chance to really know the woman, a chance her mother had never given her.

Why had her mother disliked her grandmother so much? When Kelly had posed the question as a teen, her mother had pushed her off, telling her they were staying in Boston for her. Kelly needed to make an impression with the right people to have success in life.

She called her mother.

"Hi, Mom. How are you? Have you seen Peter? How's he doing?"

"Oh, hello. How unexpected," her mother replied. "Peter? I suppose okay. The Richards keep him pretty busy when he's not working at that firm with Rupert. He seemed happy enough when I had lunch with him a few weeks ago."

"That's good. I'm glad to hear it." And she was. Peter's happiness was so well disguised it was difficult to know whether or not it existed. She took a deep breath and launched into the next subject.

"Mom, why didn't you and Grandma get along?"

"Why do any mothers and daughters not get along? You and I don't always agree."

"But we don't let years go by without talking to each other."

"I talked to my mother once in a while," Cynthia protested.

"Not like most people. I need an answer. I deserve an answer. You kept me from knowing her. Why?"

"Your grandmother was difficult. All she wanted to do was sit in those woods and write her little poems."

"She was poet laureate of Montana one year," Kelly pointed out.

"An honorary title. No one hears of poets. It's not like they're actors or politicians or anything."

Sometimes her mother's love of glitter and power got to Kelly. But there was no use calling Cynthia on it—she wouldn't begin to know what she was saying.

She waited.

"You're not going to let it go, are you?" Cynthia said.

"Nope."

"We were different people," her mother said. "She gave up her lifelong dream to follow your grandfather to that place. She was a wonderful cook. You remember."

"I do, but it seems she created another dream for herself."

"She could have been a well-paid chef."

"Well, she did put on retreats and feed attendees." In her time in the office, Kelly had found the binder that contained meal plans and recipes. Attendees had been very well fed.

"I never understood how that worked. Get a group of women together and talk. You may as well go to a nice restaurant like Craigie's and have lunch."

"Couldn't you enjoy her as she was?" Kelly asked.

"Maybe, if she hadn't try to stifle me. She wanted me to stay in that rural place, help her out, never see an art gallery or attend a symphony. I wanted regular manicures; she wanted to plant vegetables in the spring."

It was as close as Kelly would ever get to an answer. Too bad her mother didn't realize she'd done the same thing to her own daughter.

Chapter Thirty-Two

When she returned from the barn, Kelly pulled out leftovers from the retreat, a combination of salads she'd made, and fixed herself a plate. Going into the living room, she settled herself in front of the television she'd found hidden behind a cabinet door, and watched while she ate.

She tried documentaries about nature, comedy sitcoms, and even a brief start of a Hallmark love story. The last made her sadder than ever. Everyone found love on Hallmark. It wasn't true in real life.

Wanting a relationship with Ryan was ridiculous. They were poles apart. He lived a life, a life he adamantly said he wouldn't change, in a place that made her feel as in control as a leaf floating in a vast ocean. She could play the piano to her heart's content here, but what would she do with it? Her music would be as stifled here as it was in a middle school classroom.

But still he tugged at her. There was a physical draw. There always had been, she realized now, even though she would have been unable to name it as a teen. All she'd known was that when he kissed her, nothing else mattered.

The same was true in the present.

Their time together, except for their discussions of any kind of future, had been easy. He challenged her enough to look at things in a different way, even though she didn't agree with them all the time. Among her circle of teacher friends, there had always been concurrence, the same way of looking at things. She'd never built a relationship with any of John's friends or business acquaintances. She'd merely been the wife.

Why was that?

Because in spite of everything, all the years together, the kids, there'd never really been a deep connection between them. She'd told herself in the beginning that she didn't believe in soul mates. What she and John had had was good enough.

It may have been then, but apparently she'd never known her husband all that well. Would a relationship with anyone else—with Ryan—be any different?

She flipped through the channels once again, finally coming up with a crazy comedy starring Lucille Ball. There was a lady who'd kept smiling through everything. Kelly settled in to watch. When it ended, another began. She dragged herself to bed at midnight.

"Hello, Gabriella," Kelly said when she called the innkeeper the next morning. "How is Susan doing? I feel so badly that she was hurt."

"She's doing okay. I'm worried she's going to saw something off—she's trying to figure out how to use a chainsaw with one arm—but other than that, she's good. Why should you feel bad?"

"Because ... well ... she wouldn't be hurt if not for me."

Gabriella laughed. "Oh, girl, you don't have that much power. If you're talking about the retreat, that's nonsense. It was the best thing Susan's ever done. Ever since she moved here to be with me, she's been isolating, not part of the community. No matter what I tried, she resisted. When she finally decided to plunge, she went in with both feet, just like I knew she would. She's wanted to fight fires her whole life. This was a great adventure for her. She can't wait to do it again."

"Really?"

"Really. So you can stop feeling badly. How are you doing, by the way? Rumors say you and Ryan might be a thing."

"No, no, I can assure you that's not true. In fact ..." Maybe if she said it aloud, it would start being real. "In fact, I've decided to put the center and the business on the market."

"Oh, I'm so sorry to hear that. Susan said you were really good at it, almost like Henrietta was on your shoulder guiding you in the right direction."

"It's the right thing to do for me," she said.

"Well, only you can decide that. It was nice knowing you. And thank you again for what you did for Susan."

They finished up the call, and Kelly closed the phone, a sense of loss washing over her.

What did this mood call for?

Bach. Only the measured discipline of Bach would suit.

While she didn't drain herself like she'd done the day before, Kelly's arms and fingers still ached. Bach was measured, didactic. A pianist didn't stray out of the lines with Bach. There were rules, like there had been rules when she was growing up. Structure provided a simple comfort. It was the unknown that was the problem.

Still no word from Ryan.

The quilts were still in the back of the car when she headed out to the store. The wine she was going for was a simple excuse. What she really wanted was the comfort of people and news.

Alex was behind the counter when Kelly walked in. "What are you doing here?" she asked with a tentative smile.

"Maggie called in a favor," Alex said. "She's out all day at the fire site, her mother isn't feeling well, and Teagan insisted she needed to be off with Gregg somewhere. And now they can't find either one of them."

"They've been thinking some of these fires are started by an arsonist," she said.

"Yes. They even think this one might have been. But it started in such a remote place, I'm not sure how anyone could have gotten there. But there doesn't seem to be any natural reason for it to begin."

"Do you think it could be someone local?"

Alex shook her head vigorously. "It can't be. We've known each other all our lives."

The bell rang in the front. "That's good to know," Kelly said. "I'll go do my shopping. You're busy."

Alex nodded and smiled at the incoming customer. "How are you today?" she asked the older woman.

Kelly wandered the store, the possibility of the arsonist being local still churning in her mind. While the center of Promise Cove was close-knit, what about all those far-flung cabins? Hadn't the Unabomber hidden in plain sight for years somewhere in Montana?

The arsonist could be someone she'd met anywhere in town, his ... or her ... motives hidden behind a smiling face, like a serial killer. Didn't they always say serial killers were the nicest neighbors?

Concentrate. Get what's needed and get home to do some work. She needed to buckle down. Even if she went through and labeled everything for storage, trash or sale. It would be a lot of work. If Ryan were around, he'd be able to help with some of the heavier things. Maybe Larry, his friend, would help.

But she'd ask Ryan first, if he'd even talk to her.

She should ask Alex how he was doing, but she didn't want to talk about Ryan with anyone else.

Gathering her purchases, she headed back for the register. The older woman was still there.

"And they haven't found him," she was saying. "They think maybe he could have set the fire—accidently, you know, 'cause he's not too well, they say—but they can't find him. Betsy's worried to death, afraid something's happened to him, something bad."

"That's terrible," Alex said. "It must be very difficult for Betsy."

"Oh it is, it is. And you know her. She won't let anyone know how badly she's hurting. We want to help but don't know what to do. If you hear anything, let me know, please. The fires," the woman shook her head. "They keep getting worse. What's going to happen to us? What's going to happen?" She picked up her purchases and left without another word.

"Was that Betsy's son she was talking about?" Kelly asked as she laid her purchases on the counter.

"Yes. They can't seem to locate him. They've found Henry's small cabin but no sign of him. And no evidence he started the fire, either," she said, glancing at the front door that had shut behind the woman.

"That's got to be hard. This is all hard. I don't know how you people manage to live with it."

"You people?" Alex said, a slight edge to her voice.

"You know, Montanans," Kelly tried to smooth over her gaffe.

"And you're not one of us."

Reluctantly, Kelly shook her head. "I don't think so."

"I see," Alex said. "The other day you said you did the retreat for Maggie. Is that really true? Didn't some part of you want to do it for yourself? Find out why your grandmother left it in your hands?"

"I ..." She wasn't sure. Saying she'd done it for Maggie was the easy answer. She'd always done things for other people, all her life. It was easier to manipulate John into suggesting it than risk going toe to toe with him to get what she wanted.

She was pathetic.

Alex pressed her point. "Maggie and I believed doing the retreat would mean something to you. Might give you a glimpse into something that was really yours. We may have been young all those years ago, but we weren't blind. We saw how you wanted that concert career. You were really, really good, Kelly. It's too bad you caved to your mother."

"What else was I supposed to do? I loved my mother. Being a concert pianist was unreasonable. There wasn't enough time to practice and have a real life. My mother made me see that."

"Then maybe you didn't want it badly enough."

That one stung. Tears crowded Kelly's eyes. "I did," she said softly. "I did." She just hadn't known how to do it.

The front door flew open like a gale force had just blown into town.

Kelly turned away and swiped at her eyes. Pasting a smile on her face, she turned back to see Maggie bearing down on her.

"Oh, Kelly!" Maggie called. "Perfect! You're the very person I'm looking for!" She almost screeched to a stop. "What's wrong?"

"She's leaving," Alex said flatly.

"No, you can't," Maggie said, finishing her walk to the counter.

"I've given it a lot of thought," Kelly said. "It's the best thing for me."

"When?" Maggie asked, her voice cooling.

"Two weeks from last Friday," she said.

"Oh, good then. You can help me tonight. One of the subcontractors had to switch to a new fire closer to home, so we need to fill in the gap." All business, Maggie pulled out a piece of paper from her purse. "Alex, I can take over for you here. Can you do a Whitefish run?"

"Sure."

"Thanks. I'll line up someone for tomorrow."

"I'll go home and change," Kelly said. "Maybe squeeze in a nap. I haven't been sleeping well." She picked up her things. "Anyone know how Ryan is doing?" she asked in spite of herself.

"His cabin's okay so far, and he's staying put up there," Alex said. "Says he's afraid the wind will shift again. He calls in an order, then Larry picks it up for him and trucks it up there."

"Larry's house didn't make it," Maggie said. "He's staying with Ryan until he gets back on his feet."

"What will happen? Did he have insurance?" Kelly asked.

"Yes, but you know insurance companies. They sell you a cheap policy and then you only get what they think is the value of your property, never what it will cost to replace it. And they take forever," Alex said.

"A few others lost their homes," Maggie said. "When it's over, we'll get together and do some fundraisers or something. Too bad you won't be here. You'd be perfect to help in that job."

"Yes," Alex said, "she would."

Kelly's chest tightened.

"I'll see you in a bit. Right now I have to go."

The large bell clanged as the door slammed behind her, and Kelly fled the store. It was time for Beethoven again.

Chapter Thirty-Three

As she dragged herself out of bed the next morning, Kelly felt like she was living in her own version of *Groundhog Day*. Prepping food with Maggie, Teagan, and a few other volunteers had been hard work. Although everyone had been pleasant, Kelly knew she no longer had the key to the city.

Coffee. She needed coffee.

Once the brew started coursing through her veins, she took out her pad and started to make a list. She'd start in neutral territory, the sheds and cabins. Most of what was in there could stay; it just needed to be more artfully arranged to entice a buyer.

Then she'd tackle the barn. It definitely made sense to sell the business separately from the center, which meant packing all the stuff in her grandmother's office. She'd go through the rest of the space, throw out anything that wasn't useful anymore, and give the art supplies to the school.

The house would have to be last. It was the most emotionally laden space.

A piece of toast and jam sufficed for breakfast. As she walked by the baby grand, the urge to play overwhelmed her.

Just a half hour. Placing a stack of yellow books on top of the piano, she began with the long-ago warmups her teacher had given her.

An hour later she was still playing, losing herself in the discipline and love of the magic; she moved her fingers and melodies emerged.

The clock announced the hour, and she let her fingers rest. There were things to do.

Sometime in the mid-afternoon, she received a text from Maggie asking for her help. *Of course*, she replied. They may be pushing her out, but she would participate in the community to the end. Just one more phone call before she got to work.

"Hey, Gail," she said when her friend answered. "How was Japan?"

"Horrible and wonderful. Where are you?"

"Montana. I told you in that email I sent. My grandmother left me her estate, and I've been up here trying to figure out what to do with it."

"Are you ever coming home? School starts in three weeks.

They've called a meeting for us the week after next."

"Yep. I've got a flight back a week from Friday." Kelly made a quick note on her pad: Find ride to airport.

"Cutting it close. What about the kids? Aren't you dropping Peter off at school in Boston?"

"Nope. He went out early this summer to work for his grandparents. They've already got plans to send him home for a weekend, then get him settled in his dorm."

"But won't you miss that? I mean, you're his mother."

Kelly should be more upset than she was. She felt guilty about not feeling guilty she wasn't going.

What a tangled mess her head was.

"I will, but dealing with the estate ate up all the time I had."

"What's taking so long? All you had to do was put it on the market and come home."

"It's a bit more complicated than that," Kelly said.

"Did you meet a hot cowboy who's riding off into the sunset?" Gail chuckled.

Something like that.

"No, sorry, no romance here." A muscle inside her chest twisted. But there could have been, if only she weren't so afraid of fire, snow, and large animals.

"You can tell me all about it when you get home. And I'll tell you the horrors of living with my mother-in-law."

"I'm looking forward to it."

They spent a few more moments catching up, then disconnected.

How was she going to get to the airport? Would Ryan be willing to do it? She doubted it. Not after the way she left things. Everyone else was too busy. Well, she'd just have to find a limo service or an old-timer with a wood-paneled station wagon.

Some old movie she'd seen had one of those old wagons. Kelly smiled. They'd driven it into a pond. Kelly giggled. Then they'd done it again. Kelly laughed.

Then laughed again.

Laughter took over her body. She couldn't stop. Her mind released control, and she dropped to the floor, filling the room with her laughter. A kaleidoscope of images whirled: the retreat, Susan's accident, Maggie and Alex, John's betrayal.

Ryan. Dear, dear Ryan.

Her laughter broke, changing halfway to a sob before becoming a full-blown wail.

Why was she leaving him again?

Because it was what she always did. She chose safety. The known.

He was anything but safe.

He was wild, unpredictable passion.

Was it more scary to face the love he had to give her or see who she became in his arms, arms she needed right now?

The pit of her stomach caved in, and she wrapped herself around it. Crying was the only thing she was able to do. So she let herself wail. There was no one around to hear her.

Sometime later, she lay spent on the floor, silent, exhausted.

Pushing herself up, she headed back upstairs to repair the damage.

Her reflection revealed a pale woman, wide-eyed with a lack of any expression. Every aspect of her being was drained. It would be best to do rote things, to run through the chores she'd planned until it was time to go to Maggie's and help out.

Lack of emotion helped her move through the cabins more efficiently. And when she went to the store, she was a machine, with no more awareness than a robot. No one seemed to notice that she was an empty shell.

When it was almost over, she slipped away and headed back to the house.

Pouring a large glass of wine, she retrieved the FedEx envelope and placed it in the middle of the kitchen table. She stared at it for a few moments. Then she picked it up and tore it open.

Kelly,

When the phone rang the other day and I saw John's number, I realized you had found his second phone and somehow managed to get into it. John had made me promise to reach out to you if that ever happened after his death.

I did so reluctantly. I didn't think you needed any more pain. But a promise is a promise.

First of all, none of what happened between John and me was your fault. He loved you and told me about the sacrifices you'd made to fit into the life your mother wanted you to live. He told me more than once that he couldn't have asked for a better wife.

He wanted to make sure I told you that you did nothing wrong.

What was between him and me was ill-fated passion. We met before you two did. I'm a dancer whose parents emigrated from the Dominican Republic. None of that fit the criteria his parents had for his wife. We broke it off; he married you, but we couldn't stay away from each other. There was no way he ever would divorce you and leave the children. He felt he owed you all that.

So we began our affair, determined to keep it secret so you would never be hurt.

Unfortunately, you are hurt now, and I am so very sorry for that. What we did was selfish, but we didn't seem to be able to call it off, no matter how often we tried. And we did try.

I miss him terribly, as you must. Remember, he loved you too. He just was, as we all are, a flawed human being.

I wish you the best.
Lydia

Kelly reread the words, trying to make them make sense. *A promise is a promise?* The phrase outraged her. If a promise was worth anything, John should have kept his to stay faithful to her.

Of course she didn't do anything wrong. They were at fault, the two of them. *Ill-fated passion?* What was that? It was two immature people doing whatever they wanted without thinking about anyone else. She'd done what she was supposed to do. Why couldn't everyone else on the planet simply do the right thing? The world would be better off, just marching in step to the controlled fugues of Bach.

Except, without emotion, there wouldn't be the sweet caress of Chopin or the gut-wrenching passion of Beethoven or the haunting melody of Rimsky-Korsakov's "Song of India." The world would be bereft of love sonnets, Shakespeare, and the swirling skies of Van Gogh.

And what about the cultures she'd taught her students but never had time to explore in depth: the rhythms of Africa, the atonal sounds of Asia, the sensual music of the Caribbean?

But emotion needed to be contained. One couldn't just run amok doing things because the heart demanded it. John should have been truthful with her and stuck to his vows.

Could she have weathered his betrayal? Would they have done couples therapy? Divorce? Shuttled the children from one house to another?

Who was to say his solution wasn't the best? She'd spent their lives together believing everything was fine. Her children had grown up in a stable home. John had provided for everyone and attended all the important events.

Lydia had gotten the leftovers.

Leaving the letter, she went to the piano. Opening Bach, she obeyed his controlled expression on the keys. Chopin called to her. Life was not only duty. It was the full expression of love for oneself and for others. As far as anyone knew, she and John had stayed within the box called marriage. It was the bargain they'd made.

Chopin drew tears from her once again, grief for her own pain but also for the struggles her husband and Lydia must have faced. They'd chosen the wrong path, but there hadn't been anything easy about the situation.

Unlike her tears of the night before, these soothed her and washed away the remains of her angst. Finally, she ended a piece, letting the chord linger in the air, and stood. She walked to the big window and stared out a few moments before registering what she was seeing.

A good-sized black bear lumbered down the drive. He wandered around the grounds closest to the house, then headed to the hammock she'd found and strung up right after she arrived. The bear put his front paws on it and swung it back and forth a few times, his body rocking with the motion. Then he pulled up a hind leg. The hammock twisted, and he landed on the ground.

Undaunted, he picked himself up and tried again. The same thing happened.

Two more times he made the attempt and tumbled to the ground. Finally, with a big heave, he plopped himself fully on the hammock. It swung madly for a few moments, but when it settled down, he lay back and shut his eyes.

Joy flooded Kelly's body. She let her gaze expand to the land around the sleeping bear. Tinges of fall edged the property as spots of color tipped some of the trees surrounding the retreat. Most of the flower garden had faded, but the mums still held strong with their golds, oranges, and reds. Dahlias held their heads up triumphantly.

The vegetable garden could someday hold winter squashes, maybe even a pumpkin.

Fall in California meant a slight cooling of the weather; here, it was a warning. It was time to gather the last fruits before the long winter, time to find a mate, and time to prepare a home for the storms ahead.

The rawness of it woke something in her, an emotion so strong it threatened to overwhelm her. She sank into the nearest chair.

It made all the sense in the world to go. Her life was set. Her children—well, Lisa—needed her. Her story was half told already; what she did from this point in her life wouldn't matter to anyone.

Her phone dinged with an email from Ruth.

"Just a quick note," it read. "The fire messed up my plans to join the knitting group, but the women let me know they are working on projects to help those who've lost things in the blaze. So I joined up.

Haven't seen a show in a week! :-((But it's been worth it to spend time with these amazing women. Thank you!"

Kelly leaned back in her chair with a smile. The retreat hadn't been a waste of time. Susan had found the courage to do the work she'd always wanted, and Ruth had found community. Had anything changed for Julia or Alex?

It would be interesting to know.

Chapter Thirty-Four

"Ouch!" Ryan stuck his finger in his mouth and let the quilt fall to his lap. He'd stabbed himself hard enough with the needle to bleed. Nothing was working right anymore. Not since he'd stopped seeing Kelly.

But what was he going to do? Follow her to California?

Not possible. He'd tried following a woman once.

Pushing himself to his feet, he lumbered to the bathroom and bandaged his finger. Getting blood on a client project wasn't allowed.

Nope. He'd get back into the rhythm of his life, box his heart back in, and pray she never came back again.

Kelly walked the path from the driveway to Alex's front door. The cabin and workshop were tucked into the woods, and the walkway was lined with a whimsy she hadn't realized Alex possessed, including small statues of gnomes, fairies, butterflies, and birds. In between, small, river rocks curved next to the walkway.

Pretty and low-maintenance.

Alex had somewhat reluctantly agreed to meet her, suggesting she come over and see the workshop, perhaps consider a piece to take home to California.

Kelly's hand trembled slightly as she rang the bell, an inset surrounded by a copper dragonfly.

"Hi," Alex said, opening the door and immediately leading her toward the back of the house. "I made coffee. I don't have anything to go with it."

"I brought a few muffins," Kelly said, placing the box on the island in the kitchen.

"Oh, great. I've been working so much I haven't had a chance to even buy supplies." Alex was in a pair of jean overalls, her hair covered by a calico kerchief. Dust lingered on the denim fabric. "Do you want to see the workshop? The coffee will stay warm."

"Sure."

Alex headed out the back door, and Kelly followed her to the workshop, which was filled with the aromas of fresh pine, with spicy and vanilla undertones. "It smells wonderful in here," Kelly said.

"Yes. Wood is amazing. Look here—see how the grain curls through the piece? It doesn't always occur in myrtle, but it makes a piece extra special."

"How do you decide what to make from a piece of wood?"

"I sit with it for a while, let it speak to me. I imagine the different things it could be, how it might be paired with another wood for accent pieces, what it will look like when it's carved and polished." She grinned at Kelly. "I know. Very airy-fairy for practical me."

"Whatever works," Kelly said. The tension eased between them.

Alex walked to a complicated piece hanging on the wall. "This shows how different woods contrast and work together. It's a more abstract piece, kind of an experiment. It might look good in your place in California."

"Could be."

"Anyway, that's it," Alex said.

"It's wonderful. It must give you a lot of satisfaction."

"Most days. Some days nothing seems to work, or something breaks in a way that destroys what I had in mind. Those days it's easier to walk away."

Kelly nodded. There were days at the piano like that.

They took the stone stairs from the workshop to the house.

"How can I help you?" Alex asked in a professional sales clerk voice as she poured them coffee and set the muffins out on a plate Kelly recognized from ART.

"I wanted to know how the retreat benefited you, if it did at all. Susan took up firefighting, and Ruth has found her tribe of knitters. I know you said you were clearing out your husband's things, but …"

"Why do you care?"

Ah. Normal Alex was back.

"Just curious. That's all. If you don't want to tell me, that's fine."

Alex's face was serious. "Sorry for being sharp. Bad habit. It's a defense to keep other people away."

Kelly nodded. She could understand the tactic, even though she'd never employed it herself. She resorted to extra politeness to accomplish the same thing.

Alex got up from her stool and paced the kitchen, stopping to stare out the window before returning to the island. "I guess I need to tell you the whole story for it to make sense for you."

Again Kelly nodded. Her children had taught her that being quiet was sometimes the best way to get information.

"We were living in Wichita during his last deployment," Alex began. "There are good people there, and it's a nice enough place, but it's so flat. I suppose it isn't if you live there, but when you're from mountains, a small rise doesn't do it." She tore her muffin into bits.

"After I got the news that he had died, I went through the motions. You know what it's like—all that ritual. All those tears. It's worse in the military. The mourners are divided into the public, who let everything hang out, and the service people, who keep a stiff upper lip no matter what happens."

Kelly's chest ached for her friend. To be so much in pain yet not be able to express any of it except late at night when she was alone had to be horrifying. No wonder Alex had a thick outer shell. "Did you try therapy?" Friends had urged Kelly to go until she'd finally given in.

"In spades. But I'm not sure that's what really brought me back to a place where I could go on with my life." Gathering up a bunch of the small bits of muffin, Alex tossed them into her mouth, followed by a swig of coffee. "So I came home. Mom was having some medical issues, and my grandmother was aging, although you'd never know it unless it was late in the day." A smile crept over Alex's face. "She was a pistol, my grandmother."

"I think I remember her."

"Hard to forget. She was always the life of the party. Could make any problem easier than it was. Anyway, I got here right before winter set in." Alex's fingers tapped on the surface, as if trying to expel extra energy. "The doctors in Kansas had given me some prescription drugs, something to help me sleep. I started relying on them to get me through the day. There was a doctor in Whitefish more than willing to keep them going, along with a few other relaxants. But Grandma cottoned on pretty quickly. She sat me down and told me to get over myself. I still had a life to live, and my husband wouldn't appreciate it if I threw it away after he'd given everything to protect the country."

"Sorry I missed more of your granny," Kelly said.

"And your own. Henrietta is the one who eventually saved my life. She was starting her retreat business and asked me to help. She really involved me, wanted to know my opinion and took my advice. As we worked together, I absorbed a lot of her wisdom, I think. It's too bad your mother and your own life kept you apart." Alex cocked her head. "I wonder if your life would have been different with her in it."

"It's a bit late now," Kelly said. Regrets for what might have been didn't serve anyone well.

"Yeah. Well, anyway, there was a wood artist at that retreat. He turned out the most amazing art: flowers, birds, trees. I guess I kind of crushed on him a bit." Alex's cheeks pinked. "But he took me under his wing, and I went to Oregon to apprentice with him for a while."

How far had apprenticing gone?

"Eventually, I began my own work. I wanted to differentiate from him, so I veered to the more practical. We thought about working together for a while, but ... things ended, and I came home to set up my own shop."

"I'm glad your story had a happy ending," Kelly said.

"Well, the work part did. I was still frozen in grief for my husband, even though I didn't realize how much. Maggie's been trying to get me to clean out that stuff for years. But I wasn't ready. I didn't want to make an opening, no matter how small, for someone to enter my life."

Kelly started. Was she so hung up on the past—like Alex was—that she wasn't allowing room for anything—or anyone—else? What was stopping her from turning her life upside down? Her kids were grown; Peter safely ensconced under his grandparents' wing, and Lisa was demonstrating quite clearly that she was ready to fly the coup.

"Why not?" she asked Kelly.

"I was afraid. What if it happened again?"

"Oh."

It was like looking in a mirror.

"In my case," Alex said, "I had to find out what gave me passion before I could live a full life. Some people, women in particular, are fulfilled by a family. But I wasn't like that. And I don't think you are either. And I don't think being a middle school music teacher is where your heart lies."

Kelly studied the milky remains of her coffee. "I think it's a bit late to be a concert pianist."

"Could be. But there are other ways to share your music." Alex gave them each a warmup. "One of the things Maggie and I, and a few others, have talked about is how to make our artist community even more inclusive. The website is great for all of us who produce things, but what about performing artists? Wouldn't it be great to have concerts, plays, even dance?" Alex grew more animated with the idea. "Regular performances would be great draws for the town. And we could keep each other occupied in the dead of winter." Alex gave a cockeyed grin.

Kelly smiled. "But where would you put something like that on?"

"We'd have to build it, but with some money and free labor, it could be done. It doesn't have to be huge, just big enough."

"But how would you get the money?"

Alex looked at her. "You're the one with the skills."

Kelly laughed and shook her head. Yes, she could do those things. All she needed to do was stay. But if she stayed, it would mean facing Ryan.

No, correct that. It would mean facing the truth about her marriage, her own part in it, and then sorting through her feelings about Ryan.

But most of all, it meant staying here.

What if she took that momentous step and he didn't share her feelings? How could she live here, longing for a second chance at love that would never happen?

Chapter Thirty-Five

Ryan carefully cut a thin strip of brown batik. It was taking some effort to match the correct color of Kelly's hair. It contained many hues of browns and golds, and it shifted with the mood of the sky. He'd started the project after their first dinner, hoping to give it to her when she finally decided to call Montana home.

He'd been so sure she would.

He'd been so very wrong.

However, he wasn't a man to give up on things. He'd finish it and send it to her for Christmas.

"Hey, Ryan?" Larry called out from the kitchen.

"Down here."

Ryan put the fabric down and slid a sheet of draft paper over the mess.

"What's up?" he asked as Larry came down the stairs.

"Have you heard from Kelly? She called me a few days ago asking if I'd give her a hand packing, but she never called back to set a time."

"Nope. Did you try ringing her back?"

"Yeah, but it goes straight to voicemail. I even stopped by her house, but no one was there."

Odd.

"I don't know what to tell you."

"Okay. I was hoping for the work, but Mike asked me to help out a few days a week at the tavern. Seems those firefighters are a thirsty lot when they get some time off."

Ryan chuckled. The fire was pretty much done. There were just a few hundred acres burning way up in the mountains. The fire service was letting it burn out, part of the efforts to mimic the more natural pattern forest fires had before the strong suppression efforts began near the start of the twentieth century.

The only question left hanging was what had happened to Betsy's son. He still hadn't been located, although firefighters had stumbled on his totally destroyed cabin.

So much wreckage.

"That's good," Ryan said to Larry.

"Yeah. People are really being nice. It's a good place to live when the worst happens," Larry said, his loss of all he owned echoing in his voice. "Thanks for giving me a place to stay."

"No problem." It was the least Ryan could do. He'd been spared thanks to the efforts of many people. No one could really do it alone, at least not in the far places of Montana.

But what was up with Kelly? It wasn't like her to not return calls like that.

"I'm going to head down to the store," he told Larry. "Need anything?"

"I'm good," Larry said. "I got my meeting with the insurance adjuster later. They finally got ahold of the landowner in California."

"A step in the right direction," Ryan said.

"Hope so."

This end of August day was crisp and clear, the lingering smoke blowing off to the east. Hints of fall yellowed the tips of aspen leaves scattered in among the deep green pines. A marmot scurried across the dirt road, cheeks stuffed fat with forage.

Soon it would be hunting season, and the rifle shots would pepper the morning. Being a cop had made him leave guns behind, except for the handgun he kept locked away, hoping a time would never come for him to insert the key to open the box. But friends were more than happy to share their deer or elk meat. He returned the favor when the caddis hatched in the spring and he spent lazy afternoons outmaneuvering the trout.

Maggie was behind the counter when he strode into the store.

"Hey, Ryan," she called. "Charlene just brought in some of those sweet rolls you like so much."

"Thanks." He changed direction and went to the rack to grab a bag before walking back to the counter. Charlene Bird's sweet rolls made a day worth living.

"Have you heard from Kelly?" he asked Maggie, trying to make it sound casual.

"I didn't think you suddenly got an urge to come down here to see if Charlene was baking," Maggie replied.

"Got me. Well, have you?"

"Not really."

"What does that mean?" Ryan asked, tension setting his jaw.

She turned her head slightly as if to view him in a new light. "I'm not sure that it's any of your business. Rumor has it the two of you are no longer an item."

"Just tell me, Maggie," he pleaded.

"She saw Alex a few days ago. Alex didn't tell me what they talked about, and I haven't seen Kelly, but Alex thinks she's having a hard time leaving. Kelly says she is ready to go, even has her plane tickets, but Rose reported she is going on and off the point at all hours of the day and night."

"And Rose knows," he said, trying to make it light.

"Yep," Maggie said.

"Thanks." He stood awkwardly for a moment, trying to think of a topic that didn't involve Kelly. "Have you heard anything about who or what started that fire?"

"Not personally, but Amanda was talking to the fire chief—she's very worried about Betsy's son, Henry—and he told her they were looking for him, too. The fire was definitely human-caused, and it looks like it wasn't accidental."

"Why would someone do such a thing?" he asked.

"No idea."

Ryan shook his head. The world was hard enough without some fool making it worse. He stepped away.

"You know…" she began.

"What?" He turned back.

"If she's that on the fence, it might take only a little push to get her to stay."

"You think so?" The possibility gave him hope.

"I do. And I think I know just the person to do it."

"Uh-huh." If they ever had a mayor of Promise Cove, Maggie would be perfect for the job.

"Thanks," he said. "See ya."

As he walked toward the door, she called out, "Good luck with Kelly."

Without turning around, he waved his hand in the air and headed out the door.

A good long hike was the only answer to the angst he felt inside. On his way home, he'd driven by Henrietta's place. The RAV4 was there, but he didn't stop. He had no idea what he could do or say to make her stay. Was that even fair to try to manipulate her? Shouldn't she make her own decision?

He headed back to the cabin, where he filled up his water bottle, picked up his daypack, and headed north, hoping to get as far away from humanity as possible. He needed inspiration not conversation. He parked at the Swift Creek Trailhead, slung on his backpack, and headed out.

The creek trickled well within its boundaries, typical of the late summer season. Come spring, it would roar and jump, clearing everything away in its rush to get to the lake. Like the stream, he was no longer in the spring of his life. He tended to go more slowly, especially where matters of the heart were concerned.

In fact, his heart hadn't had a good workout in more than twenty years. After Lorelei had left, he'd had a few relationships, none of them serious. At some level he'd always been waiting for Kelly to return, although he'd never realized it. And he'd been standoffish at first. When he finally asked her out, he'd kept her at arm's length.

He'd been a coward.

He should have told her the depth of his feeling. He should have let her know he'd protect her, help her adapt, give her all the love he had to give. He should have rushed over all the obstacles to get to her heart.

But he hadn't.

Did he have a second chance at a second chance with her? Would she even listen to him?

He plodded up the trail, the altitude thinning the air and the effort to climb pulling at the air in his chest.

He should get a dog. Dogs loved you no matter what you did, no matter how you may have messed up the relationship. If you were scared, they didn't run away. They stuck their head on your knee and comforted you.

They also shed and needed care and companionship. The fur would play havoc with his quilts.

But how could he reach Kelly? How could he let her know that what he felt for her was real? He'd spent a lot of time not being open with her. As a boy, he'd been too shy to ask her out; as a man, he'd been too afraid to share his feelings. She'd already spent half a lifetime with a husband who'd divided his feelings between her and another woman. Ryan had to show her he was all in.

But how? Her husband had given her things but not all of himself.

John hadn't really known Kelly. He hadn't heard what Ryan had heard, the sweet passion of a young woman for the music she played.

When they were kids, Ryan used to sneak onto the property when she was practicing. He'd listen, carried away by the heart and soul of her ability. It was from her that he'd learned to love classical music, a love that had kept him sane when the rest of his world was falling apart. He'd lose himself in the rising and falling of the notes, drifting in the spaces between them.

Kelly had been so good. In fact …

A smile lit his face. He knew how to get her attention.

Chapter Thirty-Six

Kelly had taken long walks, stared at the water, read every personal journal her grandmother had written, prayed, and meditated.

Nothing helped.

She needed to move forward. Larry had left three messages on her phone, but she hadn't returned one. Even though she'd already made the decision to go back to California, she was stuck.

Maybe Alex had been right. The answer to moving forward wasn't in making the decision.

If it wasn't that, what was it?

She plopped into the chair on the front porch.

Her phone rang.

"Hey, Maggie," she said. "What's up?"

"Alex and I are staging an intervention."

"A what?"

"You know, when a person is confused—"

"I know what an intervention is. Why do you think I need one?" Kelly asked.

"Because you're wandering around town, not calling people back. Do you even know how you're planning on getting to the airport?"

"Um, no." Maybe she was in worse shape than she thought.

"Didn't think so. Be at Alex's on Wednesday at four."

"I'll try."

"If you aren't there, we'll come and drag you over. Understood?"

"Yes, ma'am."

"Good." Maggie hung up.

Since she hadn't been doing anything, she couldn't complain that they were dragging her away from important business. She may as well go. Maybe they'd inspire her to get on with what she had to do to get back to her life.

Her insides wound with anxiety, Kelly took the gnome-lined path to Alex's front door. The walk no longer seemed as benign as it had before. She was walking to her doom, or at least that's how it felt.

They were right. She was definitely lost. A great longing to stay, to begin again and find out what would happen if she did, filled her. But how could she do that with things the way they were between her and Ryan? In a big city, they could get lost from each other. But in a town of around five hundred people, that wasn't going to be possible.

Alex opened the door with a bright smile. "Here you are!"

"Yes."

"Come on. We have tea and cookies. No wine until we're done talking."

"Don't I get a say?"

"No."

Okay, then. She followed Alex into the kitchen where Maggie was bustling about.

Once they were all seated, Kelly looked from one to the other, determined not to say a word. This was their meeting.

"We think you belong here," Maggie said.

Kelly opened her mouth to protest.

Maggie held up her hand. "I know you think your life is in California, and the decision is yours, obviously."

"Obviously," Kelly echoed, trying to snatch a smidgeon of her power back.

"But you need us, and we need you."

"Remember at the retreat when you told us that all you had to do was make a decision and everything would be fine?" Alex asked.

Kelly nodded.

"Well, if your decision to go to California was fine, why aren't things humming along?"

"I don't know," Kelly said miserably. She really had believed that all she had to do was get everything ready to sell, but every time she looked ahead to the next year in the lonely house overlooking the ocean, the pit of her stomach dropped.

"The first step is admitting a problem exists," Maggie said. "Well done!"

Kelly groaned. "This isn't a twelve-step program. I just need to figure out how to get unstuck."

Alex nodded.

Kelly sipped her tea from the graceful blue mug. Art surrounded her here. Art made by people she knew and respected. California was full of bright objects, but if she examined the stickers too closely, it was clear they came from some overseas factory.

"Who are you?" Alex asked. "What gives you happiness?"

"I'm a wife … widow … and mother. My family gives me

happiness," she automatically answered, like she'd done in her school classes a thousand times.

"Yes, and...?" Maggie prompted.

"What else is there? You're a mother. You know."

"I do. And I can assure you that Teagan is not the be-all and end-all of happiness. In fact, sometimes I think she'll drive me quite mad."

Kelly gave her a half smile. Sixteen-year-old girls could be a trial.

"This is the point in almost every woman's life when they look in the mirror and ask, 'Now what?'" Maggie said. "That's what we're asking you. But first we want to tell you what Alex and I have in mind. In fact, our committee of two—three if you stay—is called the Promise Cove Renewal Committee." She banged a wooden spoon instead of a gavel. "I call this meeting to order."

Alex put her hand on Maggie's arm. "You're getting carried away."

"Probably."

"We realized when you arrived that Promise Cove was great for visual artists but has nothing to offer performing artists," Alex said. "When your grandmother held retreats, often the visual artists would donate something to ART as a gift for the support the community showed them. A writer might dedicate a work to the town and promote the website. But performing artists really have no place they could showcase their work. The town is saturated with artists, but a little variety would be nice."

Kelly nodded.

"The retreats are vital to the town," Maggie chimed in.

"Hold on. We haven't gotten there yet."

"What do you have in mind?" Kelly asked.

"We want to build a stage. Outside at first but eventually cover it over," Maggie said, practically bouncing with excitement. "There's a perfect spot of land by ART."

"As soon as the stage is built, we'd start doing concerts of local artists on weekends, beginning with you if you are here. Gabriella said she'd run specials at her inn, but there's plenty of places to camp or bring an RV around here as well. People would go to ART, to Amanda's sweet shop..."

"You don't have a nearby restaurant," Kelly pointed out.

"The fire department and rescue squad would hold an outdoor barbeque on Saturday; the youth group and school would do a pancake breakfast on Sunday," Alex said triumphantly.

"And maybe it would encourage someone to start a restaurant up here," Maggie added. "It would be nice to have someplace to go on a nice date."

"Like with the sheriff?" Kelly couldn't help herself.

"Tom?" Maggie waved her hand. "We're buds. Nothing more to it than that."

"Stay on topic, please," Alex said, although there was a teasing note in her voice.

"More seriously," Kelly said, "Where would you get the funds?"

"Labor shouldn't be too much of a problem. We have more than enough carpenters and handy people around here to help us build a simple stage. Lumber is the big expense. We'd petition the art group to expand their budget to include the venue," Alex said.

"And you could help us fundraise," Maggie said. "But only if you are staying."

"In fact," Alex said as if she were thinking of it for the first time, "Ryan would be great to head the building effort. He knows carpentry and also how to work with people." She looked at Kelly. "It would be a great chance for you guys to work together, maybe give your relationship a second chance."

Kelly laughed. "You guys are bad."

"So what's up with you two anyway?" Maggie asked.

"I'm going back to California; he's staying here. It's that simple." Suddenly, Kelly was tired of the game they were playing. She wanted to be anywhere but here.

Most especially, she longed to be sitting with Ryan on his porch, holding his hand and watching the moon rise.

She stifled her pain and strengthened her game face. "Now, can we get on with the reason you brought me here? I've got work to do."

"And there it is," Alex said.

"What is?"

"Instead of dealing with whatever is really bothering you, you bury your feelings and go right to the to-do list."

"So what? It's my life. It's how I get things done. No use worrying about things that can't be fixed. I have a life somewhere else, and I need to return to it. Besides, emotions are messy. I don't have time for messy."

"That's your mother speaking," Maggie said. "I remember her saying that very same thing: 'Emotions are messy.'"

Her imitation of Cynthia was so spot on that Kelly had to laugh.

"Look," Kelly said, "like I told Ryan, I'm not meant for this life. I like teaching at the same school for a long time, knowing where things are in my home, going to the same grocery store."

"Boring," Alex said.

Kelly shrugged. "Okay, then. I'm boring. So are a million other people."

"Not your grandmother. Not Ryan."

"That's their choice," Kelly said, her throat tightening on the words.

She mashed the muffin crumbs on her plate with her fork and stuck it in her mouth. What they were saying was too close to home. She'd been living her life following a script her mother had handed her. No wonder she didn't think her story mattered.

It wasn't her story.

What if …?

Her lower lip began to tremble, so she bit it to keep it still.

"Give yourself a chance," Maggie said, her hand closing over Kelly's.

"We'll help you," Alex said, grasping Kelly's other hand.

It was tempting, so tempting.

But Ryan didn't really care, did he? He'd never said he did. And he was way too willing to let her go.

She shook her head, grabbed her purse, and left. She needed to get away from this place, these people, this life.

Chapter Thirty-Seven

Kelly paced the great room of her grandmother's house, her insides in turmoil. How dare they? How could they possibly know what she was feeling? They knew nothing—nothing! —about her. They hadn't even seen each other in more than twenty years. They had no right to tell her she belonged in this country bumpkin town in the middle of nowhere, filled with danger everywhere a person turned.

Packing. That's what she needed to do. She stalked to the bookcase. Books were easy. Flat with edges. No need to protect them from breaking. She squatted down. Yellow piano books stared back at her.

Jerking upright, she looked around. Emotional time bombs. Everywhere.

The kitchen. That was it. Difficult to pack, but most of it would be going to a yard sale. She'd hire someone to do it after she left and donate the proceeds to ART. That should satisfy the women who'd once been her friends.

Whirling, she marched to the kitchen and began with the far cupboard, pulling things out and stacking them on the counter. Once she had a fair number, she began to sort. She didn't even know what half these things were. Her grandmother must have been very talented in the kitchen.

She grabbed a box and sorted through what she had pulled down. Placing a few items of interest in the box, she moved the remainder to the kitchen table, trying to lay things out in some sort of order so she could maximize the space.

Then she repeated the exercise with the next cabinet. And the next. Robotic movements. The only time she stopped was to slide a disc of the Metropolitan Opera's latest version of *Aida* into the CD player and crank it up.

Darkness finally descended around nine o'clock. Exhausted, she hauled herself to bed and tumbled into a deep sleep, not stopping for a shower, pajamas, or even a glass of wine.

Return to Promise Cove

Her muscles ached the next morning when she finally roused herself after eight. She dragged herself into the shower, dressed, then returned to the kitchen to search for breakfast. If things weren't as they were, she'd head to the store to see what Elaine had on the grill.

Instead, she started the pot of coffee and searched the mess for a mug.

The day was blooming bright, so she took the mug to the porch, along with a throw kept in the mudroom for that purpose. Wrapping herself in it, she drew her knees to her chest and stared at the beauty beyond.

As she gazed, a memory by Melpomene's cabin began to focus. She'd seen something there once. Two people kissing.

Two people who shouldn't have been kissing.

There was only one person who could tell her whether or not her memory was accurate.

It was about time she talked to her mother anyway.

"Are you coming for Thanksgiving?" her mother asked almost immediately.

"I haven't even thought about the holidays," Kelly said. The previous year she'd bowed to Cynthia's wishes and brought the children to Boston for both the long weekend and Christmas holidays. With John so recently gone, the trips had made more sense than rattling around the house with the ghost of her husband.

"Well, you need to plan, you know. It was so late last year, it was amazing we got those plane tickets at all. Peter will already be here, so it will be easier this year."

Easy sounded nice. But she wasn't going to get to easy until she finished with the retreat center.

"I'll figure out what to do by the end of September."

"That's too late," her mother protested.

"Nonetheless, that's when it's going to be."

"Oh." Her mother seemed taken aback.

"Mom," Kelly began, unsure of how to begin the conversation. "I know you said we stopped coming to Montana so I could participate in important things in Boston, but was there another reason?"

"You mean other than Henrietta and I never got along?" Cynthia's tone was sharp.

"Yes."

Cynthia sighed. "There wasn't much to do in Promise Cove. Great if you're a kid, but not as a teenager. Besides, you were never there in winter. You never knew how deadly boring it could become. Anything you wanted to do outside meant snow and cold. Brrr."

Kelly had to laugh. "I get the point."

"I wanted to contribute to the arts. When I graduated, I worked for the Boston Museum of Fine Arts for a while, but then I met your father, and he convinced me I could have more impact by serving on boards. With his income, there was no need for me to work. And he was right. Is that what you needed to know?"

"Somewhat."

"There weren't any other reasons." Cynthia sounded wary, which spurred Kelly to ask about the memory that had surfaced."

"I remembered something," she began. "I need to know if it was true. No judgment on my part, but I want to know the truth."

"I'll do my best."

"That last summer we were here. I seem to remember … well, I thought I saw you kissing someone. Did you?"

Silence.

Kelly waited. If one of her children asked her the same question, she would have to think about how to answer as well.

"Ah. I guess you're old enough now. It was someone I'd known—dated—in high school. Your father and I were going through a rough spot. I saw this man I'd had a crush on in high school, and all my old feelings took hold. It was stupid. It didn't get very far. I realized what I had to lose and ended it."

"That's really why we never went back, isn't it?"

"No, no. I did it for your sake," her mother protested.

"Truth, Mom."

"That is the truth. Maybe the other was an influence. I didn't know. I've never been into the deep self-analysis you seem to be intent on doing. Tell me. Why is it so important?"

Good question. Why was it so important?

Then she realized. Her mother had physically separated herself from temptation. Kelly was about to do the same, except in her case, she was running away from the potential pain of living near someone who didn't want her.

"This is about Ryan, isn't it?"

"What? How did you know about Ryan?"

Her mother laughed. "I always knew about Ryan. The two of you were like open books; you only thought you were hiding how much you cared about each other from the rest of us. It was a cute puppy love. At least at first. But as you two got older, it only intensified. You weren't interested in dating any of the boys you knew in school. I began to worry. I wanted someone better for you."

"Like Dad."

"Your father's a good man."

"So is Ryan."

"Yes. He was a good kid. It seems he's grown up well. His quilts are famous—there's one on display at the fine arts museum right now."

"How did you know it was him?"

"It wasn't hard. How many Ryan Svobodas from Montana can there be?"

Kelly had to chuckle. "You've got a point." But then she sobered. "That's why you didn't come back."

"Like I said, I did it for you. You needed to be exposed to everything life has to offer you, not only a pretty lake in the middle of the forest in summertime. Life can get rough. Winter shows up. You needed someone by your side who was dependable."

John had been that, almost to a fault.

"Maybe I was wrong. I don't know. I let my past experiences prevent me from letting you have your own. But I did what I thought was right."

"I know, Mom." Cynthia's good intentions had shaped her life up to this point. But now it was Kelly's decisions that mattered.

"So are you and Ryan in a relationship?" Cynthia asked.

"No. We ... I thought ... but no."

"That's too bad."

"Really?" Kelly asked.

"Like I said, he was a good kid. He might be right for you now."

"But that would mean moving to Montana," Kelly pointed out.

"He won't go to California?"

"Nope."

"I guess that answers that. A woman shouldn't uproot her life for a man."

"Definitely not," Kelly agreed.

"That doesn't only mean going somewhere to be with a man." Cynthia's voice was wistful. "It also means not twisting yourself in knots to avoid one. I wish ... well, never mind. That decision is in the past. Only today counts now." There was a pause on the line. "How's Lisa doing?"

After a few pleasantries about the children, they ended the call, leaving Kelly more unsettled about her decision than before.

Kelly pulled into the post office parking lot. She had only fifteen minutes to pick up her mail and get the postage stamps she needed before the small office closed. When she got to the desk, she was surprised to see someone other than Betsy behind the counter.

"Is Betsy okay?" she asked the man filling in.

"Yep. Better than okay. Her son's been found."

"Oh, that's wonderful. Is he okay?"

"A little worse for wear, but seems to be. He got himself trapped up behind the fire lines and couldn't find a way back. Then when he did, he was so upset that he'd lost everything, he just wandered around for a bit."

"Oh, that's not good."

"Betsy's got him. She'll fix him up good. I'm going to fill in for a bit so she has the time." The man stood up a little straighter, as if proud to be of service to the community.

"Thank you," Kelly said and took her stamps. She headed out but stopped when Maggie entered the small space.

"How was your trip?" Maggie said as she slid her key into her box. "Did you get everything?"

"Pretty much. The rest I can order online. Good news about Betsy's son."

"Almost."

"What do you mean?"

"Tom told me the feds think he might be responsible for the fire, that he committed arson to see the flames or something like that. They think he's mentally ill."

"That's horrible! It can't be true."

"I hope not. It's such a terrible thing. I thought they had Gregg in their sights, but they shifted as soon as Henry surfaced, and they went after him."

"Sounds like they've got some bias."

"Yep. We're going to start a fund for his defense."

"Count me in," Kelly said. "See you. I've got to get home and get stuff unloaded before it gets dark."

"Bye."

As she walked out, Ryan's truck pulled into the remaining space, and he got out.

There was so much to say, but she wasn't ready to say it.

Instead, she waved.

He nodded and continued on his way into the post office.

Chapter Thirty-Eight

The road south to Whitefish was bright with promise. Cloudless blue skies delineated the tips of lodgepole pines and the bright islands of aspens. Cottonwoods dominated the skyline along streams that flowed from the snowpack to the lake. With most of the past winter's deposits gone, the water flows had turned to trickles.

The classical playlist she'd made provided the perfect background music to the scenery.

Just a few more tasks to be done and she'd be on her way back to California, just in time to get ready for the school year. She'd accomplished a great deal in the past week. Larry had come to make the few final repairs and was happy to have his pick of the stack of things she was giving away.

The piano had sat unplayed, and Kelly had pushed aside any desire to stay in Montana. She wasn't going to uproot her stable and successful life to satisfy a whim ... or a man. She wasn't running away from Ryan. She was simply leaving.

Someday, when the time was right, she might move on to a second relationship—or third if she counted whatever went on with Ryan. Time would allow her to relegate John's continued infidelity to the past where it belonged. Her long-ago crush on the man in Montana could be delegated to the land of fantasy, where it obviously belonged. An aging handyman quilter determined to live a quiet life in the woods was obviously not the man for her.

After weaving through the morning streets of Whitefish, she headed to the attorney's office, where he had some final papers for her to sign.

"Good morning, Kelly," he said when she arrived. "Coffee?"

"That would be wonderful."

"So you've decided to go back to California," he said once they were settled.

"Yes."

"Henrietta would be disappointed. She had great dreams of you taking over her work."

"I'm not suited for it, I'm afraid. And definitely not ready for life in the big woods."

He chuckled. "It's too bad you'll miss fall, though. It's a really magical time of year. The tourists are mostly gone, and we have Glacier back to ourselves. The animals seem to know they're protected there, and there's more chance of seeing something very unique. You haven't lived until you hear an elk bugle!"

There was one thing to be said about Montanans. They loved their state.

"I'm sure," she said. "You said there were things for me to sign."

"Yes. They're here in this folder."

He guided her through the several pages of legal documents, explaining them as he went. When they were finished, he smacked the edges on the desk several times and put them back into the folder.

"You have sixty days to change your mind," he said. "After that, everything will be filed and the place put up for sale."

"You can do that if you want, but I'm ready to let it go as soon as I get on that plane next Friday."

"It's what Henrietta wanted."

"Okay, then." She rose and held out her hand. "Thank you for all your help. It was an interesting trip. I look forward to getting everything finalized."

He gripped her hand with both of his for a few seconds. "I hope you'll be happy in California. Good luck."

"Thank you."

She should have felt elation at being done when she left. Instead, a whisper of sadness claimed her.

Walking back to her car, she decided to take one last stroll around Whitefish, maybe pick up lunch before she headed back to Promise Cove. Maybe she'd stop at the same restaurant she'd gone to with Ryan, reinvigorating one last memory of what might have been to take home with her.

She was being stubborn and more than a bit afraid. Impulsive decisions had never been a factor in her life, so making the decision to return to her own life made all the sense in the world. If only it didn't feel so wrong, like she was losing out on something wonderful because her comfortable rut felt safer.

Her comfortable loafers didn't make a sound on the wooden sidewalks that lined a part of the main street. Overhangs gave the place a Western feel, not that it needed it. The tall, granite-topped mountains surrounding the town provided that. An outdoors vibe, similar to that of Vermont, made its presence known in ski, hiking, and outfitting shops. A few galleries and tourist shops were interspersed with restaurants. A distillery was tucked around a corner.

She paused here and there, trying to imagine what some of this charm would do to a place like Promise Cove. Maggie was determined to put the cove on the map, turning it into a destination instead of just a pass-through. Would that save it or ruin it?

The idea of a performance space was solid, but the town would need more infrastructure to support it: a few more restaurants and nice places to stay overnight. Not everyone was fond of sleeping in a tent.

The skills she'd built up raising money for charitable causes and serving on boards over the years would have been valuable to Maggie's efforts. But like staying in Montana for a man, staying here to support someone else's cause didn't make sense, did it?

But what was she going home for?

She wandered into an upscale tourist shop. Paintings and photos lined the gray planked wall, while cute carved bears, native-made soaps, and other creative souvenirs stood on rustic wooden shelves. A photo caught her eye.

It was Promise Cove. The view was one she'd seen many times from her grandmother's property. She stared at it, tears beginning to form in her eyes. This was the view she'd just signed away, the one her grandmother had created and done her best to keep going in order to pass something on to Kelly.

But she'd refused the gift.

Her heart ached as she picked up the photo. She turned it over to identify the photographer: Pamela Cuzins. The name sounded familiar. Oh, yes. Pamela had been proposed for her mini-retreat.

Kelly checked the price on the photo and was surprised at the cost. It was way too low for the quality of the work.

She took the print to the cashier and paid for her purchase. "This is really a steal," she said to the cashier, who'd identified herself as one of the owners. "The artist should be charging much more for this type of work. I'm from California, and we'd easily pay twice that price for something this good."

"Oh? Really?" The owner pulled out a notebook, checked it, and nodded. She scribbled something on a sticky and stuck on the page. "I'll check into that. We like to see that our artists are paid fairly. Thank you."

Kelly smiled as she left the store. Score one for Promise Cove.

Finally! Ryan held up the cassette he'd never lost in all his travels but had somehow buried in the most remote closet in his cabin. He'd always kept a small player with him. Technology had definitely improved, and now was the time to transfer the contents to something more permanent.

Using the computer, he cleaned up the sound and transferred the recording to a CD, then created a cover from a picture he'd taken a long time ago.

Now the only question was when and where to give it to Kelly.

Would it do what he needed it to do? And if it didn't, how far would he go to get her love again?

Maybe they could work out a duel state life: warm weather season in Montana, winter in California. Lots of people did that. There had to be solution. Kelly was too vital to his life to let her go again. He just had to convince her to give them a chance.

Kelly was hearing things. Somewhere, a Berlioz piece was playing. It had once been a favorite of hers.

Then she heard the same mistake she always made.

Putting her grandmother's journal down, she stood from the rocking chair, causing it to thud back against the wall. She walked around the side of the house to the porch by the kitchen. A small speaker sat on a table near one of the Adirondack chairs. Next to it sat a CD case. Picking it up, she stared at the cover. The title overlay a picture of her from a long time ago. It said simply: *Kelly, The Inaugural Album.*

There was only one person who would have a picture like that. The squeak of a board made her turn.

Ryan stood with a bouquet of flowers, a hopeful smile on his face.

Kelly's hand went to her mouth.

"Did you do this?"

He nodded. "These are for you." He held out the flowers, a shy teenage boy in a man's body.

She took them and breathed them in deeply.

She should say something. But what?

"Whenever you practiced, I was nearby listening." He pointed to a group of aspens at the back of her grandmother's house. "I think Henrietta knew I was there, but she never let on. One day I decided to make a recording so I could listen to you all winter. I wanted the feeling you were close, even though you were almost a continent away."

"I used to look out my window—it faced west—and imagine we were together somewhere, floating in space between two worlds." The longing to be with him had been incredible. Where had it disappeared to?

She picked up the CD and stared at it, her heart bursting with the memory of playing her heart out for an imaginary audience. It turned out the audience wasn't totally in her mind.

Ryan stepped closer.

"I've been an idiot. I never let you know how I felt as a kid, and I sure haven't let you know how much I feel now."

"And what do you feel?" she asked.

He hesitated, then seemed to gather himself. "I love you." He went silent, as if he were a stunned by the words as she was.

"But how ... you hardly know me."

"I know what's important. I know you from your music." He gestured to the CD. "And I know your heart from how you played and how you lived your life. Even though it wasn't the one you wanted, you were steady and true. That matters. You matter." He took the flowers and CD from her hands and laid them on the table.

He clasped her hands in his. "I'm hoping you believe in third chances."

Did she? This was sudden. Too sudden. Her mother's training kicked in. They hadn't been dating long enough. They'd barely dated at all. He lived too far away. They'd never make it work.

Then she looked into his eyes.

This was Ryan. She'd known him once, and she knew him still. He was dependable, trustworthy, and set her pulse racing whenever she saw him, although she'd never admit that to anyone else.

"How ...?" she began.

"We can live in California in the dead of winter if that suits you."

"But what about my job?"

"We'll figure it out."

He was trying to meet her halfway. She needed to try.

"I could try to run the retreats," she said, a quaver in her voice.

"You could, but either way, I think there is an answer. Provided, of course, that you love me. You haven't said."

Did she?

Would she allow herself?

"Yes," she said. "I do."

"Then that's all that matters. The rest of it are just logistics. And speaking of logistics ..." Dropping to one knee, he pulled a small box from his pocket and opened it. "Will you marry me?"

For a nanosecond, the old rules hammered at her. It was too soon. He was the wrong type of man. What would her children think?

She kicked them to the curb.

"I will."

All smiles, he slid the ring on her finger, a silver setting with a polished blue stone that reflected hidden depths, like the man who gave it to her. "It's a yolo sapphire," he said. "It's Montana's stone."

"I love it." She looked up at him. "But not as much as I love you … or the idea that someone will keep me warm in the winter."

He laughed. "I've taken care of that, too." He indicated an envelope stuck in the flowers. "Open that."

Eagerly, she tore it open.

"Hawaii!" she yelled.

"Yes, my love. Hawaii in February when Montana's at its coldest. Or if you are teaching, we'll change the tickets and go when California is at its wettest and you are on winter break. As long as you're with me, that's all that matters," he said.

"I'll be here for the rest of your life." She wrapped her arms around him and coaxed him toward her for another kiss. "I love you," she whispered again. "It was always you." She slipped her arms around his neck and tugged him closer.

She sighed as their lips touched. At last they were together.

Chapter Thirty-Nine

Maggie was deep in conversation with the sheriff when Kelly walked into the store a little after noon the next day. Good, maybe she was giving the poor man a chance. He obviously liked her.

Kelly sniffed the air in the store. Elaine was definitely cooking up something delicious today. The sweet aroma of caramelized onions contrasted with the bitter tang of garlic. Everything smelled good this morning.

She and Ryan had talked long into the night, finally coming up with the outline of a plan. She'd go back to California to her teaching job, and he would join her in a few weeks. They'd make the next step from there.

In the morning, she'd called Bruce to put the sale on hold. Her grandmother had thought she was good enough to run the high-end gatherings. It was time to stop restricting her options.

Heading back to the tables, Kelly was happy to see Alex sitting at one, nursing a cup of coffee.

"I'm surprised to see you here," Alex said.

"I wanted to touch base with you and Maggie. Things have changed a little."

"Oh?"

"I want to wait until Maggie's here." Kelly glanced over at her friend and Tom. "What's up over there?"

"I'm not really sure," Alex said. "Tom came in a bit ago, and they've been talking ever since. I heard something about Gregg and Teagan, but I'm not sure what that's about. Maggie will fill us in, I'm sure."

Kelly nodded. "Any word on Betsy's son?"

"Betsy's back at the post office, so he must be on the mend. As far as we know, no one's charged Henry with anything."

"That's good. I hope it stays that way."

"I do, too. There's no way he's responsible, at least intentionally. And the US Forest Service investigators were pretty sure the fire was deliberately set. I don't know why they're chasing this new theory."

The front door thudded shut, and Maggie appeared, a whirlwind of color and motion. Today she'd dug up a tie-dye shirt from some ancient pile to pair with her jeans and tennis shoes.

"Mom's trying a new recipe, and since you're both here, you're her taste testers," she said as she settled into the seat.

"If it tastes as good as it smells, it's a winner," Alex said.

"And why are you here?" Maggie asked Kelly. "Shouldn't you be packing or something?"

"Like I said, things have changed." She slowly drew her left hand from her lap and put it on the table.

"A yolo sapphire?"

"It's on her ring finger," Alex pointed out. "Her *left* ring finger."

"Hallelujah! Ryan finally made his move!" Maggie shouted.

"Shh. The whole town doesn't need to know," Kelly said.

"Oh, yes it does," Maggie said.

"It took him long enough," Alex added.

"So when? Does that mean you're staying?"

"I'm still going back to California, at least for the short term," Kelly said. "Ryan's going to join me. Then we'll see what happens. We'll definitely be back here next summer."

"Oh," Maggie said, her shoulders drooping.

"But I'm going to do another retreat," Kelly said. "And I'll help you with your plans for the performance space. Fundraising in the summer when the tourists are here will be a lot more productive."

"Good." Alex nodded.

"But she's leaving," Maggie whined.

"She's coming back. Give Montana a little more time, and she'll hook Kelly good." Alex flashed Kelly a confident smile.

"That will have to do," Maggie said.

Kelly laughed. Living in two states for a while might be a challenge, but at least there were friends in both places.

"What did Tom have to say?" Alex asked.

"It's good news," Maggie said. "Well, kind of. I'm going to wring Teagan's neck when I get ahold of her."

"Why?"

"It seems Gregg's determined to find out who set the fire. Apparently, one of his close friends was seriously hurt in an arson-caused fire a long time ago. When they announced this was probably the same cause, he was determined to find the culprit. And ... And ..." Maggie's voice rose with her agitation. "He dragged my daughter into danger with him!"

"But they're both okay," Alex said calmly, placing her hand on Maggie's arm.

"Yes."

"Good then. So have they caught the person?"

"They think so. Remember that old tan pickup they'd seen?"

"Yep," Kelly said. "I thought it was someone looking for work."

"Well, they got suspicious when they realized he'd been hired on at a couple of different locations across the state right after the fires started near there."

"And that's strange? I'd think a temporary firefighter—or whatever they call them—would naturally be at different locations. He has to go where the fire is."

"Not that close to the start of the fire. Anyway," Maggie continued, "Gregg—I'm going to ring his neck, too—started watching this guy. He took a look in the back of the pickup once and saw a gas can."

"That's not unusual around here," Alex protested. "A lot of folks do that in case they run out in the middle of nowhere."

"But that wasn't all. There were some gadgets with timers. Gregg said they could be set to start a flame and self-destruct once the fire really got going. They're almost impossible to find."

"But they found one," Kelly guessed.

"They found a few." Maggie nodded. "And with Gregg's information, they were able to find the guy and charge him."

"So Henry's off the hook," Alex said.

"Yep."

"That's good. I'm glad," Kelly said. Her little community was almost back to what it was before the fire started.

"Here you go, ladies." Elaine balanced the tray on the edge of the table and gave them each aluminum-wrapped packages. "Spicy chicken and onion wraps. Perfect for a cool fall day, don't you think?"

None of them answered. They were too busy unwrapping the aromatic food. Murmurs of satisfaction was all Elaine was going to get.

Kelly let a purr of satisfaction escape.

Life was good.

Ultimately, the decision to sell the California house and move her life was easy. As promised, Ryan came down to the coast a few weeks after Kelly began teaching. Living in Montana, even for a short while, had changed her. She longed for the quiet and solitude of a long afternoon. She missed the drive and purpose of her friends to make Promise Cove the best place it could possibly be. Even practicing the piano, which she'd taken up again once she was settled, wasn't quite the same.

Although having Ryan sit on the couch, hand-sewing his latest project with a smile on his face had made it easier.

So she'd tendered her resignation, ending her teaching career after the midterms and made plans for Christmas in Montana. Over the two-week school break, her family would celebrate, and she and Ryan would get married in the barn. They'd take the honeymoon in Hawaii after her work ended.

Cynthia declared it was all happening too fast, but Kelly told her the timing was perfect.

The Friday after Christmas ...

Romantic classical music played as Lisa walked down the makeshift aisle in the barn. Alex, Maggie, and Ruth had enlisted others to set up chairs and decorate the space with Christmas wedding flowers, ribbons, and twinkling lights. Peter, whom Ryan had convinced to be his best man, stood awkwardly to one side. Kelly's parents watched from the front row. They'd arrived a few days after Christmas, loaded with presents, even a few for Ryan.

Kelly smiled at the memory. After an initial hesitation, Cynthia had given her future son-in-law her traditional air kisses, then taken him aside to lecture him on exactly how her daughter needed to be treated.

Kelly smiled up at the man beside her as they waited for Lisa to get to the front of the room and turn. There was no need for her mother to worry. In the few months since they'd made their commitment, he'd proved to be a loving partner, ready to work through the inevitable issues of a newly intimate relationship.

As she waited, she took in her wedding setting. Her friends had created beauty from almost nothing. The scent of pine filled the room from the green boughs that hung from the ends of the rows of chairs, twinkling lights strung among them. They'd created a small arbor from poinsettia plants, white wicker, and greens from the forest around them, along with more twinkling lights.

Kelly's heart filled with joy and pulsed in waves for the small community she'd grown to love. So many people were here, accepting a general invitation she'd sent out that was passed person to person until everyone knew they were welcome. And they had come, decked out in jeans, button-down shirts, flowing dresses with cowboy boots. Next to her, Ryan stood tall in a dark blue suit with a red tie. The same red was reflected in the accents to the white Christmas dress she'd chosen. Her small bouquet added a touch of green for the season.

Finally, the music she'd chosen for their walk began. She took Ryan's arm, and they started forward, the crowd standing as they passed. When they finally reached the front, Betsy smiled at them. She'd turned out to be an ecumenical minister and had agreed to lead them through the vows they'd written and the exchange of rings.

All Kelly was aware of during the ceremony was the promise in Ryan's dark brown eyes. His words flowed over her like a loving baptism. Once their vows were exchanged, they turned toward the side, where Julia Leonard, the singer-songwriter who'd attended the retreat, sang a sweet song she'd created for them out of gratitude for the strength she'd found during the retreat.

When the singer finished, Kelly and Ryan exchanged rings. Then, with a triumphant blare from the sound system, they headed back down the aisle. At the rear, they held an impromptu reception line while dozens of people rearranged the barn area into small table groupings and set up a bar and a space for dancing. The caterer lined tables with food that soon set Kelly's stomach rumbling. At the far end of the food table, Charlene's contribution of a wedding cake sparkled with green and red trim.

They spent the next few hours talking and dancing. They'd taken their turn as the first to dance, their choice of song a slow melody they'd both been fond of in their twenties. But as long as she was in his arms, the song didn't matter.

At one point, she noticed the sheriff and Maggie in a deep discussion. Maybe her friend would finally give Tom a chance.

Susan and Gabriella were rarely off the dance floor. Susan's arm had healed well, and she'd become well-known in the town.

Kelly looked up at the man she'd married and smiled. "I love you."

"I love, you, too," he replied. "I can't believe how lucky I am."

She snuggled closer to the man who'd stolen a piece of her heart decades ago. Henrietta had been right to bring her home to Promise Cove.

It was where she belonged, right beside the man she loved.

The End

I hope you enjoyed this story. *Spring in Promise Cove*, the next book in this series, is available in print at your favorite online bookstore or your local bookstore can order it through IngramSpark.

Author's Note

As I neared the end of my women's fiction series, I knew I wanted to try my hand at something different. I enjoy contemporary romance, some more than others. When I looked at the common denominator, I found they were more about older heroines and the story involved more than the romance.

I thoroughly enjoyed writing this story. I live in an RV that we move from place to place. This story began its journey in Kentucky and ended its journey in New Hampshire. Everywhere I go, I find I have the most interesting discussions while doing laundry, and I almost always find women who like contemporary romance.

I hope you enjoyed this story. I look forward to writing the next one. To learn more about my travels on the road, learn about upcoming releases and free books, please go to www.caseydawes.com and sign up for my mailing list
Sincerely,
Casey Dawes
P.S. P.S. Want to learn more about Henrietta? Go to https://bookhip.com/VAKFSWN to get a free novella: *Promise Cove Beginnings*.

~ ~ ~

When you join my mailing list, you'll also receive
a free novella set in Promise Cove.
Go to **https://bookhip.com/VAKFSWN**
to claim your free copy!

Other Books by Casey Dawes

Promise Cove Romance Series
Return to Promise Cove
Spring in Promise Cove
Hope in Promise Cove
Winter in Promise Cove
Promise Cove Wedding (coming spring 2023)

Beck Family Saga
Home Is Where the Heart Is
Finding Home
Leaving Home
Coming Home
Starting for Home
Finally Home

California Romance Series
California Sunshine
California Sunset
California Wine
California Homecoming
California Thyme
California Sunrise
California Coast Romance Series (5 books)

Stand Alone Stories
Keep Dancing
Chasing the Tumbleweed
Love on the Wind
Short Stories for Women (And Some Men)

Christmas Titles

A Christmas Hope
Sweet Montana Christmas
Montana Christmas Magic

About the Author

Casey Dawes writes non-steamy contemporary romance and inspirational women's fiction with romantic elements.

Her women's fiction series, Rocky Mountain Front, explores the five siblings from a ranching family living in Montana, the people who love them, and the characters in the small town in which they live. Previous to that she wrote a five-book contemporary romance series about friends and family on the Central Coast. Her latest series features love between "seasoned" heroes and heroines in a small Montana town.

Currently, she and her husband are traveling the US in a small trailer with the cat who owns them. When not writing or editing, she is exploring national parks, haunting independent bookstores, and lurking in spinning and yarn stores trying not to get caught fondling the fiber!

Are you enjoying Promise Cove? Go to
https://bookhip.com/VAKFSWN
to get a free novella set in Promise Cove! You will be added to my newsletter mailing list: On the Road to Your Next Read ...

Printed in Great Britain
by Amazon